I0628582

EMENDARE

R. E. Bradshaw

Rainey Bell Thriller Series:
Rainey with a Chance of Hale (2017)
Relatively Rainey (2016)
Carl of the Bells (2015) (Short Story-ebook only)
Colde & Rainey (2014)
The Rainey Season (2013) Lambda Literary Awards Finalist
Rainey's Christmas Miracle (2011) (Short Story-ebook only)
Rainey Nights (2011) Lambda Literary Awards Finalist
Rainey Days (2010)

The Adventures of Decky and Charlie Series:
Out on the Panhandle (2012)
Out on the Sound (2010)

Sand Letters:
Book 1: Silly Love Songs 1976-1977 (2018)

Hiding Hearts: An Appletree Swamp Romantic Escapade
(2018)

Molly: House on Fire (2012)
Lambda Literary Awards Finalist

Before It Stains (2011)

Waking Up Gray (2011)

Sweet Carolina Girls (2010)

The Girl Back Home (2010)

EMENDARE

R. E. BRADSHAW

Published by
R. E. BRADSHAW BOOKS

USA

EMENDARE
By R. E. Bradshaw

© **2019 by R. E. Bradshaw. All Rights Reserved.**
R. E. Bradshaw Books/April 2019
ISBN-13: 978-0-9989549-9-8

Website: http://www.rebradshawbooks.com
Facebook: https://www.facebook.com/rebradshawbooks
Twitter @rebradshawbooks
For information contact rebradshawbooks@gmail.com

No part of this book may be reproduced or transmitted in any form or by any means, electronic or mechanical, including photocopying, recording, or by any information storage and retrieval system, without permission in writing from the author and publisher.

Warning: The unauthorized reproduction or distribution of this copyrighted work is illegal. Criminal copyright infringement, including infringement without monetary gain, is investigated by the FBI and is punishable by up to 5 years in federal prison and a fine of $250,000.

This is a work of fiction. Names, characters, businesses, places, events, and incidents are either the products of the author's imagination or used in a fictitious manner. Any resemblance to actual persons, living or dead, or actual events is purely coincidental.

Dedication

Deb.

"This thing that men call justice, this blind snake that strikes men down in the dark, mindless with fury, keep your hand back from it, pass by in silence."

Maxwell Anderson, 1935
"Winterset"

1

Let's start here...

"Do you know why they call this Doe's Ferry?"

A middle-aged bottle-blonde in need of a root touch-up held a camera to her eye. Struggling with the weight of a giant telescoping lens, she clicked away at the deepening colors of the sunset over the Albemarle Sound and glanced at her male companion between shots.

"It's a charming tale," she went on.

Blondie spoke in a thick Northeastern North Carolina accent—a confluence of Virginia drawl and coastal twang. I noted the amateur historian layered the southern sugar on a little too thick to be genuine, while she lilted her way through the tourist trap mythology of the abandoned ferry dock. Her companion looked bored as hell. I just wanted them to go away.

"It's said, back in the colonial days, a doe—as in," the woman paused to sing, "doe, a deer, a female deer."

The tall gentleman with her, wearing skinny jeans and working too hard to be hip, nodded impatiently. "Yeah, yeah. I got it without the Julie Andrews," he said.

Maybe that's what he said. He pronounced only the essence of his words, abandoning the hard consonants on the ends and allowing vowels to swim about in his cheeks. I thought he'd be more at home in a pub somewhere along the Thames. English explorers peered over this expanse of water for a glimpse of the mainland more than four hundred years ago. The historic landscape remained virtually unchanged but unimpressive to this modern day Englishman.

The blonde lowered the fancy digital camera from her eye. "You're cheeky, Richard. Do you need a snack?"

The Englishman's hands popped out of his pockets and up into the air. He screeched, "What? I understood it was a feckin' deer, Helen. I'm not a toddler in need of a nap. Finish the bloody story."

"Isn't the sunset beautiful?" The woman seemed willing to ignore her companion's worsening attitude.

"Bit like lookin' over Saint George's Channel, innit? Same ol' sun at evenin' tide."

In response, Helen raised the camera again and took a long burst of pictures. I couldn't tell if she was letting the snide remark pass or plotting her date's demise. I would have gotten up a head of steam and pushed him off the dock, but that's just me.

The setting sun painted the prismatic rippling surface of the water with the full expanse of the color wheel. I'd come to the water to "do dusk," as my dad used to call it. He'd roll one up and burn it down, then head out to the dock to enjoy his buzz in peace. I had a few cannabis edibles an hour ago when I crossed the county line and had been basking in the familiarity of this particular falling of the sun. Richard and Helen were a distraction, but I couldn't help being amused at the train wreck it was becoming.

Richard's skinny jeans must have been squeezing his tiny brains. He certainly wasn't using his big one. He kept up the provocative attitude, apparently looking to end the date abruptly. He chided the photographer as she continued to snap away.

"The silent treatment is a childish ploy used by cowards. At least that's what my ex-wife's therapist told her to tell me."

Richard chuckled a little, in an attempt to assure his audience that the recollection was meant to be humorous. Stand-up comedy was not his forte. Helen was not amused.

She lowered the camera and glared at the man she had liked until about five minutes ago. "Fuck you, Richard."

"Not likely with that attitude," he answered back.

"I don't see any need to continue this charade. You're not having much fun, are you?"

"Well, now that you mention it, you've had me in a car all day, runnin' about the countryside peerin' at," he made air quotes around, "antique things."

Helen looked and sounded genuinely surprised. "Your profile said you loved relic hunting."

The date already a disaster, Richard laughed. "This rubbish is far from old. The foundation of my grandmother's barn was growin' moss when they built that expatriate jail you're so proud of."

2

Richard pointed over his shoulder at one of the first jails erected in the region during the late 1700s. The original lost to fire, the jail standing now was built in the early 1800s on the old foundation with the addition of an adjacent county courthouse. Our English visitor had spotted the bait and switch in the tourism marketing team's wording of "colonial foundation." But why bother with that factual detail?

The county erected a set of replica stocks for photo ops on the courthouse lawn and let the colonial legends take flight. The lore was part of the tourist draw to a county desperate to replace the waning traditional agricultural and watermen economies. Albemarle County wasn't on the main route from the north down to the Outer Banks of North Carolina, so it had to work to draw visitors off the faster four-lane highways. Now that the bypass bridges were built and the ferry route closed, the people of Doe's Ferry couldn't be faulted for a white lie or two.

Richard continued, "Show me evidence of Viking exploration or ancient Native American relics and we'll talk about old things. You New World yanks act as if you were the first ones here."

"I'm not going to take colonization insults from a British imperialist. I think this date is over," Helen replied, with no trace of the sugary veneer left on her drawl. She headed for the driver's side door she'd left open in her excitement upon arriving.

"Aren't you going to throw tea in the harbor before the revolution?"

I stifled a laugh. Okay, maybe Richard had a future behind the microphone. Helen, again, was not amused.

"Well," Richard said, following her, "now you're withholding information just to be cunty. How American of you."

Helen whirled to glare at him and spat out the romanticized fable of Doe's Ferry. "During a hurricane, a doe washed up here with her baby on a small raft of storm debris. It's probably a lie, just like your profile suggested you were an English gentleman with a passion for history."

"I am," Richard argued. "I'm sure it's a lovely story. Although it does lose some of its historical quaintness when told through gritted teeth."

Helen reached the car, tossed the expensive camera on the passenger seat and climbed in. The door slammed with force as the engine turned over. Helen wasted no time and left no doubt Richard would need a ride home. She peeled away, sending gravel flying in a plume of trailing tire smoke, but didn't go far. The courthouse stood less than one hundred yards from the old ferry dock. The North Carolina highway patrolman waiting to pull out of the parking lot had only to flip on his blues and slide in behind the angry blonde for the first ticket of his shift.

"Fuck it all," Richard complained. He pulled a cell phone from his jacket pocket and began waving it about above his head, in search of a signal. It was at this moment that he realized I had witnessed the entire scene.

I had been sitting on the picnic table next to the dock's tiny public restroom doing dusk, floating up and down memory lane—or the memory docks, as it were. The Brit and Helen were just the latest to interrupt my reflection on the innocence of childhood and how quickly we discover we've been fed a line of crap since day one. Bad men win because they do not play by the rules. Rules are for suckers. The myth of triumphant decency could be found in the last national election and in the number of cable news satellite trucks hovering about Doe's Ferry.

Multiple photojournalists shooting B-roll of the Albemarle Sound had come and gone from the dock during my short time of observance. Everyone wanted to be first on the scene when the President cut the shortlist for the next nominee down to one. If one believed the rumors, my childhood neighbor was next in line.

I felt my old friend nausea returning and popped another twenty-five milligrams of medicated chocolate into my mouth. My stomach had been in knots since I arrived. Past mistakes churned against my stomach lining, eating it away. I knew I'd die of a bleeding ulcer if I remained in Doe's Ferry long.

My movement drew Richard's attention.

"Oh, hello," Richard said, taking a few steps in my direction.

If I ever possessed the southern hospitality gene, I killed it on a peyote quest with some old hippies in the Black Hills in the late 80s, far from here. It was then that I decided my motto would be "fuck people." I'm so glad I thought better of getting that tattooed on my neck after I came down. Even behind dark sunglasses, my lack of interest in social engagement must have registered with Richard.

He stopped his approach and asked, "I don't suppose they have car service this far from civilization?"

I raised my eyebrows so they could be seen above the rims of my glasses. Lowering my chin and curling my upper lip into a sneer, I maintained a "Do Not Enter" perimeter with nothing more than body language, a skill picked up in prison.

4

"I'm sorry," he said. "That sounded worse than I meant it to."

People get hung up on my stint in prison. It is hardly the most thrilling or mysterious part of my story. I took my first breath in a high school locker room not far from the ferry dock. Fifty-eight years later, I had come full circle—back to the land of my people.

As Richard noted and the desperate waving of his cell phone at the sky emphasized, we were far from civilization. Cultural advancement lagged on this stretch of sand and swamp sandwiched between the mainland and the coastal counties on the Atlantic Ocean. The pobocra—longstanding Carolinian slang for white trash—gripped tightly to the deeply planted roots of white supremacy. The haves told the have-nots that the have-nothings were stealing everyone blind, while the haves got richer and fed the fires of social unrest. The mask of civility worn by the God-fearing, law-abiding, deeply rooted citizens of Albemarle County slipped on and off as quickly as their drawls and drawers.

"Grandma, last one in is it," a child's voice drifted on the breeze into my thoughts.

On the old dock to my left, two children ran out in front of a middle-aged woman in a white beach wrap and hot pink flip-flops. The cut of her blonde hair—an excellent dye job—held captive by a white visor, the rhythm of her gait, the glimpse of her profile, all hints of a woman I used to know. She had a phone pressed to her ear, but listened to her grandson.

She held up one finger, finished her call, and then challenged, "Marco!" She dropped the phone in her pocket and removed the wrap to expose her hot pink bathing suit. Grandma was still a hottie, but she knew it, making her less attractive and leaving my "selfish bitch" opinion of Cindy Spencer unchanged.

The kids yelled, "Polo," and jumped into the water.

Doe's Ferry faded back to a memory.

2

Sin is always attractive...

"Jane Doe, you know I can't kiss a black boy. It's in the bible."

"It's 1972, Cindy. No one cares about what it says in that old book about black boys kissing white girls. Don't y'all study Civil Rights in sixth grade?"

William Malachi Blount, Jr., the black boy in question, was my friend and my third-half-cousin. It's complicated. Malachi and my dad shared a great-great-grandfather, but not a great-great-grandmother. Skin colors and races meant a lot more to other folks than it did to two kids grown from birth together. I was barely a month older than Mali. We hadn't known there was a difference between us until we started school. Now, at age eleven, it had been made clear to us that people didn't see the world like Mali and me.

Cindy Spencer was having none of my argument. "Civil Rights means Mali can ride our bus and go to school with us. The bible still says we are not to mix the races."

Malachi spoke up, "Actually, it says—"

"Marco," Doodie shouted, coming to the surface about ten feet away, eyes squinted shut.

Hains said to him, "We're not playing anymore."

Doodie opened his eyes and rubbed the brackish sound water out of them. He tried to focus on the rest of us. "Man, I was down there a long time, probably ten minutes at least."

Hains disputed Doodie's fantastic claim. "No way, man. One minute tops."

I continued trying to convince Cindy to sacrifice her morals for the cause.

"Well, you kissed me, and I'm a girl. I'm pretty sure that's in the bible too." I shoved Malachi toward her. "Go on, Cindy, kiss him."

Cindy ignored Malachi, stepping around him to preach at me instead, "It just says boys can't lie with boys. Besides, girls can practice kissing on each other. My brother said so."

Hains nodded, agreeing with Cindy's older brother's pronouncement because J.P. Spencer was already in college and Hains thought that made JP the expert on everything.

"It's okay because girls can't get each other pregnant," he said with mock authority. "It's safe for them to kiss and stuff."

"I don't think kissing is how you get a baby, Hains," Doodie said, pointing down below the surface of the water to his crotch. "It happens down there," he mouthed. His cheeks flushing red, Doodie was overcome with giggles.

"Shut up, Doodie," Hains, ever the alpha male, barked at his toady. He slapped the surface, sending an arch of water into Doodie's face.

Malachi looked kind of scared. He had never kissed a girl—let alone a white one. He wasn't as enthused as we were about the prospects and agreed with Cindy that this was a bad idea. His daddy was all the time hollerin' after us, "That white girl is going to get you in trouble."

I focused on Cindy, arguing, "If girls kissin' was okay, you wouldn't tell me we had to keep it a secret. We can keep you kissin' Malachi a secret too."

Cindy rolled her eyes and whined, "Well, it's not a secret now."

Doodie covered his mouth to stifle another giggle, but Hains still said, "Shut up, Doodie," and splashed him until he dove under to escape the onslaught.

The five of us waded in chest-deep water just off the deep channel used by the mainland ferry. Sometimes we slid dangerously close to the sandy edge of the frequently dredged chasm. Even good swimmers were wary. In the cold black water under the ferry dock lived a creature that dragged kids beneath the surface to their deaths.

We knew of one high school kid who dove in and wasn't found until his bloated body floated up a week later. We all saw him, bobbing there on the surface, while the Sheriff's men tried to grab onto him with a gaff hook. They said he got caught up in some tree branches sunk down in the channel. But we could clearly see claw marks on his

7

back when they pulled him out, making the ferry dock creature more plausible in our minds.

Doodie resurfaced close enough to the abyss to require a frantic backstroke away from the reach of the ferry dock monster, which we'd all decided looked a lot like the creature from the Black Lagoon. Only Malachi had insisted on long octopus-like tentacles for fingers because we had all felt the icy grip around an ankle, just the tip of something slipping by, and seen a shadow in the darkness recoiling away. Of course, it could have been a fish or an eel, but the mere possibility it could be a monster negated dismissing anything unknown as benign.

Cindy sought another way out. "Why does it have to be him? Why can't it be Hains?"

"I told you. The clue says only a male Doe kissed by a virgin is protected from the curse."

Popping up from the water between Cindy and Malachi to demonstrate how little he knew about genetics, Doodie said, "What about me? My mom is your momma's sister, Jane. Doesn't that make me part Doe?"

Doodie's real name was Brian Duty. His last name, as pronounced by his peers, unfortunately, rhymed with a euphemism for shit. Our socially awkward pal was unaware of boundaries and slow to catch on to this fact. He was almost as tall as Hains and thickly muscled, also a bit uncoordinated and clumsy. He barely made the cut to be in our grade, which made him almost a year younger than the rest of us. An only child, spoiled and overprotected, he matured a little slower. These facts made him the lowest ranking in our group dynamic.

Though goofy and awkward, Doodie actually read a lot and made good grades. He was a nerd-filled with random facts and our loveable teddy bear. Being Doodie's friend was like handling a hot biscuit as it dripped butter down the back of your hand. The mess was worth it; even if it required a thorough clean up afterward. We loved him and helped him try to fit in, though our methods were sometimes harsh. We were children, modeling behavior demonstrated for us by adults in our lives. The most famous character on TV was a crude, ignorant bigot. People thought it wasn't reality, but they didn't live in Doe's Ferry.

"Shut up, Doodie," the four of us said in unison.

The "courthouse kids" ruled Doe's Ferry. We were given the label, not for our delinquency, but because we all lived within shouting distance of the county seat. Malachi lived next door to me, and our houses backed up to the Albemarle Sound on the north side of the mainland ferry dock. Hains lived by the courthouse on the southern side of the dock. His lawn sloped down to a short sandy beach with a long wharf paralleling the ferry channel. Doodie lived across the canal from Malachi's house on the north side.

Cindy's house was the biggest and newest. It sat across from the ferry dock next to the longstanding Swann place. The petite pretty girl foil to my solid-bodied tomboy athleticism, Cindy, already twelve, had completed the sixth grade where the rest of our cadre headed in the fall. She also had boobs, which made me, the only other local girl for miles around, invisible.

The road we lived on followed an old wagon path to the courthouse, where we all had ties. Cindy's father was the district judge; Hains's father, the Sheriff; Malachi's mother, the custodian; Doodie's mother cooked for the jail, and his dad was a jailer. My father, whose ancestor lent his name to the original colonial trading post now known as Doe's Ferry, was a frequent guest of the county's drunk tank. According to my grandmother, I would be too if I didn't change my ways. I was eleven, hardly a hardened criminal or a drunk, but there was time.

"Look," I said, trying a different approach with our stubborn virgin. During Cindy's bible study, she had missed several of the seven deadly sins. I appealed to her vanity and greed. "If this clue leads us to Bonnet's treasure, you can move to New York and be an actress. Like you said you would if you had the money."

"I'm not sinning for financial gain. You cannot serve both God and money," Cindy complained loudly, with full Southern Baptist preacher inflection.

This was the same girl that would share a stolen cigarette with all of us and had been known to sip a beer, at least that one time when I took one from my dad's cooler. We chased it with orange soda. Damn the temporary reformation qualities of vacation bible school.

"You know, you get like this every summer when you come back from staying at your grandma's. That church camp makes you mean."

"It isn't mean to follow the Lord."

I pointed at Malachi's deeply tanned bare chest and said, "But Mali isn't any blacker than I am. He's brown. Besides, we're cousins. So, what does that make me?"

Cindy refused to listen. "Bertie's daddy was a bastard son of James Doe. That doesn't make you cousins. It makes him an abomination according to the word."

"Goddammit, Cindy. Just stop quoting the bible and kiss him so we can get on with it."

9

Cindy turned and walked away, calling over her shoulder, "I won't be your friend Jane Doe if you're going to take the Lord's name in vain."

"Fine. We'll find a virgin somewhere else."

She wheeled around, red-faced. "I don't believe that stupid pirate's map is real anyway."

"When we're rich, we'll send you a postcard from Hawaii," I said, pretending not to care if she stayed.

Cindy glared at me and then went for the kill. "Aren't you a virgin? Why don't you kiss him?"

Cindy knew why. She was just being hateful now. I wasn't about to lose my chance at finding the "Gentleman Pirate" Stede Bonnet's treasure over a technicality. We found the map and accompanying directions to the cache in an iron-strapped wooden box. It was buried in the woods behind the salvage yard attached to my family's service station up on the new road. The new road had been there since the early 1800s, but as long as there was an old road, it would always be the "new" one. The fenced lot filled with rusting wrecks towed in off the county byways was part of our playground. The courthouse kids roamed freely in the twenty acres between the sound shore and the busy highway.

I hollered after Cindy, "I'd rather go to hell than kiss you again, anyway," and then kissed Mali on the cheek.

We all stared at the sky when it rumbled a warning of the coming summer squall.

"God is going to get you for that, Jane Doe," Cindy yelled at me.

Already out of the water, she ran toward her house. The rest of us scampered for the shore when lightning streaked across the sky.

Mali shouted over the sound of our legs churning against the shallow water, "Jesus, Jane. You've cursed us all."

"Do you think God is about to strike us down?" I said, laughing at the thought.

I wasn't the typical god-fearin' churchgoer that my peers were. My grandmother's response to my irreverence was to say she thought I read too many of my father's books while he was overseas. She complained that the preacher didn't come by as much after I started talking.

Mali, who had heard my take on the "good book," said, "No, not that bible stuff—the pirate curse. You ain't exactly pure. Maybe you just put a hex on us."

Having been raised by two devout Methodists and one avid atheist's book collection, I got a kick out of what people thought unseen forces could do to you, but I believed with all my heart in pirates and pirate treasure. We could see the evidence of their existence all around us. Pirates built wharves for unloading spoils in what was now my backyard. The ancient pilings were still there. We dug up artifacts all the time. My grandpa had a flintlock pistol he found when he was cleaning out the ditch that drained the low spot across the road.

Malachi believed in pirates and pirate curses. He picked up his pace.

Hains added his take on the matter. "I guess we should have found a real virgin."

Doodie tripped and fell face first while trying to say something, "Lightning travels on the surfa—" Splash. Splash. "Dang, did you see me step in that hole?"

The air filled with the smell of rain. Another flash and thunder pounded against my chest. We pushed through the shallow water, arms pumping at twice the speed of our knees. Our legs fought against the dense milfoil, an invasive aquatic grass that grew near the shoreline.

Mali looked over at me with his dark chocolate eyes and smiled. "It's just God making sure you don't get any ideas about kissing a black boy again."

"Yeah, that's probably it," I said, laughing as the sky opened up.

We could no longer hear each other over the roar of the rain pounding the surface of the Albemarle Sound behind us. Lightning cracked across the sky. Danger loomed. In our youthful innocence, fear only made us laugh louder and run faster. The storm would pass, and we still needed to find a virgin. Our original plan kept the treasure and map within our trusted gang of five. Cindy's reaction would force us to seek help from outsiders.

I couldn't figure why Cindy was so hung up on kissing Malachi. He had near as much white blood as I had. Mali and me, we were both naturally tanned; like coffee with cream, only I got an extra splash of half and half. Cindy and Hains were blonde and blue.

One time when my dad was home on leave, he called them the "evidence of European expansionism." I laughed, even though I'm not really sure what he meant.

Mali and I were on the other end of the color scale, with our dark black hair and deep brown eyes ringed in amber. But in the summer, when we wore little clothes and browned every exposed inch of our bodies, Malachi turned a deeper bronze that amplified his father's

11

ethnic roots. His head was full of shiny black curls while mine lay flat. He was the prettiest person, boy or girl, I'd ever seen. I wasn't alone in my thinking.

Earlier that morning, we had passed some women I knew from Grandma's bridge game afternoons. With teased hair and bows carefully centered behind identically trimmed short bangs, the evidence they had the same hair stylist was overwhelming.

Hains stopped, as the rest of us ran past. Ever the gentlemen or politician—both in his nature and genetics—he said, "Good morning, Mrs. Sprague. Good morning, Mrs. Dowdy."

"Thank you, Hains. What a polite young man," Mrs. Sprague said.

We plopped onto the creaky porch steps of Swann's store with our grape sodas and cheese nabs.

The women stopped on the porch above us, not knowing we could hear them or just not caring if we did.

Mrs. Sprague said, "That mulatto boy is so beautiful."

Mrs. Dowdy answered, "Sin is always attractive, Beth."

I glanced at Mali. He just shrugged and turned up the soda for a long swig. After several cooling gulps, he pulled the bottle from his lips and let out a loud, "Ahhhhh," so the women would notice. He smiled up at them, dimples in full charming rascal position, and boldly winked.

Grown women blushed and covered their mouths because an eleven-year-old black boy winked at them. Mali was just learning the power he wielded with his looks. I laughed when he turned that magical smile on me, as the women scurried away.

Malachi never cared what people said about him. He probably should have.

3

Howdy, Sheriff...

Malachi's smile faded from my memory, his image replaced by the Englisher's silhouette. Richard blocked the last rays of sunset and my chance to appreciate them. He attempted to communicate through sign language, managing to convey only gibberish with his hands. He also spoke his words deliberately and loudly, which I've never understood. Why yell at a person who can't hear you?

"Can you hear me? I require assistance."

"Might I be able to help you, sir?"

To my rear, a friendly male voice offered a way out of having to deal with Richard. Skinny jeans man looked over my shoulder and sighed with relief. He stepped around the picnic table to greet the new member of our ferry dock party.

"Hello, officer. Chuffed to see you."

"I hope that's a good thing," the officer responded.

Richard laughed. "Yes, an excellent thing. I seem to have been left without transportation. I can't locate a cell signal and need assistance."

I had a good idea to whom the approaching voice belonged without looking. I could also imagine Richard indicating me with a tip of his head or glance of the eye, he may have even pointed at my back.

He lowered his voice and informed the new arrival, "I think she's deaf and dumb."

My former playmate said, "Who, Jane Doe? I've never known her to be shy."

Richard responded like the rest of the world. "Her name is Jane Doe? Really? You aren't joking?"

"Yes. Her father's name was John Doe. Her mother's last name was Smith. Jane Smith Doe, that's her. Her dad said he guaranteed her anonymity for life. Thought it was funny."

"Probably hard to get a bank card," Richard said, "or use one. Merchants must suppose them some sort of sample sent through the mail."

"TSA is a real bitch, I imagine," my friend added, chuckling audibly.

My head bobbed slightly, as I involuntarily agreed with both men.

Richard should have stopped there, but he didn't. He mistook the locals' amusement as a sign to continue.

"I imagine sticking your child with that name would serve as a family jest among the ancestral progeny of the lawless colonial coast. Wasn't this place run amok with pirates and people who wished not to be found?"

"Yes, sir. We are part of the pirate coast."

Richard should have stopped, but he continued, "The chances are one's DNA might lead to a life requiring anonymity. Still doesn't explain why she won't acknowledge a person in need."

Intending to be entertaining, Richard's comments showed the familiar disregard held among people living north of the Virginia/North Carolina border for those living south of it. William Byrd surveyed the line in 1728 and wrote of the fitness of the land and its people only for the husbandry of pigs, pinning forever the label of simpletons struck by laziness to those living in the Carolina colony. After his disparaging remarks, Byrd bought a broad swath of the land straddling the border and founded a family that would make its way to the highest offices in the nation. The chip on our collective Carolinian shoulders had grown with the weariness of our hick reputations. I could hear the resentment in the Sheriff's response.

"It's Sheriff, not officer. I work for the county. We don't have any city police officers around here."

I was thinking we didn't have a city or a town. The best we could muster was a blinking caution light at the only major crossroad and a bunch of colloquial village names where old families happened to settle together. If there were enough people, the government had made whatever name the villagers settled on official and gave them a post office. It still didn't mean we were ignorant swamp dwellers, at least not all of us.

I'm pretty sure Richard heard the change in the Sheriff's tone, too. He took a few steps back. Able to see his lower legs in my peripheral vision, I watched as he shifted his weight nervously from foot to foot while the Sheriff spoke.

"It's probably a turn of your luck that ol' Jane there decided to give you a pass. Your date is waiting for you with the patrolman." There was a pause and a chuckle before he sent Richard on his way. "Be nice. At least until you get back to Virginia."

"Thank you, Sheriff."

In the practiced style of one whose department budget depended on tax dollars generated by tourism, the Sheriff regained control of his emotions, and let his schmoozer pitch follow Richard down the sandy path by the road until he was beyond earshot.

"My pleasure. Y'all come back when you can stay longer. Stop and get some of Miss Edna's pie on the way back. Her place is just about a mile north on your right. It'll put the sweet back in your sweetheart. You'll come back for more, guaranteed."

Then my blood brother, sealed in a ceremony inside a candlelit boathouse fifty years ago, turned his attention to me. My shoulders were probably still visibly moving, as I tried to subdue the laughter at his hokey delivery of Edna's sales pitch.

I heard him take a step closer, before he said, "What's the word of the day?"

"Reditus."

"I'll have to dig my old Latin dictionary out."

"It's a returning, a turning back."

"Appropriate."

"How'd you know it was me, Hains?"

"You've been sittin' here for two hours, according to my deputy. By the way, he's on to you. He's certain you're a risk and should be reported to the feds."

"I'm the last person you anticipated finding in Doe's Ferry, I expect."

"I don't know. With all that's going on, it isn't all that surprising to find you here. I know it's the last place you could be anonymous, name or not. So, you aren't hiding from anyone."

"I forgot how quickly strangers who linger are singled out here."

"You're not a stranger, Jane."

"Oh, I've been that from the day I was born, but tell me this, what prompted the Sheriff to personally check out the report?"

Hains moved around to stand just in my peripheral vision, an old cop trick to make a suspect turn or remain uncomfortable. "My deputy's description of the stranger down at the ferry dock: female, forty to fifty." He paused to say, "You should thank him for that." And then continued the description from memory, "Short, five-three or four, salt and pepper gray hair, tattoos on inside wrists that read 'No Justice' on one, and 'No Peace' on the other, muscular build, probably works out. Awfully accurate I'd say."

"Put that clerk at Swann's on the payroll. She's the source of the detail, not your boy."

"Oh, so you met my confidential informant." Hains laughed. "She's as nosy as they come. Her radar pinged because you gave that guy directions to the marina. That's a local kind of thing to do."

"Are you sure it wasn't because she saw the name when I opened my wallet to get out some cash?"

Hains chuckled. "You're too smart to have let that happen unplanned. I figured you wanted to see who would come looking."

"Now, why would I do that?" I smiled to myself, knowing he was absolutely right. "Is everyone's hypervigilance because of Judge Spencer's pending nomination to the Supreme Court? Were you waiting for me, Hains? Are you here to have me state my business?"

Hains chuckled. "Your business is no concern of mine until you break the law. Promise you'll be a good girl?"

"Commitment and I have an on again off again relationship, so I'm going to keep my options open. Besides, I have 'Rebel Without Cause' tattooed on my ass. Omitting the 'a' was purposeful."

"Wow, it's like a time warp. Jane Doe, sarcastic to the point of arrogance, living on the edge of the blade, tilting at windmills, you haven't changed." He paused to consider his tactics and settled on a different approach. "I was right there with you most of the time, so I can't say much. I know we survived more often than we had a right to."

"Some of us didn't."

My flatly delivered cynicism directed at his attempt at levity resulted in what felt like backing up to our respective corners. Hains needed to reassess his opponent. The pause gave me a chance to slow my heart rate and swallow the adrenaline. Don't show your hand.

The leather of his utility belt creaked when he sat beside me on the picnic table. Clouds floated by on the surface of his polished black boots. Ironed to a razor's edge crispness, the crease of his pants stood perfectly straight up to his bent knee. He used to smell like his father's Old Spice. Today, he'd chosen for his scent—a hint of birch, pineapple, and musk—a signature blend of an expensive men's cologne. It went well with his underlying bouquet of tea tree soap, leather, and gun oil.

I made my living reading people. Hygiene could tell you a lot about a person. Expensive products hinted at disposable cash. Knowing real money from the cheap knock-off was essential to my success as a…well, they don't really have a name for what I am. We'll get to the details in a bit. My nose was telling me the Sheriff was either making some cash on the side, or he was still the same guy women were willing to spoil for his attention. Growing up, it was like watching the virgins bring offerings to the prince.

Next to the words "ladies' man" in the dictionary should be a picture of Hains Lawton Forster, III, with emphasis on the plural nature of ladies. The secret of his conquests lay not in his natural charmer status, but in the size of his penis, or so I've been told. According to Malachi, Hains's dick acquired legendary locker room status at age twelve, when the county boys began playing sports in middle school and had to start taking showers together. Mali swore the rumored measurements were not exaggerations. I'd never cared to find out. Cindy, however, declared Hains's penis her property in high school. I was already gone when they married and really didn't give a damn what happened to either of them by then.

Hains eventually let out a disarming chuckle, a tactic he had used to defuse confrontation since we were in diapers together. It seemed almost reflexive this time, meant to cover emotions brought on by my presence and the memories I awoke within him.

In his warm baritone, he said softly, "No, some of us didn't make it, that is true. I don't know if it's because I'm closing in on sixty or a longing for simpler times, but I think of our little gang often. You were all part of the happiest days of my life. I miss us, together, taking on the world. I've missed you, Jane."

"That's surprising. The last thing I remember you saying to me before today was 'Fuck you, Jane Doe,' when I called you a coward. Have your feelings on the issue changed?"

"We were kids stuck in a mess created by adults. Our parents made decisions for us. I'm sure we all said things we wish we hadn't. My therapist says you have to let go of the past and live in the now."

I turned to see that time had been very kind to Hains Forster. He had grown sexier with age, more distinguished, with a little gray in his closely cropped beard and a bit of salt and pepper at the edges of his hatband. He made eye contact with me and grinned. His blue eyes still sparkled with mischief, just as they had when we were too young to know all the shitty stuff life would dump on us.

"Are you fucking your therapist?"

17

"She's not my type. I think she plays on your team."

"My team? Are you assuming I'm a lesbian because I was never all over your legendary dick."

Hains shook his head, chuckling again. "No, not because of your lack of interest in me sexually. I saw you and that girl from the campground. Her name was Mary, I think."

"Maria."

"Yeah, Maria. That's her. I saw you two in the boathouse one night, the summer before our senior year."

What he might have seen flashed through my mind. It was my turn to chuckle. "Oh, that summer."

"Yeah, you were 'unavailable,'" Hains made air quotes, "for most of July. Then she left, and you were miserable."

I studied his expression, remembering that I had loved him before I hated him. We had all loved each other. We were more than childhood friends. Malachi, Hains, Cindy, and me, we formed some kind of love quadrangle. Doodie seemed to love the idea of us as a whole. The five of us swore loyalty to the end. The end came sooner than we expected.

I smiled involuntarily. I couldn't help it. Hains hid a gentle strength behind a swaggering grin. My weakness would always be for the wholesome athletic type, the boy or girl next door. I studied myself as much as I studied others. In Hains, I recognized the source of my lifelong infatuation with lean athletic muscle and clean-cut handsomeness.

I acknowledged his good deed all those years ago. "You never said anything. You could have tormented me with that information."

Hains turned to look out over the water. "You were hurting enough."

We sat quietly for another moment. I'm sure his thoughts raced, as did mine, through our childhood bonds.

Finally, I said, "Well, I've given up women at least five times since that summer, so your assumption is informed, but incorrect. I'm not a lesbian or any other pigeonholed label. I'm not a single dot on the sexuality spectrum. For the most part, at this stage of the game, I lean toward stable humans with jobs. Body parts are less important than a lack of drama and a paycheck."

He nodded, "What's that they say? 'There are no wrong holes if you love someone.' That's what my fourteen-year-old grandson says anyway."

"Wow, a teenaged grandson. You're old, Hains."

"You forget I started on my eighteenth birthday. Our first was conceived the day I became old enough to be held legally responsible for her."

"How convenient for Cindy."

"Hey," he warned me with a frown.

"I see Cindy is still off-limits for criticism."

Hains stiffened. "Cindy is my wife."

This response came so quickly, I knew it was reflexive and one he'd repeated to the point of muscle memory. He forgot I knew this rehearsed tone. We sat together for twelve grades. I knew him better than he knew himself. I had known he'd marry Cindy if she got pregnant. She did too. That's what pissed me off.

He continued defending his wife. "It took both of us to make that baby. Our daughter wasn't planned, but I've never regretted having her in my life."

"Shit happens. Just because it worked out, doesn't make it less shitty."

"Okay, I'll give you that. Her name is Emily, by the way. She is a nurse, like Cindy, with kids of her own. We have a son too. He's nineteen, a bit of a wild child and tempered like his mother."

"I read about him in the paper last year. How in the hell did y'all get those charges dropped? I love how sexual assault is just boys being boys. 'Athletic hazing' I think they called it. I hope the younger boy is okay."

"You of all people should know how things can be blown out of proportion."

"I didn't fuck a kid in the ass with a broomstick."

"Let's just drop it, okay?"

I couldn't without saying, "From what I saw, he's JP with your build. Basically my worst nightmare. And you can stop blaming yourself. You had a fifty-fifty chance of hatching a bad seed."

Hains decided to ignore my digs, another of his social tactics. He said, "I love my kids and grandkids, Jane. It wasn't a bad life."

"That sounded final. I think we have a bit to go, don't you?"

"Yeah, I was just saying…anyway, I love my children, even when they aren't likable."

I noted he didn't say he loved Cindy, but I let it go. We sat in silence for a second or two.

Hains seemed to let the 'what ifs' settle down in his brain, before asking, "So, you haven't set foot in Doe's Ferry since 1979, what finally brought you back?"

"Do I have to answer that question?"

"You didn't come home when your father died in 2000. With your history, you can see why this sudden appearance would concern me."

"My history? Which part? The part where we were cradle to grave friends, all of us, or the part where one of us died, three of us lied, and one of us went to prison."

"I'm assuming that means this isn't a nostalgic trip home."

"No point in pretending I've made peace with the total fucking-over I received in that courthouse at the hands of men covering their own asses."

Hains turned to look at me, really look at me. I stared ahead at nothing, as I learned to do when a corrections officer had me against a wall.

"I went to see you. The prison officials wouldn't let me in. My name wasn't on your list."

"There were no names on my list."

Hains chuckled. I wondered if he knew this mechanism had gone from charmingly disarming to an anxiety tell. Maybe it always had been. He tried his concerned tone next, another interview technique. I had trusted Hains with my life at one time. Now, even if I wanted to, I couldn't. My game plan involved trusting no one.

"How much time did you do?"

"I did the whole five. Got out in '84."

"Five years is a long time to go without seeing anyone who cared about you. Why the whole five? No time off for good behavior?"

I turned to look him in the eye, before I said, "To get time off for good behavior, I would have had to be good. Also, they required that I show remorse for a crime I did not commit."

"Come on, Jane. You were guilty."

"Your father caused it by turning a blind eye." I paused the appropriate amount of time for effect, before adding, "And you had done exactly what I did on multiple occasions. So, don't play innocent with me."

"You got caught by the feds. You can't blame my dad for that."

"Who planted that pot on me? And who sent them to a little bar in the middle of nowhere looking for drug traffickers, Hains?"

"I don't know, and my dad is dead. So we can't ask him."

"I was set up and the people that should have helped me lied or looked the other way. Nobody wanted to know the truth."

Hains tried more therapy crap. "Maybe we all told the truth as we saw it."

20

"Bull shit! Every one of you told the story that had the least negative consequences coming home to roost."

"Are we talking about you or Malachi, Jane?"

"It's the same thing, Hains. That's been my contention all along. I went to prison because I wouldn't accept all the lies. I couldn't turn my back on a friend and so my friends turned their backs on me."

Hains turned to look past me toward the courthouse. He seemed to desire my ire return to smoldering ash from raging red coal. I followed his gaze, watching as the parking lot lights blinked on. Streetlights lining the old road filled the late dusk gloom with an amber halogen glow, as the mist rolled ashore.

The light fixtures outside the ferry dock restrooms buzzed to life. The one by the women's entrance began to strobe slightly. The fluttering light reflected in the gold badge on Hains's hat. My head started to hurt. I closed my eyes and rubbed my left temple. When I opened them again, I realized too late that Hains was looking at me.

He decided to steer the topic away from my incarceration. I couldn't blame him. I wouldn't want to talk to me about fucking me over either.

"So, where've you been since you got out?"

"Anywhere but here. I see the apple didn't fall too far from the badge. From the next Roger Staubach to Andy Griffith. How does that happen?"

"My freshman year at State I took a hit during a mop-up preseason appearance, broke a vertebra and pretty much ended my hopes of an NFL career, or college for that matter. Another hit like that and I wouldn't be walking they said. I had it fused, and that was that. I had a wife and child to support. I couldn't join the military with pins in my back. I got an associate degree in criminal justice and took a job in the department. I ran for Sheriff after my dad died. Been in office for twenty years now."

"Bet that screwed Cindy's plans of leaving here and never looking back."

He glanced over at the home where, as it turns out, he had spent his entire life. The lights were on in almost every room. Silhouettes of people moved behind the closed blinds.

"We even live in the old house. This was the last place she thought we'd be, across the street from her parents, back in Doe's Ferry for a life sentence."

21

"Whoa, that's a bit poetic. Try not comparing your comfortable, if not ideal, life to one in a penitentiary. I assure you your burdens were easier to bear."

"Everybody's got their own version of prison."

"Damn. When did you become so deep? Are you sure you aren't fucking that therapist?"

"I'm positive. Blame it on podcasts and long drives up and down these country roads. I've evolved. Besides, I told you I'm not her type. I should introduce you two. How long you going to be here?" He waited for an answer.

"Nice try and no thanks."

He grinned. "Are you going to tell me why you're here, or are you going to make me figure it out on my own?"

I had a decision to make. Up until I was eighteen, Hains would have been the first person I reached out to in a situation like this. He was our white hat hero, the guy we counted on to lead us out of danger. I wondered who Hains had become. Was he anymore estranged from the man he thought he would be than I was from the dreams of my childhood? Was he contemplating the same thing about me? I decided to dodge his question with one of my own.

"Do you remember when we went looking for a virgin?"

4

We need a virgin...

"Y'all are forgettin' I can't swim if it's over my head," Malachi said, with his toes dangling in the water beneath the boathouse.

Hains chuckled. "You ain't swimmin' if you can still touch the bottom. That's wadin'. I don't know why you're so scared of deep water. It's the same water in the shallow part."

"The water don't scare me. It's the drowning that does."

The courthouse kids had a fort in the thicket between the salvage yard and the back of the church. Our tree house was in the patch of woods behind Doodie's parents' place, overlooking a shallow canal where we went frog gigging. But we practically lived in my boathouse.

Abandoned by the adults in my family, the boathouse became our headquarters when we were old enough to turn the knob on the weathered gray door. Here we shared and kept each other's secrets, plotted our adventures, and hid from the outside world when necessary. This was where we sliced our fingers and mingled our blood, three blood brothers and a sister. Cindy said the ceremony was unsanitary and refused to be blooded.

At the moment, Malachi had the floor. "And my daddy said if I kissed a white girl, the white man would set a dog after me. So that ain't happenin' either."

Malachi's father, William, drove a truck and wasn't around much. I was glad, because he was mean and when he was drunk he was meaner.

I had heard him tell Malachi, "Civil Rights ain't going to stop them from throwing niggas off bridges 'round here. You might look more pleasin' to them white folks with your creamy skin, but mess with their women and you is black as me."

My family treated Malachi like the family he was. I ran in and out of Aunt Bertie and Uncle William's house following behind their son. I wasn't really their niece, but that was what I always called Malachi's parents. We were rarely apart, except church, where believing or not, I was forced to go. I could go to Malachi's church and did on occasion. The raucous gospel sounds made my heart sing. I loved going to church with Mali because it felt like a party. He couldn't come to mine, even if it was across the street from his house. The church was where I first experienced racism.

I figured I didn't count as the "white folks" Uncle William complained about. I thought my family different from other racists in the south. When Malachi, Hains, and I found the white hood and some old Klan papers in a box in my attic, I knew the history I had imagined for the Doe family had been blindly misinformed. My two friends and I vowed never to speak of what we'd found. We also promised to change things when we were old enough. Currently, we had more important matters to deal with.

Malachi continued his protest, interjecting reason, which the rest of us were ignoring. "I've had time to think about it now, too. How did the pirates know the ferry dock would be where it is two hundred years later?"

Minnows schooled beneath the old shad boat suspended above the water in the stall across from where we sat. The boat hadn't moved since my grandfather had a stroke. My dad was too busy at the service station or too drunk to spend time on the water. My grandmother only cared that I bathed, showed up for regular feedings, and ran a brush through my hair at least every other day. My mother, well that's another story. The empty boat stall on the left became our private pool, a fishing pier, and a place to float in a scavenged old rubber raft we patched with a bicycle tire repair kit and tied to the boatlift.

Hains had the perfect answer to Mali's reasonable observation. "The Doe's Ferry area was used by the Indians to haul out canoes and fish traps. It's been a busy waterfront for hundreds of years."

We rode out the afternoon storm in the boathouse, eating lunch prepared from our stash of bread and peanut butter. We were generally allowed to run from dawn to dusk unfettered. After checking-in for dinner at home, we reconvened outside until the streetlights came on in winter. In the summer, we had more freedom and a longer nightlife. Malachi and me, we spent most evenings together, until his mom called

24

him home. I slept in the boathouse sometimes. Nobody in my house missed me.

We waited for the rain to taper off. The thunder and lightning had moved on ahead of the storm an hour ago. We knew it was time to go when sunbeams cut through the shadows in the water under the shelter. The weather no longer an obstacle, our search for a virgin was back underway. We needed a kisser, but now Malachi refused to be the kissee.

"I don't care if you find a virgin, I ain't diving into that water at the ferry dock," he insisted.

"The virgin's kiss will protect you from the monster," I reassured him.

"I ain't worrying about the monster. I'm worried about sinking to the bottom. I can't swim. We all know it. I've tried, and I just can't do it."

I nodded that I did know, but said, "It's because you tense up as soon as you think about how deep it might be. You would float if you relaxed, but you freak out."

Malachi threw his hands up in the air. "Because I cannot swim. Are you deaf?"

Hains had thought this through. "You don't have to swim. We'll tie a rope to you. Doodie and I will be on the other end so we can raise and lower you."

Malachi shook his head. "You are crazy. How are you going to know when I need to come up?"

Doodie emerged from the waist-deep water, spitting out his snorkel. "Hey, look. A quarter." His nose was pinched under his goggles, giving his voice a cartoon quality in the cavernous boathouse.

"Any luck finding my earring?" Cindy asked.

We let her in the boathouse when the storm eased up and her previous tantrum had passed, only because she brought still warm cookies made by her housekeeper, Malachi's Aunt Lutie. We had our priorities in order. Lutie's warm chocolate chip cookies trumped nearly everything else.

"No, I didn't find it, but I'll keep looking." Doodie handed Cindy the quarter and dove again.

"Malachi is right," Cindy said. "We need another male Doe. How about asking your dad, Jane?"

I laughed. "John Doe is not chaste of heart."

"How do you know?" Malachi asked.

25

"I looked up chaste in the dictionary. Drinking until you pass out every night is the opposite of what that means." I thought for a second and then stated the obvious aloud, "We need a nice kid who can swim and is kin to me on my dad's side."

Cindy demanded, "Let me read the clue again." She held out her hand.

Hains handed her the piece of tanned deer hide with the hand-inked riddle on one side and a map to the ferry dock on the other. A crude skull and crossbones flag marked the spot where the treasure lay in the deep hole by the shore, with the words "Here it Be" written beside it in fancy script.

Cindy read aloud, her voice taking on an eerie quality, echoing inside the old cedar walls.

"Tell no one, or the curse befall ye.
Do as you're told and reap the bounty.
The Beast guards what lies in the dark.
The map is but a wee part.
Let not a word of this riddle be missed.
The male Doe must be chaste of heart
And by a virgin be kissed.
Thus protected from the Beast of the deep
The treasure he will find and keep.
If the Doe dives without the purest kiss
Never will he return from the black abyss."

Cindy stared at the riddle and then announced, "I still think this is a fake. Jane, did you make this? It looks homemade."

Hains snatched the riddle back from Cindy's hands. "Of course it looks homemade. The pirates made it."

Malachi chimed in. "Besides, there were five old coins in the box as proof."

Cindy wasn't convinced. "They look like the coins they sell at Pirate's Cove gift shop at the beach."

I ignored Cindy and addressed the task at hand. "Okay, if Mali won't do it, we have to find someone else. I can only think of one boy I know, but it'll be dangerous going to get him."

Doodie, who was climbing out of the water and up the ladder said, "Cool. Where are we going?"

5

My dad is gonna kill you...

"So who is this kid?" Doodie asked.

"Olin Doe Walker is my dad's cousin Olive's boy. We never hang out with that part of the family."

Cindy asked, "How come?"

"Some kind of land dispute. Goes all the way back to my granddaddy's granddaddy."

"And they still don't talk," Malachi added. "That's why we can't tell anyone where we're going."

"I told my mom. I had to, or I couldn't come," Doodie said.

"Man, Doodie, why didn't you just say you were going to my house? She never checks," I complained.

"Why did you go home? You knew she was there," Malachi chimed in.

"I had to go get dry clothes."

"You're going to ride in a boat. You're going to get wet again."

"Yeah, but I get a rash if I wear wet clothes for a long time."

"So you told her where we were going?" I said, shaking my head.

"You know I can't lie to her. She says my ears turn red when I do," Doodie said.

We all laughed when Hains said, "They do, red as a beet."

Doodie covered the sides of his head with his hands.

"Here, take this," I said, still laughing as Doodie's ears turned scarlet.

I handed him an Army surplus PRC 6 walkie-talkie. My dad was concerned about me on a sober day and gave me one of a pair of radios so we could stay in touch during my ramblings. I swiped his handset on a not so dry night and used the pair to communicate with my friends. Dad never asked about it.

Hains took over the planning, as he usually did. "Okay, since Doodie's mom said he can't ride his bike on the highway and Malachi won't get in a boat, you two are taking your bikes. Doodie and I will take my skiff. We'll wait for you at the campground docks."

Cindy, who was staying behind for a scheduled piano lesson and because Judge Spencer's daughter wouldn't be caught dead in Marshland Trailer Park, asked me, "Are you going to tell your dad you're going by the marina?"

"Nope. What he don't know, he can't stop me from doing."

"You should leave one of those radios with me, so I can get help if you need it."

I saw right through her game. "No way I'm leaving you a radio. You wouldn't shut up the whole time."

"I couldn't talk during my lesson." Cindy reasoned.

"Then what good are you as an emergency contact?"

Hains stepped in. "I'll keep the radio."

It was settled, or so I thought. The alpha male had spoken. I turned to leave.

"See ya at the docks," I said to Hains. "Don't be late."

Hains, the fastest of our crew, took off running, spurring a stampede as he called over his shoulder, "Last ones to the campground docks have to lick an eel."

#

"I could go meet them. You can wait here," Malachi offered.

He and I had rolled to a stop about fifty feet from the back door of the marina. It was a mile from the courthouse by road and half that by boat. The shallow water grasses slowed Hains's little twenty-five horsepower Johnson outboard and the wind was against him today. Our chances of winning the race to the campground docks were good. But the way there required we pass close to the marina.

"If I don't go, they'll make us eat eels."

"Lick eels," Mali corrected me and laughed.

"Whatever. Old man Poyner doesn't scare me," I said, though the hole in my stomach grew deeper with every passing second.

Mali stood on his pedals, balancing the bike without touching the ground. I pushed off and started slowly propelling myself down the worn dirt path behind Poyner's Marina.

Mali fell in with me, offering words of encouragement, "Maybe he won't be there today."

"He's always there," I said.

The odor of the salt marshes baking in the sun followed the breeze off the water. The smell funneled down the tree-lined path mixed with the pong of fish, both fresh and in a state of rot. Gulls laughed above us, scavenging for the bits that produced the most stench.

People had bought bait, stored boats, cleaned fish, mended nets, loaded crab traps, filled fuel tanks, and spread gossip at this marina long before either Mali or I was born. There had been a long line of men called old man Poyner, some good, some bad. My dad told me he and his friends had run-ins with the modern version of Mr. Poyner back when he was our age. Dad warned me to watch myself around the old coot.

Poyner lived at the marina with his mother. A snaggletooth old man in a dirty ribbed tank top undershirt and stained khaki pants, he was the embodiment of evil to us kids. These days the old man walked with a limp and wore a patch over one eye, for which he held me responsible. I was, in a way, but he shouldn't have touched me.

#

Two years earlier, with Hains gone to football camp, Doodie at his grandmother's, and Cindy on a trip with her mother, Mali and I were left on our own. On that particular hot August morning, we decided to pick our way along the shoreline down to the marina for a frosty Dr. Pepper. Everyone knew the marina had the best drink box around — so cold it formed frost on the outside of the bottles. The best part was they kept the candy bars in the dairy cooler.

I'd been to the marina with my grandma, but never on my own. It would have been more convenient to walk to Swann's store across from the courthouse or over to the Doe service station, where my dad would have probably given us the drinks and candy for free. At nine years old, the adventure made the spoils taste so much better.

We were too young to ride our bikes on the highway. That was about our only restriction. No one knew where we were going and, as far as we knew, no one cared. It took all morning to travel the half a mile by shoreline. We explored and lollygagged along the way. We arrived at the marina just before noon. We had saved our pennies until we had enough to buy two drinks and a candy bar to split plus the tax, sixty-eight cents.

"Vado: to hasten, to rush," Malachi repeated.

"Yep, that's the word of the day," I said, my feet dangling off the end of the dock.

"I think it's cool how your dad learns a Latin word every day. He's been home for almost a year. That's nearly three hundred and sixty-five new words we learned too."

Malachi's legs were longer. His feet swung back and forth under the edge of the dock and skimmed the surface of the slick calm bay. We watched trails of water fly from his toes on each swing, while we waited for our clothes to dry. A big sign on the marina store door read, "No Wet Bathing Suits."

I picked at the weathered gray dock board and asked my lifelong friend, "Have you ever looked at that Latin dictionary my dad carries everywhere, I mean really looked at it?"

He answered, "No, he always has it in his back pocket."

I lowered my voice so as not to be overheard, although there wasn't another soul in sight. "It has blood on it."

Malachi lowered his voice too, asking, "Real blood?"

"Yeah, I think so, and other stuff," I whispered.

"What kind of other stuff?" Malachi winced, anticipating my answer.

I leaned in and mouthed the word, "Brains."

Malachi's eyes widened. "Whose is it?"

"I'm not allowed to ask my dad about Vietnam or how part of his foot got blown off. Grandma says to leave him be."

"It's been kind of weird since he came home."

"What do you mean?"

"We don't really know him. He's only been here a few times since we were born."

"He was in the Marines. He couldn't be home, but he sent cards and letters to Grandma and me."

"He doesn't act like a dad."

I nodded because I knew what Malachi meant. "Yeah, he's cool and all, but he's more like an older brother than a dad, like JP and Cindy."

"He's still stuck in the suck. That's what Doodie's dad said, whatever that means."

"He screams a lot at night. Grandma said that's why he drinks so much. Says we got to give him time to adjust."

"It's been almost a year, Jane. How long will it take?"

I sighed and stared out over the vast sound waters. "I hear him crying sometimes."

30

"Hey! What are you two doing down there?"

We both flinched when old man Poyner's gravelly voice pierced the quiet.

We scampered to our feet, while I explained quickly, "Hey, Mr. Poyner. We're drying off before we go in to get a drink."

The door to the marina store opened and Mrs. Poyner, the old man's mother, stuck her head out to yell to her son, "I'm going upstairs for my nap now." She paused, waiting for a reply. When none came, she called out, "Eldon, do you hear me?"

He waved in his mother's general direction. He continued to glare at Malachi and me, his eyes bouncing from one to the other. He finally answered, "Yeah, yeah. I hear you."

Mrs. Poyner didn't acknowledge Malachi and I were there. I'm not sure she saw us. She disappeared into the shadows behind the creaking wooden screen door.

As the door slapped shut, old man Poyner smiled down at me. Cavernous darkness surrounded his one remaining upper front tooth. He had partials, false teeth that filled the voids, but rarely wore them. I saw him sporting a full set of ill-fitting fake choppers at a funeral my grandma dragged me to. He looked like a different man that day, clean and smiling. Apparently, cleanliness and his teeth weren't necessary while working on the marina docks. Neither was sobriety. His stench surrounded us before we reached him.

"Well, get on in there and take care of your business. I don't want no children playin' 'round here. You fall in and drown and my insurance goes up."

We hurried ahead of the old man. Malachi yanked the door open.

"Where do you think you're going, boy? Ain't no coloreds allowed in the front door. Been that way for over three hundred years. Don't see no need to change 'cause some man in Washington put his name to a paper. He don't live here." He shooed Malachi off. "You go on around back. I'll serve you out the walk-up window like the rest of your kind."

At nine years old, we didn't argue with adult rules. We mostly did as we were told. Malachi let the door handle fall from his hand. The spring snapped the door closed with a slap. We jumped down from the small porch and headed around back.

"Where you goin', girl?"

We stopped. I turned around to answer, "I'm going around back, so you can serve us at the window."

"That window is for coloreds. White people don't get served there."

31

"But Mali and I are cousins—"

Old man Poyner laughed. "It don't work that way girlie. Go on in the door there. Boy, you go on 'round back."

I squinted against the sun and back at the old man's silhouette, unable to see his features. "Why can't he wait out here for me?"

"I ain't havin' no colored boy hangin' out on my porch like he's waitin' on a handout. Others'll git ideas."

"Can I pay for his and he can wait around back until I call for him?"

"I don't care how the money comes, just so it does. And out back is where he'll go if he wants to stay here."

Confused, but bound to retrieve the ice cold drinks we came for, I took the little change purse Malachi had kept in his bathing suit pocket, and we separated. I went to the front door.

Malachi disappeared around the corner, yelling over his shoulder, "I'll be right back here."

By the time I got to the door, the old man was holding it open for me. I almost gagged when I had to dip under his arm to enter the small store. Made of wide hand-hewed planks, the floor creaked beneath my feet. My grandmother said that part of the marina store was there when she was a girl. I headed straight for the refrigerated box with the frosty drinks inside.

Poyner said, "I need to get the change box. Find what you want and put it on the counter over there. I'll take your money for the drinks when I come back."

He went through the store and exited into the depths of the marina. I grabbed two Dr. Peppers, making sure each had just the tiniest bit of ice forming at the surface of the liquid. Since no one was looking, I licked the thin coating of frost on the sides of the bottles.

I closed the drink box and walked over to the dairy cooler to dig out the Milky Way we had decided to split. The tall two-door unit stood in the back corner, near the hall that led to the newer parts of the marina, where old man Poyner had vanished. Down that hall were the shops for fishing and hunting gear. At the far end of a run of buildings, they sold marine equipment and motor parts. The marina had anything a fisherman, from commercial to weekend enthusiast, could need.

I heard a thump, like something fell up against the hallway wall, but outside. Muffled voices followed. Then more thumping, turning to banging, and then I heard it loud and clear.

"Jane! Help! Jaaaaane!"

The cry screamed through a crack somewhere down the dim hallway. I ran toward a slanting beam of light on the opposite wall, followed its source, and found a door to the outside. I dropped the bottles of soda at my feet. They clanked together. One of them exploded into a fizz cannon, soaking everything in reach including me. I fumbled with the lock and yanked the door open.

Blinding brightness filled the darkness. I jumped down the two steps to the ground, shielding my eyes, trying to focus. I could hear Mali.

"Stop it, you old freak!"

When I could see again, I saw Malachi's face pressed against the wall. The old man, his dick in his hand, was trying to shove it into my friend's naked ass. Mali's swimsuit was pulled down to his knees. Tears streaked his cheeks.

"No!" he screamed and struggled to free himself.

"You'll take it boy and keep your mouth shut about it, like the rest of 'em. You hear me?"

The old man was so focused on the squirming nine-year-old in his grasp, he forgot about the other one. I reached back into the doorway, grabbed the still full bottle of soda, and charged ahead before I could scare myself out of it.

"Ahhhhhhhhhhhh!"

Old man Poyner turned just in time for me to slam that bottle across his right brow. The bottle broke and sliced a gash from his eyebrow to his cheekbone. Poyner's hand flew to his face. He pulled it away and looked at the blood dripping through his fingers. His eyes rose to meet mine, then he roared—really roared like a lion or a beast from down below.

"Run!" I screamed at Malachi, who had fallen to the ground wrestling with pulling his wet swimsuit back up.

I should have yelled after I started running, not before. I made only one step before Poyner grabbed my arm in a vice-like grip.

"Let go of me."

The old man's stink wrapped around me as he pulled me against him and clamped an arm over my chest.

"Let me go. My dad is gonna kill you. He's crazy. He killed all kinds of people in 'Nam."

Mali made it to his feet but froze, staring at me, eyes wide with terror.

"Get help, Mali. Vado! Ru—"

33

Poyner's blood-covered hand covered my mouth and nose. I kicked at his legs and screamed against his palm, but I was no match for this grown man. Even though he was small of stature, Poyner's strength was too much to overcome. Mali disappeared from sight as the old man dragged me back into the store. I don't remember much about what happened next. I don't try to.

The next thing I do recall was walking down the dirt path toward the road when my father met me in his wrecker with Malachi on the seat beside him. I was naked, my bathing suit having been ripped off in the struggle with the old man, my body painted with handprints in dried blood.

A dust cloud enveloped me when the wrecker slid to a stop. In seconds, John Doe flew out of the cab of the truck and limped toward me as fast as his half a foot would allow. He pulled his tee shirt off over his head as he approached. He checked me head to toe. I had a few bruises and scrapes, a black eye and a cut lip.

He asked, "Where is all this blood coming from?"

Malachi, now out of the truck, said, "It's the old man's. She cut his face with a bottle."

Dad pulled his tee shirt over my head and helped me get my arms through. He looked into my eyes, searching for life it seemed. I still had not spoken.

"You're okay, Jane. You're safe now. He'll never hurt you again."

"He's a bad man," I said, and that was the last thing that came out of my mouth for weeks.

Malachi, however, was full of ideas. "Are you going to kill him?"

My dad picked me up and told Malachi to get back in the truck. He carried me to the driver's side and slid me across to the middle. He reached over me to the glove box and took out a pistol. He turned to look at us. His focus bounced between our frightened eyes. I could smell the trace of alcohol on his breath. It was ever-present, like familiar cologne to me by now.

"Lock the doors. Stay here until I come back or the sheriff comes. Do not get out of this truck."

He left the truck running and turned up the radio. We stayed put until my dad came limping back to sit in the cab of the wrecker with us and wait for the law to arrive because they were coming. Sirens wailed in the distance. Sheriff Forster, Hains's father, stopped to talk to us through the window and then continued down to the marina alone.

When the patrol car returned to where we were sitting in the wrecker, the Sheriff said, "Looks like someone locked a couple of wild cats up in that little store. The ambulance is on its way to pick up that dirty old man back there. I don't know which one of you did the most damage. You go on and take Jane to Dr. Mead's office and get her checked out. He's waiting for you. We'll discuss that accidental discharge of your weapon when you get back home."

Afterward, I stayed silent about all of it. My grandmother would say it was the only time in my life I wasn't talking someone's ear off. What Malachi had to say should have been enough, but a black boy doesn't count for much when testifying against a white man, even a bad one. Sheriff Forster spoke to the District Attorney and Judge Spencer. That was the end of it.

"We could have put him away, John, if you hadn't shot him in the foot," the Sheriff told my dad. "We had to make a deal to keep you out of prison."

When I did start talking again, I never spoke of the time inside the marina store. Two years had passed, and I still had told no one what transpired between that old man and me. The vagueness of my story left much to the collective imagination of the county, hence my shaky virgin status and our current quest to find a real one.

#

"Monday Night Football. This is The Flip Wilson Show. Do you read? Over."

We went by our favorite television shows for code names. Of course, the boy who wanted to be the next great NFL quarterback loved the new football night on TV. All of our must-watch shows changed as often as the seasons' new offerings. Malachi liked variety shows and bounced between Flip Wilson and Carol Burnett. I had recently switched to Alias Smith and Jones from Ironside.

"This is The Mary Tyler Moore Show. I have the radio. Over."

Malachi and I had stopped our bikes in the bushes on the creek behind the marina store, out of sight. We could see Poyner on the marina docks. If we broke out of the bushes and headed for the campground docks, he would certainly see us. The ends of both structures were close enough to step from one dock to the other. If he decided to finally follow through on one of his many threats since the Doe family scarred and lamed him for life, we'd be sitting ducks on that dock.

I forgot we were trying to be quiet when I grabbed the walkie talkie from Mali's hand and shouted into it, "Why in the hell do you have the radio, Cindy?"

"Use code names, please. And say over. Over."

"Why in the hell do you have the radio, Mary? Over."

"Identify yourself. Over"

"Oh, for the love of—"

"Just do it. You know how she is," Malachi said.

"This is Alias Smith and Jones asking why the radio she gave to Columbo and Monday Night Football is still back there with you?"

We heard nothing but static for a few seconds. It felt like minutes, but it could have only been seconds. It was long enough for Cindy to answer us.

"Mary Tyler Moore Show, are you there?"

"You have to say 'over' when you're done talking. Over."

I rolled my eyes for Malachi to see. "Mary Tyler Moore Show, this is Alias Smith and Jones asking how you having the radio is supposed to help us communicate with the other party on this reconnaissance mission? Over."

"I'm your backup. Over."

"I thought we talked about this. Over."

"We decided you were wrong. Over."

"I'm going to kill her one day," I said to Malachi.

He laughed. "You always say that, but you end up doing what she wants. Cindy Spencer has a way."

"I'm still going to kill her."

The radio crackled. "Are you there, Alias Smith and Jones? Over?"

"Yeah, I'm here, and now I'm going away. We'll call if we need you. Over."

I turned the radio off before Cindy could say anything else. I handed it back to Malachi.

He suggested, "We could wait here. We can see them land the boat."

"We have to meet them on the dock. You know they'll say we were last."

Malachi straddled his ten-speed bike beside me. "My mom said the judge told Poyner he had to stop threatening us kids or the deal they made was going to be torn up. Maybe he'll go away when he sees us coming."

"Yeah, and maybe a snappin' turtle will turn you loose if you ask it nicely."

Poyner's head turned as if he heard us. We took a step deeper into the woods. That's when we heard the campground kids laughing as they rode toward us on bicycles. There were three of them today, all boys. I recognized one of them, Simon. He'd been coming down to stay with his grandparents at the campground since he was a little kid.

Simon Corby was Cindy's age, a year older than the rest of us. He didn't come up to the courthouse anymore. His grandparents thought we were too wild for Simon to play with after the incident with old man Poyner. I hadn't seen him in the two years since, but there was no mistaking that cowlick of red hair above his forehead. The three boys slowed in front of us.

One of Simon's fellow riders asked, "Did you see that old freak out there staring at us."

"He's still staring at us," the other one said.

"He's psycho." Simon encouraged his companions, "Let's go down to Swann's store at the courthouse."

The smallest of his companions said, "Simon, I can't go on the highway."

Simon smiled back over his shoulder, and said, "Then don't be on it long." He pushed down hard on the right pedal, his butt rising above the seat, as he shouted, "Last one there has to pay a quarter to the first one."

Malachi looked as if he was about to draw Simon's attention to us, but I tugged on his arm and shook my head. I saw Poyner turning, coming toward the marina store, the one we were hiding behind.

We let Simon and his pals disappear around the bend in the path before I said, "Come on. Let's go."

I didn't always lead, and Mali didn't always follow, but most times, when one of us felt strongly about something, the other went along without question. It had worked for us since we broke out of the playpen the first time when I followed Mali over the top rail at his urging.

We emerged from the bushes and headed for the campground docks. I didn't look toward the marina where Poyner had been. I pedaled as fast as I could on the hard-packed path. My skinny ten-speed tires dug into the occasional powdery soft spots. Malachi stayed with me, pedal for pedal.

Just past the end of the dock, we could see Hains and Doodie in the skiff. We skidded to a stop and ran onto the dock, mere seconds before the bow of the boat gently tapped the protective bumper. Doodie threw a rope up to Malachi.

"I think it's a tie," Hains said.

I did not agree. "We were here a while. We had to hide from old man Poyner."

37

"Only folks needs to hide is thieves and liars. The nigger's the liar, so that makes you the whore thief."

Poyner had come onto the campground dock, stinking of whiskey, his pants unzipped, wearing the same nasty tee shirt he always wore. He'd been saying since day one that Malachi lied. His excuse for my injuries was that he caught me stealing and I fought him when he tried to wrestle the candy from my grip. The snarling pervert in front of me was the only person who believed the beating I took was over a handful of candy.

Hains leaped onto the dock. Graceful like a deer, his athletic prowess was a wonder to behold. However, Hains most incredible asset was his calmness in the heat of battle. Poyner had not known Hains was there, or he wouldn't have confronted us. He was too much of a coward to mess with the Sheriff's kid.

Hains stepped between Poyner and the rest of us. "Mr. Poyner, we don't want any trouble. You need to just go on back to your dock, and we'll go about our business. There's no need to have my father come out and explain how this is going to go again, is there?"

At eleven and a half, Hains was already five feet six inches tall. His dad stood six feet five inches. Hains and Doodie, side by side, made a formidable pair. Doodie wasn't as tall, but he was thick and what my grandma called country strong. He'd managed to finally make it up the dock ladder and stumbled to Hains's side.

He panted for air, while he said, "Yeah, we don't want any trouble."

Poyner's pupils floated in a bloodshot pool of yellow, barely visible under drooping lids. He looked past Hains, focused on me. He was a grown up and we were kids, but he was a little guy. I heard Hains's dad say Poyner suffered from "little man complex." He was mad at the world for being a squirt.

The coward Poyner could overpower one of us, but the four of us could handle him easily. One good rush and we could send him into the water to cool off or sober up—or drown. I prayed every night that he would stumble off the dock in a drunken stupor and free the world of his stink.

Malachi said that I have a twitch in my jaw muscle when I'm about to say something I'll regret. He must have seen it. He whispered at my side, "Let him go, Jane."

"Hey, Hains. What's happ'nin'?" Jeremy Bartlett, one of the trailer park boys, pedaled up to the dock on a banana seat bike with apehanger handlebars. His brother Johnny trailed behind him with the Pine twins, Randy and Sandy, all on bikes modified with borrowed parts.

Johnny, the older Bartlett brother, slid to a stop, throwing sand at the old man's feet. He was thirteen and had hair on his chin and chest. He always wore a bandana tied around his bushy mane. Johnny was handsome but always seemed to be covered in dirt or grease. I read "The Outsiders" and thought Johnny Bartlett would have been a Greaser with a nickname like Biker Johnny or something. He could be our friend or our worst nightmare. We never knew how it was going to go.

"Is this pervert botherin' you again, Jane?"

Happy day! Johnny was going to be on our side this time. Poyner might have thought about the night or two in jail he would get if he messed with the Sherrif's kid, but the threat of an ass-kicking the extended Bartlett family could bestow—the trailer park was full of them—carried a heavier weight. Poyner began backing away immediately, but he was too much of an asshole to retreat quietly.

"One day, I'll find you alone, girl. I'll finish what I started. You'll pay for what you done." He made a slashing gesture across his patched eye down to his chin. "You'll pay in kind."

Malachi's hand grabbed my arm before I could react, but his grip did not slow me. My brain had done the math, and I saw my chance. I pulled away and pushed through Hains and Doodie to face my nemesis.

I glared back at the old man. "They should notch your ears like a sow and throw you in the pig wallow. You smell about like one."

"I ought to teach you what I taught your momma about her mouth."

Anytime someone mentioned my mother, I got kind of prickly. I didn't know her. She left me on my father's doorstep and went to Virginia Beach. The closest thing I had to knowing her was my Aunt Joyce, Doodie's mom, and from that, I knew I didn't care to know much about the rest of that side of my family. I loved Doodie, but his momma made my skin crawl. I never understood why. I just avoided her if I could. I tried not to go in Doodie's house if I could help it. It might have been the pictures all around their home of my mother's family. The worst were the ones of her and Aunt Joyce when they were kids, happy and smiling. It just gave me the creeps.

I took a step forward and repeated what I had heard said about me, "My grandma said I ain't nothin' like my momma, 'cause I don't run from trouble. Neither does my dad. If you want him to take another shot at you, I bet he doesn't just shoot you in the foot next time. I hope he gets your balls." I sneered intently, adding "They're so small, I bet he can get both of 'em with one shot."

Malachi couldn't control himself and shouted, "And your tiny dick too."

Poyner thought about taking a step toward me but then thought again as Johnny stepped up beside me. Hains and Doodie stood on one side, Johnny on the other, with the rest of the boys joining us on the dock.

"You've touched your last kid, old man," Johnny said, laughing in Poyner's face. He leaned a little closer and spoke in a whisper, so the old man had to turn his head a bit to hear, when Johnny warned, "You touch one of my little brothers and I'll skin you alive myself."

The old man turned and limped away.

Johnny said, "Doe, someday that old man is going to find you alone."

"I'll kill him if he touches me again," I said. I had not hesitated and delivered the threat with the coldness I felt toward that pustule of a man.

"Whoa, big talk for a little girl," Johnny replied. "I hope Poyner doesn't call your bluff."

Malachi turned to head toward the spot where we discarded our bikes. He told Johnny, "What makes you think she's bluffing?"

Doodie followed and chimed in, "Yeah, don't make Jane mad. She holds a grudge."

Hains chuckled. "She's patient too. Jane will wait until you forget she's after you and then wham, out of nowhere, you get a water balloon to the face."

Doodie agreed. "It's even worse when she puts food coloring in the water."

Johnny ignored the others and looked into my eyes. We exchanged a look of empathetic knowing. I believed Johnny understood the kind of feral hatred I felt for Poyner. The white circular scars on his arms were healed cigarette burns received from his mother's boyfriend, who went by the infamous name of Porky. A pot-dealing domestic abuser, Porky went to prison for charges stemming from a giant fight between the entire family, Johnny included. Unfortunately for Porky, he was splitting up a pound of homegrown when the shit hit the fan. Johnny's mother still visited her man every month behind bars. Yeah, Johnny understood the kind of loathing I had for old man Poyner. Porky would be coming home soon.

"Don't provoke that old drunk," Johnny warned. "He'll die soon enough."

"Today is not soon enough," I said.

Jeremy asked, "So, what are you doing down here at the campground?"

Doodie answered, "We're looking for Jane's cousin, Olin."

Randy and Sandy repeated in unison, "Olin?" Then Randy asked, "What do you need him for?"

Doodie would never make it as a criminal. He couldn't keep a secret. "We need Olin to kiss a virgin."

Johnny shook his head. "You what?"

Malachi tried to cover Doodie's blunder. "We need Olin for a...a...Dammit, Doodie. Man, you just can't help yourself."

Hains must have decided a lie wouldn't work at this point. He explained, "We need a guy kin to Jane that will kiss a virgin and then dive for a treasure at the ferry dock. The kiss will protect the diver from the monster."

Johnny laughed. "There ain't no monster down at the ferry dock. Just trees and stuff gets pushed into the channel. People get hung up and drown."

"How do you know?" I asked.

"If you don't believe me, I'll go jump off the ferry dock right now."

Sandy said, "You can't jump now, the ferry still has a couple of more runs."

We played all over that ferry dock, but only when the dockworkers were gone for the day. The ferry ran during daylight hours and overnighted on the mainland, so the last run was at least an hour before sunset. Our limited dive window approached, and we still had no virgin.

"Wait, did you say treasure?" Jeremy had been paying attention.

Johnny laughed. "Kids games. Check ya later." He jumped on his bike and pedaled away.

The other three trailer park boys were not ready to dismiss the treasure adventure so easily. They stayed with us as we moved our bikes to the big tree at the end of the dock and stacked theirs with ours.

"Have you seen Olin today?" I asked Sandy as we walked toward the trailer park on the other side of the campground.

"Yeah, he had to cut the grass at the park today. He should be done by now."

41

Olin's parents owned the trailer park and lived in the big double-wide out by the road. The land, a part of the Doe family's original grant, had been the source of the dispute between my side of the family and Olin's. We found him driving the riding lawnmower back to the shed.

"I can't go with you. I still have to finish the ditch up by the road with the push mower. Mom said she'd tan my hide if it weren't done by the time she and Dad got back from town."

We had explained our mission, and Olin seemed willing, but his mother was formidable, and he wasn't about to cross her. Not many would. Olive Doe Walker stood six feet tall and weighed three hundred and fifty pounds. She seemed mad at the world because of it. Her husband, Delbert Walker, weighed one-fifty, maybe.

Jeremy and the Pine twins huddled together and then called Olin over to them. They spoke for a few minutes and then turned back to us. Jeremy acted as their spokesperson.

"Olin will do it if you guys mow the ditch. We have three mowers. It'll get done faster, and we can get to the docks right after the last ferry leaves, while it's still light. Oh, and we want a fifty-fifty split."

"Sixty-forty," Hains offered in return.

"Deal," Jeremy said.

Hains shook Jeremy's hand and declared, without consulting anyone else, that we would accept the terms. "Deal. Now, where are the mowers?"

I had no intentions of cutting grass with that many boys around to do it. Brain, not brawn, my dad would say. I didn't give anyone a chance to argue with me.

I started walking away and said to the group, "I'm going back to the campground to look for Maria."

Doodie, who wasn't a real fan of manual labor, volunteered, "I'll come with you. In case those campground boys give you any trouble."

"We saw them earlier. They went to Swann's. I want to find Maria before they get back. Meet me by the bikes when you're done."

Maria Larking lived in Lynchburg, Virginia during the school year, but stayed with her family at the campground all summer. We had known her since we were old enough to walk this far from home, about six years. Maria was pretty, with sandy blonde hair and brown eyes, but not prissy like Cindy. All the boys loved Maria. I liked her too. In fact, Cindy was the only person I knew that didn't think Maria was cool.

Of course, the campground boys would guard their princess against neighboring young males who might challenge for her attention, but maybe they wouldn't notice me, and we could get the kiss done without anyone else discovering our quest for the treasure. I thought I could talk Maria into kissing Olin just one time. He wasn't gross. Olin was kind of cute when his acne was under control. It wasn't too bad today. I had an idea about how to make kissing him a more manageable proposition to sell to Maria.

As I ran off in the direction of the campground, I called back to Malachi, "Clean him up, Mali. Make sure he smells good."

He yelled back, "Watch out for Poyner."

I wasn't scared of that old man, but I stopped to pick up a sturdy stick before I reached the campground.

#

I found Maria on her parents' back deck, sprawled in a lounge chair reading Jonathan Livingston Seagull. She was twelve and going into seventh grade like Cindy. Decking surrounded the family travel trailer on three sides. The wooden structure stayed the same, but the camper had changed several times. She smiled when she saw me approaching.

"Jane Doe. I haven't seen you all summer. Did you find a boyfriend to keep you busy?"

I still could not understand why girls' worlds revolved around finding and keeping a boyfriend. It just boggled me. Boys surrounded me all the time.

"That's not it. I just haven't been around, that's all."

"Where have you been?"

"Down home, mostly."

"Well, what are you doing here now?"

"I need you to do something for me."

Maria grinned and closed the book, "What?"

"What if I told you that after you do it, you get to kiss Hains?"

Maria wrinkled her nose. "Is that supposed to be a reward?"

"I thought you liked him."

"That was last summer."

My plan to appeal to Maria's crush on our resident stud was crumbling.

"Who do you like now?"

Maria put the book on the little table beside her chair and stood. She indicated I should follow her. We walked to the edge of the deck and leaned on the railing facing the water.

"I like this guy I'm not supposed to. My parents don't like his parents, so I'm not allowed to be with him. It's very Romeo and Juliet."

"Who are they?"

"You don't know who Romeo and Juliet are?"

"No, are they from Lynchburg?"

Maria laughed at me, which felt kind of weird in my stomach.

"No, silly. They're from Shakespeare," she explained.

"I don't know where that is," I said, and then got on with my quest. "Where is this new boy and are you still a virgin?"

"Jane!" Maria laughed again. "Of course, I'm still a virgin. I haven't even kissed him yet. What a strange thing to ask."

"It's for a thing. Anyway, where does this guy live?"

I was hoping he didn't live here, because what he didn't know wouldn't hurt him, and I thought I could still talk Maria into kissing Olin to save him from sure death at the hands of the ferry dock monster. I didn't care what Johnny said. Some evil force lurked in that dark water. I had feared it my entire life. I could swim like a fish, but I wouldn't dive off the ferry dock, no way!

"He lives here," Maria said and dashed my hopes, but then she kept talking, "People don't really know him like I do. He's shy and sweet. When his face clears up, he'll be adorable, I think."

"Olin? You like Olin Walker?" My heart jumped with joy.

"Yes, but you can't tell anyone. My mother hates Olive Walker."

"You and Olin Walker. Wow," I said, unable to fathom our luck.

"He's nice. He brings me flowers and leaves notes for me in our secret place."

"That's cool, Maria."

I think she thought I was approving of her romantic interest in Olin. It was cool because it made my job easier. She smiled at me, and I remembered why everyone loved Maria. For just a moment, I wished I were the Doe she was about to kiss.

She asked, "What did you want me to do, anyway?"

It was my turn to laugh. "You're not going to believe this."

6

Who thought this was a good idea...

After promising Mrs. Larking that we would bring her daughter back before dark, Maria climbed into the boat with Doodie and Hains. We had about an hour to complete our quest and return the virgin unscathed. Mali and I led the bicycle contingent down the highway toward the ferry dock. We rushed to make preparations before the virgin arrived on her royal barge.

Jeremy and the Pine twins went to the ferry dock with Olin, while Mali and I broke off to retrieve the big pulley and some rope we had gathered for lowering our "male Doe" into the abyss.

"Jane, if Johnny said there's no monster, why are we going through all this to break a curse that don't exist?"

Malachi was thin and not as strong as Doodie and Hains. He wasn't even as stout as me, but he said God made me tough and him pretty. He got the better deal. I carried the massive head block on ahead, while Malachi struggled with the thick coil of rope, dragging it up the hill to the ferry dock from the boathouse.

I dismissed his concerns about the monster's existence. "Better safe than sorry, Mali. Do you think Doodie remembered the waterproof flashlight?"

"Yes. I saw it in the boat. Ugh," Mali grunted against the weight of his burden. "We have too much rope."

"Do you know how deep the ferry dock hole is?" I asked and watched him shake his head. "Neither do I. No one we know has ever touched bottom and come out alive."

Our conversation stopped as we crested the little hill and heard the disturbance. The ground vibrated as the last ferry's propellers gathered speed and rumbled away, while a rumble of another kind had begun on the dock. The campground boys had run into the trailer park boys.

I looked at Mali. "Is there ever a time when boys don't pick sides and fight?"

Mali smiled. He rarely caused trouble and floated between social groups with ease.

"Only when there is someone they can fight together. So don't give them a reason to make that someone us."

"That has to be why they invented football, to keep y'all from killin' each other all the time."

As we approached, we heard Jeremy say, "Go home to your mommy, pussy."

"At least my mom doesn't get her dresses from Omar the tent maker, like Olin's mom," replied one of Simon's friends.

"Oh, yeah," Olin shot back, "well, your mom is a campground tent tramp."

Bikes hit the ground, and tempers flared. Boys and their mothers— I doubted I would ever understand them at all. Ignoring Mali's advice, I intervened.

"Hey, fellas. My mother left me on my grandma's doorstep an hour after I was born and just took off. She forgot to see if anyone was home. It was November. I could have frozen to death before someone found me. My pecker froze off, and now I'm a girl. I win the worst mother prize."

Malachi's eyes widened. He could never believe it when I would tell people that story. I loved the shock value of it. My frozen pecker embellishment depended on the audience, but the rest was totally true. Mothers who would do what mine did unnerve people. Although everyone had a mother, very few had one who would wrap a newborn in a tee shirt with a bloody umbilical cord still attached and stuff it into a canvas gym bag she pulled from the trash behind the high school, complete with crusty socks and a dirty jock strap.

Joan Smith had me in the girls' locker room, walked across the road to deposit me on my dad's doorstep, and then waited at Swann's store for the next Greyhound out of town. Knowing the Smith family as I did, I was fortunate that Joan chose to leave me with Virginia Swann Doe, my grandmother, who knew exactly what to do with a wild child like me—let her run. Joan had not been back to North Carolina again, as far as I knew. I heard she lived in Tidewater Virginia somewhere, but I didn't care to know more than that. She could live her life. Mine was going along fine without her.

My worst mother ploy worked. The boys focused on me long enough to distract them from their testosterone infused squabbling.

I asked the Pine twins, "Hey, can you help Mali pull that rope up the hill?"

They hesitated to leave Jeremy and Olin alone to stand off Simon and his two friends. I kept moving until I was standing in the middle of the two factions.

"Hi, Simon. Whatcha doin' at the ferry dock?"

Simon smiled now. We had always gotten along. "We came to Swann's. Old man Poyner was watching us at the marina, and no one was around to keep him from being a pervert. Whatcha doin' with that rope and stuff?"

"We're going to tie Olin to the end of the rope and drop him off the ferry dock to see what he can find down there."

It wasn't a lie. I just failed to mention the treasure.

The older of Simon's companions asked, "Cool, can we watch?"

A station wagon slowed to a stop on the road.

All our heads turned when the driver yelled out the open windows, "Robert Wright, I'm going to skin you alive."

The smaller campground kid turned pale. He must have been Robert.

The woman with a red scarf tied around her beehive hairdo crooked a finger at her son and said, "Let's go! I'm following you back to the campground. And you two, Wilson, Simon, your mothers said to bring you home with Robby."

I saw the skiff approaching. While being followed home by a station wagon with its hazard lights on and driven by a housewife in a red scarf had to be humiliating, I was glad Robby's mother showed up when she did. Our luck was holding so far. Just a few more minutes and the treasure would be ours.

Simon shrugged. "I guess we have to go. See you 'round."

We all said some version of "Yeah, see ya later," and watched the embarrassed campground kids pedal away. We wasted little time on pity for their humiliating pedal down the highway and quickly returned to the task at hand.

"Help me hang this from that cable over there," I said, and handed the pulley to Jeremy. "Randy and Sandy, help Mali get the rope laid out and get Olin tied up. You need to make a seat, like a breeches buoy. We got to hurry."

"Well, I see you found your male Doe," Cindy said.

I hadn't seen her approaching. All the boys except Malachi turned to mush in her presence. She was holding up progress.

I interrogated her, "What are you doing here? Where's the radio?"

"I thought you still needed a virgin to kiss him and the batteries died because you wouldn't answer."

Mali filled her in. "We got another virgin."

The hum of Hains's skiff motor approached the ferry dock. Cindy smiled when the sound reached her ears. She had staked claim to Hains Forster. I knew that when she saw Maria sitting on the seat beside him, it wasn't going to be pretty.

"Hey, go get the radio. We need it to communicate with the boat."

I hadn't made the request soon enough. Cindy walked closer to the water and saw the boat approaching and then turned on me.

"You went to get her? You didn't need Maria Larking. I would have kissed Olin. He's not that bad."

Olin shifted his weight from foot to foot and turned bright pink, accentuating the pimples as blood rushed to the surface of his skin. Mali had done a pretty good job of cleaning him up. His shirt was different and didn't have stains on it, and the grass clippings had been combed from his hair. He smelled like freshly mowed lawn, gasoline, and Old Spice.

"You had your chance," I said, as I climbed the creosote-soaked piling to hang the pulley Jeremy held up to me. "Hand me the end of the rope," I said to Mali, "so I can thread it through."

"I can't believe you, Jane Doe. You know she hates me."

I gathered rope into my hands as my thighs and feet gripped the pole. I was sure I'd have a rash from the sticky creosote, but I was willing to sacrifice for the cause and to keep from losing my footing. I wasn't afraid of falling in the water. It was crashing into the structure below me that caused the most concern. While trying not to die, I answered Cindy.

"I don't think she hates you. I don't even think she knows who you are."

That was mean, and I knew it. Cindy had been a pain throughout this whole ordeal. She deserved some crap.

"You want Hains to like her. I know you do," she whined.

"This is bigger than you and your obsession with boys, Cindy. Go get the radio. We need it."

Cindy bargained, "Tell her to go home and I will."

Malachi played peacemaker. "Cindy, you said no. We found someone who said yes. Now, if you want to help, we need the walkie talkie. The sooner we get done, the faster she goes back to the campground."

It worked. Cindy stomped away. We all went back to our respective jobs. Hains pulled the boat up close to shore and let Maria out. She climbed the hill up to the dock.

"Hey, Olin," Maria said.

Olin turned absolutely crimson. I thought his zits might start popping.

"Hey, Maria," he mumbled.

"All right. Let's get this done. Kiss Olin so we can finish tying him up."

"Out here?" Maria apparently wasn't into public displays of affection.

Thinking quickly, Malachi led the kissers to the restrooms. I suggested the women's bathroom would be cleaner, after Maria balked at the men's room door. I promised to watch the door and they went inside to do the deed.

Doodie, whose mother took him to movies the rest of us had not seen, did his much-loved routine from "MASH" with a bit of editing, so the lovebirds could hear clearly.

"Oh, Olin. Oh, Olin. My lips are hot. Oh, kiss my hot lips."

We all giggled and wondered what was happening in there. Already the mysteries of human sexuality were beginning to pique our interest.

With his audience enjoying the impressions, Doodie went for his recent favorite. "He's got a real pretty mouth, ain't he?"

This quote from the new movie "Deliverance" was unknown to us except through Doodie's explanation because his mom had to pay the ticket man extra to sneak her eleven-year-old in. We only laughed because we thought we were supposed to. The giggles faded and waiting began to feel uncomfortable.

"All right. The sun's going down," I said, and stepped up to bang on the door. "That's enough. He won't be chaste if he stays in there much longer and you won't be a virgin."

That got a laugh.

When Olin reemerged, he smiled a lot and acted dazed. The boys made a rope seat that looped around each of Olin's legs and then wrapped around his waist a few times. His arousal made the rope seat uncomfortable, and he adjusted his crotch with his one free hand continuously. Maria clung to the other hand right up until the last possible moment, like a war bride warding off impending doom. She even worked up some tears.

I called down to Doodie and Hains. "Okay, we're going to lower him to you. He'll need to stop at the boat to get the flashlight. Do you have it?"

Doodie responded, waving the flashlight at me, "Got it."

I looked at Olin. "Are you ready?"

Olin seemed to realize the magnitude of this adventure. If the kiss worked, he would be the boy who defied the ferry dock monster. If not, he'd be its next victim.

"Are you sure you read the clue right, Jane?" Maria asked with the concern a fear-stricken girlfriend should exhibit.

I hated the drama girls created over boys. There were plenty to go around, I thought. I had little patience with the wilting flower routine.

"Yes, I read the clue right. Guys, grab the rope. We have to pull him up first and then swing him out over the water. Ready?"

There were mumbles of readiness before Olin said, "Let go of my hand, Maria. I have to hold on."

Maria stepped back. We tightened the slack, and I gave the order.

"Pull!"

I don't know what scared us all the most, the siren or the blood-curdling scream Olin let out when we pinched his balls in our makeshift rope lift.

"Drop that rope," Sheriff Law Forster yelled out his car window as he whipped his cruiser into the ferry dock driveway.

We had already lifted Olin high enough that he had begun to swing like a pendulum. We all let go on the Sheriff's order, which happened to coincide with an outward swing.

"Oh shit," were Olin's last words, before gravity took hold and he splashed into the water tangled in the now loose rope we had dropped as ordered.

The Sheriff jumped out of his vehicle and ran past me to look over the edge of the ferry-loading ramp.

"Hains, what in the hell are you doing?" The Sheriff looked back at me. "Never mind." He yelled down to his son, "Hey, get that boy out of the water and take the skiff home."

The Sheriff turned his full attention on me. I was always to blame if any of us got in trouble. I'm not sure why Hains's dad thought I was the mastermind on our capers, but I always took the responsibility without informing on my friends. Nobody was going to punish me; at least nothing horrible was going to happen to me. The worst I got was grounded until I drove Grandma crazy and she let me go just to be rid of me.

"Jane, who thought this was a good idea?"

"We were just going to dip him in the water and see what he could find down there."

Still not a lie, but explaining our true mission seemed counterproductive at the moment.

"The judge mentioned a treasure map. There is nothing valuable buried here. This place has been dug more than any other spot in the county. Archeologists cleaned out anything worth much back in the fifties when the state leased the land from your grandfather and built this ferry dock. Stop being numbskulls and risking your friends' lives over made up stories."

I quit listening at the word "judge." Cindy had ratted us out to her dad. I looked past the sheriff to see her standing at the edge of her yard, arms crossed defiantly. I stuck my tongue out at her.

"Hey! Cindy probably saved the life of that boy you had trussed up like a hog. Suppose he got tangled up in some of the trash that sinks down in there? You guys need to start using your heads for blah...blah...blah..."

I tuned out the latest adult lecture I'd endured in my lifetime and focused on why our plan failed. Cindy had ruined our chances at retrieving the treasure. We didn't often ask permission, but we rarely defied a direct command, especially from Hains's father. There would be no way I could talk the rest of them into helping me find the treasure now. I figured I'd have to wait until Malachi learned to swim or a male Doe cousin came to visit. Anyway, the treasure hunt was over, and we were sent home to lick our wounds.

#

"I can't believe she told on us," Hains said.

"I can." I was thoroughly disgusted at Cindy's betrayal. "Hand me the lantern."

Hains handed up one of the lanterns we built with old channel marker lights and batteries. This one glowed red as I hung it in the cupola at the top of the boathouse. It was a signal we used to gather the troops when needed. If I put up the green light, it just meant I was in the boathouse and all was well. We couldn't get the treasure tonight, but I still needed my friends for a mission—all but Cindy. She couldn't see the signal light and had to be properly summoned like the princess

51

she thought she was. On that night, no one wanted her along, least of all me.

"My dad wasn't really mad," Hains said. "I heard him laughing when he told mom about it. He didn't even punish me."

"Did he take Maria home?"

"Yeah, and he even let her out behind the marina so her mom wouldn't see him."

"That's cool. I'm glad you could come with me. I just didn't want to go down there tonight by myself. I saw JP and his friends walking that way."

JP Spencer terrorized us kids whenever he was home. He was eight years older than his sister and basically an all-around dickhead. We had all been ecstatic when he went away to college.

"Yeah, I saw 'em, too. Looked like they already had a few."

"Mr. Tommy called. He said Dad is having a rough night and the crowd was rowdy. He thought I ought to come get him before things went south."

John Doe came home from Vietnam in 1969, at least physically. Before that, he spent almost a year in a hospital, where they tried and failed to save his mind and most of his foot. For the first nine years of my life, my father had been enlisted in the Marines. A young man with a child had little choices for steady income. My grandparents raised me for the first eight years. I saw John Doe rarely in that time, but he was a constant in my life. My grandmother saw to that.

"It's weird how he'll do what you ask when he ignores everyone else," Hains said of my father.

"I guess 'cause I don't try to fix him." I climbed down the ladder from setting the light, answering Hains as I descended. "Everyone else wants him to smile and be happy. He's sad. Something bad happened to him. People need to just let him be."

After our treasure quest was foiled, we had all gone home for dinner and watched our respective guardians plop down in front of the television for a night of primetime sitcoms. We were able to roam about until around ten o'clock when the stadium lights went off on the baseball field at the high school. The school was just down from the courthouse and across the main road. The glow from the ball field could be seen from our homes and served as our curfew indicator. Fifteen minutes after the sky went dark, my friends were expected to be home. My curfew was breakfast. My grandmother kept track of me by the meals I showed up for.

The ballgames at the high school were our excuse to hang out after dark. When we turned twelve, we'd all join the county league and play on teams. Until then, we could go to the field and play cup ball behind the bleachers with our peers from around the county, or say we did and find some other mischief to occupy our warm summer nights.

The door to the boathouse opened. Malachi walked in with Doodie right behind.

"Momma sent this," Malachi said, holding out a plate covered in tin foil.

Taking care of John Doe had become a neighborhood project. Bertie, Malachi's mother, loved John like a brother.

"She said to feed him before we put him to bed. Said if we had any trouble call her on the walkie talkie. I left it with her. You got yours?"

"Yeah. It's over there on the shelf."

Doodie picked it up. "Can I carry it this time?"

I exchanged looks with Mali and Hains. After a mutual nod, I answered, "Yes, but keep the antenna in until we need to use it. You 'bout beat me to death with it last time you carried it."

Doodie saluted. "Aye, aye, captain."

I shook my head. I loved the guy, but he was so goofy sometimes. I unplugged the light, opened the door, and led my friends out of our innocence.

#

Because John Doe was a functioning alcoholic, he did two things every day, work and drink. I suppose I should have been glad he restricted his intake to beer. Dad told me once that liquor made him crazy. Since I had seen what beer could do, I was thankful he abstained from stronger things. John Doe didn't do hard drugs like a lot of veterans. He said he'd watched heroin destroy people. I guess Dad couldn't see what the alcohol was doing to him. He smoked weed when he could get it— said it helped him sleep—but the daily salve for the open wound that would not heal came from a cold red, white, and blue can.

My dad worked hard and was a genius with motors of all kinds. The garage bays were always filled, and a list of customers waiting in line hung by the phone at the station. John Doe made enough money to pay the bills, and I didn't need anything that wasn't provided for me. Dad was a sucker for hard luck stories and was owed more than he was paid most months. He went to work just after sunrise every morning, as sober as the sleep he got left him. The big breakfast Grandma always made the two of us helped too, I guess.

He worked all day without a drop of alcohol; exchanging beer cans for little green soda bottles while the station remained open. When the roll-up door on the garage came down at the end of the day, John Doe popped open his first beer. He would walk home for a shower and dinner. By the time he was finished eating, he'd have downed a six-pack and showed no signs of slowing. Some nights, Dad drank in front of the glow of the television, not watching, staring off to some distant memory. Or he'd sit on the bench in the backyard smoking a joint and jump every time a screen door slapped shut, or a car backfired out on the main road. He would stumble off to bed after a while and do it all over again the next day.

Sometimes Dad went down to Hunter's Pub, just five hundred yards from our front door. Tommy Hunter was the next in a long line of Hunters to own and run the pub. The dark, smoke-filled bar catered to the outdoor sportsman who came down to hunt and fish in our woods and waters. A pool table and a few pinball machines occupied the rear of the pub. There were long tables, where rich men told fish tales and smoked cigars over pints of beer. A jukebox played tunes of the day and a lot of oldies.

The pub allowed wealthy gentlemen to forget their manners without recourse unless they crossed Tommy. Locals knew better. Mr. Tommy loved my dad and took care of him. Having spent a year in the jungles of Vietnam, Tommy seemed to understand what my father was trying to drown with alcohol. He also knew when it was a night I'd need to walk my father home.

The first time I went to the pub with my grandmother to fetch John, I had just turned nine, and he had been out of the hospital for about two months. Tommy had him outside waiting when we walked up. Dad argued about being asked to leave. He ignored his mother when she told him it was time to go, but when I said, "Come on, Dad," he stopped resisting and took my hand. We walked home like that. From that day forward, if I showed up, John Doe would take my hand and walk back home with me without a second thought. I never knew why.

"Fuckin' fairy-boy!"

We had just passed old man Swann's daughter's house when we heard the shout. We were just south of Swann's store and across from the post office where Miss Susie worked the window. Susie Swann Ferrell had older kids with kids of their own. Her grandchildren were too young to hang out with us, but we did play in the patch of woods beside her house. During the daylight hours of winter, when all the undergrowth had sunk back, and the leaves had fallen out of the way, it was possible to see through to the other side by the highway. On a summer night with all the vegetation in it's growing season splendor, the vastness of that little patch of woods could be imagined endless.

"Kick his ass!"

The encouragement preceded more name-calling.

"What are you doing in my county, you dick suckin' queer?"

Hains put a hand on my shoulder and lowered us all to a crouch. His finger to his lips, he motioned for us to be quiet and follow him. We slipped into the patch of woods and crept closer to the disturbance. JP and his two friends encircled a young man, a stranger to us. It was a small county where we all knew each other. I'd never seen this guy before. He could have been older, but I guessed him to be late teens, twenty tops. It was hard to tell. His face was bloody, and one eye was beginning to swell shut. Plus he was on his knees, which made estimating height difficult.

"You want to ask the judge about that," he said to JP, before spitting blood at his attacker's feet.

JP kicked the young man in the stomach, while yelling, "Lying faggot."

Enraged, he looked around and grabbed a fallen pine limb. He broke it over the kneeling guy's back, only because the guy moved in time to avoid a direct hit to the head.

"Hey, what's going on?"

I recognized that slur immediately.

JP turned to answer my drunk and stumbling father. "Go home, John Doe. This isn't any of your business."

My dad kept coming closer. As his mind registered what he saw, he appeared to intervene in a memory. We watched in silence as he approached the man on his knees.

"Private Barnes, is that you?" He looked around at JP and his friends. "What's happening here?"

"My name ain't Barnes," the guy on the ground answered through swollen lips. He breathed in short gasps, as he continued, "But you can call me anything if you can stop these boys from breaking another rib."

One of JP's friends kicked the guy in the back, sending him face first into the dirt.

My dad moved pretty fast for a drunk man with part of a foot. He was at the injured man's side in a flash, standing off the other three men.

He warned them, "Back off. Get back to your bunks."

JP and his friends stared at him.

"I said back to your bunks, privates. Move. And be quiet. There's VC just outside camp."

Dad bent down to help the injured man.

The tallest of JP's crew said, "Look at this guy. He thinks he's in 'Nam or something."

"Yeah, John Doe spent some time in the jungle," JP said.

The other guy with JP asked, "His name is John Doe? Really?"

"Yep, there's the namesake of the village, Doe's Ferry."

"He's a fairy too?" The tall friend asked. "Let's whoop his ass then."

At that, my father turned from helping the injured guy to facing off JP and his friends. I'd never seen that particular look in his eye before, and I hoped instantly to never see it again. He took a step closer to JP's tall friend.

"You want a piece of me? The last sons of bitches that tried didn't kill me. You sure as hell won't."

Hains whispered in my ear, "Let's go get my dad."

I couldn't move. I heard the sounds of my friends retreating, but I stayed frozen in place, watching Staff Sergeant Doe appear before my eyes. Fixated on the tallest of JP's friends, he continued to advance.

My dad wasn't a big man. Just under six feet tall, he wasn't thick like me, but he wasn't skinny either. His work made him strong, and he was in pretty good shape for a shot up twenty-nine-year-old Marine with a bit of a limp. His adrenaline overcame the drunkenness, momentarily steadying his gait. The alcohol, however, clouded his thinking. Staff Sergeant Doe didn't seem to care that there were three of them.

"Do you think I'm afraid of you maggots? I've killed better men than you. Y'all ganged up on one man. Fucking cowards, all of you."

The guy on the ground said, "Junior thinks daddy might be bringing his twinks a little too close to home." He spit more blood. His eye was completely closed now.

JP growled, "Shut up, cocksucker," and kicked the downed man in the gut again.

His tall friend took JP's action as a sign the beating was to commence and shoved my father in the chest.

"Let's go, tough guy," he taunted.

John Doe stumbled, gathered himself, and then charged forward with a primal scream. He didn't swing at the guy with his fist. He caught him across the jaw with an elbow punch that sent the larger man sprawling backward. The smaller of JP's friends attacked my dad from the rear, while JP kept punching the bloody guy on the ground.

I don't remember deciding to leave my hiding spot. My scream joined my father's primal roar, and out of the bushes I came. I landed on the smaller guy's back, giving my dad time to shed his attacker. I could hear Doodie behind me. He hadn't run with Hains and Malachi.

"Miss Bertie, come quick," Doodie yelled into the walkie talkie. "In the woods beside Miss Susie's house. We need help."

I heard Doodie cry out about the same time the guy I was clinging to threw me off his back. I saw JP knock the radio from Doodie's hand as I flew through the air. Everything went into slow motion. Doodie and I landed on our backs close together. One exchanged look, and we were on our feet again. I lunged for the radio. My dad was fighting two of them. Doodie charged at the small one, who swung him off without much effort.

"Bertie, get the Sheriff!" I yelled into the walkie talkie.

JP snatched at the radio. I flailed about wildly, the antenna swinging through the air like a whip. When JP grabbed me from behind, I don't think he expected the wildcat reaction he encountered. I'd been manhandled before. I scarred that man for life. What was one more?

I was told later that the growl I heard came from me, but I don't recall making the sound. I can't bring up the image of how I escaped his grasp. I just know that within seconds of JP Spencer putting his hands on me the antenna sliced through his chin. I was prepared to swing it again when Sheriff Forster's voice rang out.

"All right! All right! Enough!"

Blood dripped through JP's fingers, as he held his injured face. He pointed at me with his other hand.

"Arrest that little bitch. Look what she did to me. And her drunk father. Put them in cages like the animals they are." He kicked the guy on the ground again. "Take this fucker, too."

The Sheriff barked, "Knock it off, JP. Go get that face taken care of."

JP looked at the blood pooling in the hand he held under his chin. "Come on," he said to his friends. "I think I need stitches. Let my father deal with this white trash cocksucker and his rescue party."

I was eleven. I sowed the seeds I'd reap right then and there.

"You mean Judge cocksuckee?"

The bloody guy on the ground tried to smile through his grotesquely swollen face, when he said, "Actually, he likes it the other way around."

7

Treasure in each other...

"We started on a childish treasure hunting adventure that day and ended the night in a bloody brawl. Nothing was ever the same after that, Hains. That night changed my life forever. From that moment on, we were all on borrowed time."

Night had fallen on our picnic table, but neither of us seemed to want to go anywhere. Hains and I slipped back into our friendship, filling in the details of each other's stories as if the years between our last conversation and this one had vanished with the sun.

"By the time Malachi and I got back to the woods, Miss Bertie was loading you guys in the bed of Mr. William's truck," Hains said. "That was the first time I saw Asa. He looked a lot different when he healed up."

The bloody guy on the ground ended up at my house that night. Bertie and my grandma tended to his wounds long after I had gone to bed. My dad had a few bruises, but JP's big friend looked a lot worse the last time I saw him. I had a cut or two, but nothing permanently scarring. Doodie had a black eye by the time he left to go home.

He had beamed at me before Malachi walked him out the door. Grinning from ear to ear, he said, "We make a pretty good team."

"Thanks for sticking with me, Doodie. I owe you one."

"That's what cousins are for," Doodie answered.

"What's your name, son," my grandma asked the boy with the bloody face.

"Asa Speight."

Bertie laughed. "Your momma named you ace a spade? She sure 'nough put a hex on you."

"It ain't exactly spelled the same, but I'd agree with the hex part," Asa said, speaking softly through swollen lips. "If I knew where she was, I'd give her a piece of my mind."

Bertie couldn't believe it. "You don't know where your momma is?"

"Last time I saw her, I was twelve. She left me standing outside the Byrd Theater in downtown Norfolk, Virginia. They called it the 'pervert theater,' you know, where the old men troll for the young stuff. I guess you could say she helped me get started in the business."

"Shh, hush now," Bertie said, glancing over at me. "Stop that talk. These children don't need to know more than they already had to learn this evenin'."

I was tired and sore, but I couldn't tear myself away from the kitchen table where they attended to the broken boy. In the glare of the overhead light, I could see now that he barely had hair on his chin.

I asked, "How old are you?"

"I'll be nineteen next month. How old are you, and what's your name?"

"My name is Jane Smith Doe."

"Really?"

"Yes, really. I am eleven years old and going into the sixth grade this year."

"Well, Jane Smith Doe," Asa said, looking at me with the one eye that remained open, "I want to thank you and your friend for helping me out. That was very brave of you."

"I wasn't helping you. I was helping my dad."

"I'll be sure to thank him when he wakes up," Asa said, and then leaned back and let the women take care of him.

Hains brought me back from the memory of that night by asking, "Have you seen Asa since you were released? I know your dad saw him regularly until he got too sick to make the trip to Raleigh."

I wasn't ready to talk about Asa, not yet.

"Do you remember what happened the next day, when my dad called us all over to the service station?"

Hains nodded. "Yeah, I do. Every time I hear Jackson Browne's 'Doctor My Eyes,' it takes me to that exact moment in time. It was playing on that little radio your dad kept on his tool caddy. It's weird how a song can make that happen. I swear I can smell the grease."

#

60

"That's a nice shiner," my dad said to Doodie when we entered the garage.

"Thanks, Uncle John," Doodie answered, smiling from ear to ear.

I noticed the guy I now knew as Asa in the back corner of the garage. He still looked horrible. He moved slowly as he cleaned tools with a faded red shop rag. He wore one of my father's sleeveless tee shirts, which showed off the ace of spades playing card tattooed on his upper left arm.

"What's he doing here?" I asked.

Dad smiled down at me. "He needs our help until he heals up some and we're going to offer it, okay?"

"Yeah, okay." I didn't see why not.

Dad added, "Turns out, Asa is pretty good around motors, and I could use a hand. There's more than one man can get done around here."

Asa smiled, sort of. He did the best that he could with one side of his face still disturbingly swollen. The red wounds looked painfully feverish. I felt sorry for him and kind of admired him for standing upright. He waved slowly and went back to what he was doing.

"Looks like he's going to fall over," Malachi said.

"That's one of the reasons I sent for you," Dad went on. "Asa is going to be staying in that travel trailer out back, so he can rest when he needs to. Y'all need to get your stuff out of there and clean it up."

"Yes, sir," I answered for all of us.

We had thought ourselves clever and undetected acquiring the key to the Winnebago. Dad had towed it into the salvage yard for lack of rental payment at the campground. No one came to get it. It was practically new, and of course, we were not supposed to play in it.

Hains echoed my statement. "We'll clean it up, sir."

My other two companions nodded in agreement.

"Ah, there you all are," Judge Spencer said, accompanying Cindy into the garage bay.

He came straight over to my dad and shook his hand. "Good afternoon, John Doe. I've come to apologize for my son's behavior. He and his friends had too much to drink—no excuse, I assure you—but I'm sure as a man who has served with young men, you can understand how they can overindulge from time to time."

The judge glanced over at Asa but turned his attention to Doodie and me.

"I see young Brian took quite a hit. Is this your first black eye, son?" The judge tussled Doodie's thick hair.

Doodie beamed under the attention. "Yes, sir. First one."

Judge Spencer turned to me. "And this is your antenna wielding defender."

"I didn't mean to—"

The judge cut me off. "Sh, sh, sh, child. You were defending family. Never apologize for that, dear girl."

"Is JP okay?" I only asked because I wanted to know how much trouble I was in.

Cindy answered, "He had to have fifteen stitches."

The judge smiled down at me. I wondered if he knew his smile was more of a condescending sneer than a disarming comfort.

"JP will have a permanent reminder of the consequences of his foolishness. It certainly was not the behavior of the gentleman he was raised to be."

Asa coughed. I was sure he was covering the pain of holding in a chuckle with broken ribs.

"And you, Mr. Speight. I had no idea when I picked up a young hitchhiker that we'd meet again. I must apologize to you most especially and offer any financial assistance you may need with medical bills or with continuing on your journey to wherever that may be."

In that instant, I fell for Asa's dimpled grin, even though only one side of his face could participate. He turned to show it to the judge, giving JP's father a good look at his son's handiwork.

"Thank you, Judge, but I'm going to be staying around. John's family is taking good care of me, and I've been offered a job less likely to get me killed than my last one."

"Asa's a pretty good mechanic," Dad said. "Diagnosed a timing problem by ear this morning."

"I see. Well, maybe I can swing a job or two your way." The judge moved toward Asa. "I've got some classics out at the old homeplace."

My dad positioned himself between Asa and the Judge, as he said, "Since I got that county contract, I believe I can keep us both busy. But Asa's free to do as he pleases."

"I appreciate the offer, Judge. That's kind of you." Asa's one dimple deepened painfully, but he seemed to relish in it. "Everyone here is so friendly, except for that little misunderstanding last night. I think I'm going to like living in Doe's Ferry."

"Well then," the judge said flashing his phony smile, "welcome to our community. I hope you'll enjoy your time here." He nodded to my father, "John. I guess I should be getting back to the courthouse. Cindy, are you coming?"

"Judge, if you don't mind," Dad said, "I'd like Cindy to stay for a minute. I have something for the kids."

"Okay, then. Again, my apologies for JP."

"Thank you, Judge."

The judge shook Dad's hand before he left for the courthouse. Judge Spencer would spend the rest of the afternoon sitting in judgment of other men's sons and daughters, for whom an apology would not have sufficed as punishment for beating a man like JP had done. Nothing was going to happen to Cindy's brother or his friends. Even as a preteen, I began to understand the unfair advantage of power and privilege.

Dad gathered us around the counter in the front part of the station.

"The Sheriff told me you all were treasure hunting yesterday, trussed some boy up to deep dive at the ferry dock. Would that have anything to do with this?"

He lifted our pirate treasure clue box from the floor behind the counter. (Evidently, my father did go in the boathouse from time to time.) After placing it on the countertop, he opened the lid of the box, exposing the contents. The map with the giant red X lay on top. He started laughing. Dad didn't do that often. In fact, he was in the best mood I'd seen him in since he came home from the war.

He looked over our heads and smiled. I turned to see Asa was leaning in the doorway that separated the front part of the station from the garage bays. He wiped his hands on an oily rag and winked at me with his one good eye.

"Folks," Dad said, regaining my attention, "I know all about this treasure."

There were gasps and a couple of audible "Cool" comments.

"See, I told you we should have asked your dad," little goody-two-shoes Cindy said.

"Shut up, Cindy." I chastised her. "You caused us to get caught."

"Hey, hey," my dad reprimanded me. "Cindy did the right thing. That's why I wanted her to stay. It doesn't matter if you're the only one that thinks a thing is wrong, you have to keep standing up for what you know is right."

I argued, "She didn't tell on us because she thought we shouldn't do it. She saw Hains with that Maria girl and got jealous."

Cindy huffed and put her hands on her hips. Hains feigned shock, while Doodie and Malachi nodded in agreement with me.

"Well, for whatever reason, she did the right thing. As for the other four of you," Dad began.

I figured we were about to get a lecture, but that's not what happened.

Dad continued, "I commend your loyalty to each other. The word of the day is amicities. It means friendship."

We repeated the word, as we did each day he chose to teach us one, but I was bursting to know, so I asked, "But what about the treasure? You said you knew about it."

He ignored my question and reached into the box. He pulled out the five pirate coins. The coins now had holes drilled in them and were attached to rings. The rings were suspended on necklaces made from a spool of beaded chain that Dad used to make key fobs for the vehicles people left at the shop. He laid the five necklaces out on the countertop with the backs of the coins facing up. Dad had used his steel die set to personalize each one with our names.

"Cool," Doodie said.

"Yeah, cool," echoed Malachi.

"When I was twelve years old," Dad began, "I had a crush on a girl down at the campground. I thought up this elaborate scheme to get her to kiss me. I made a map, made up a curse to fit the monster we all know lives at the ferry dock." He paused to wink and grin at us. "Then I put some fake pirate loot I got down at Nags Head in a box with all the other stuff and buried it."

Hains asked, "Did it work?"

"No," Dad answered. "Mainly because I forgot where I buried it and never found it again."

Doodie shouted excitedly, "But we did."

"See, I told you it was all phony baloney," Cindy said, with a smirk. "There isn't any treasure."

"Oh, but there is," my dad corrected her. "These are the best days of your lives, and these are the best friends you'll ever have. No one else will believe you when you say a monster grabbed your foot when you got too close to the ferry channel. No one else will follow you on crazy adventures, pursue dreams with you simply because you dreamed them. You will never fully trust others like the friends standing here with you now. Your treasure is each other."

He handed each of us our own engraved fake pirate doubloon necklace. I was the last to receive mine.

As he placed it around my neck, he indicated my friends with a nod of his head and said to me, "Keep them close, honey. Good friends are hard to come by."

#

"Do you still have yours, Hains?"

"What, that coin necklace? Yeah, I do. It's in my sock drawer, where it's always been. Do you?"

"I left mine hanging in the boathouse. As far as I know, it's still there."

I pulled one of the necklaces from my back pocket and held it out in front of him.

"I got this one in the mail a week ago."

I watched his eyes follow the doubloon as it swung on the end of the chain. I knew what he was looking for—the name stamped on the back.

"It's Mali's necklace, Hains. I always assumed it was at the bottom of the ferry channel. Now how do you suppose it ended up in my mailbox?"

"May I?"

Hains held out his hand. I laid the necklace in his palm. He looked it over for a few minutes and then asked, "How do you know it isn't a copy?"

"I thought about that. Even if it is a copy, there are only four people left in this world who would know the significance of this necklace. Look at the chain. It's broken, stretched apart. It was torn from Mali's neck according to the marks it left. That's quite a detail to replicate."

Hains let the doubloon spin, catching the glow of the restroom lights as it wound itself up on the chain and then unwound again.

"I assume you tried to track where the package came from," Hains said, after a long pause.

"It originated in a FedEx drop box in Chesapeake, Virginia. Paid for with a gift card. Gift card traced to a cash purchase and a kid who kept the change and dropped the box for an online customer. The kid has a gig mailing anonymous packages. He's rethinking his business model after I pointed out he may find himself in a criminal investigation."

"That's pretty thorough for a civilian."

I smiled. "With the right favors done and due, a person can find out damned near anything you want about anyone."

"I thought you were a bartender."

"I thought you didn't know where I've been since I got out."

Hains chuckled again. "Like you said, a person can find out damned near anything." He handed the necklace back to me. "What do you think it means?"

"I don't know."

"Who do you think sent it?"

"Did you, Hains?"

"Am I not doing a good enough job of looking surprised?" Hains chuckled. "Seriously, who would want to stir this up again? It makes more sense that it's you that has the motive to do that."

"The person who had Malachi's necklace, knowing it was evidence, had to have a special attachment to keep it for forty years. I wonder if they even know it's missing from its hiding place. If they don't know by now that I have it, they will soon enough. The question they will be asking is which one of us betrayed them. It sure as hell wasn't me."

"I suppose this is why you came home."

"That and some other things," I replied. "Mali's necklace wasn't the only thing in the package. There was a notecard containing one word."

"What did it say?"

I pulled the card from my other back pocket and handed it to him.

"Emendare," Hains read. "What does it mean?"

"To make amends; to correct; to restore."

I stood from my perch on the picnic table, stretched and stamped my feet to get the blood flowing. We'd been sitting for several hours, reminiscing. Hains unfolded to his full height. I'd forgotten how small I felt beside him.

"Jane, suppose someone is just setting you up for trouble."

"I thought about that. I've been looking to get into some shit for a while now. I've had this itch since I found out that asshat might be nominated to the Supreme Court."

"You know he'll come after you."

I smiled up at my old friend. "It's been long enough, Hains. An innocent man is locked in his own mind. A guilty one sits on the bench. It's time to set it right."

"I can't help you," he said.

"If what you said during the investigation was true, then you really can't help. Why should you change your story now?"

"I wouldn't. I told the truth."

"Then here we are again on opposite sides of the story, my old friend. May the truth will out."

Hains chuckled. "Good luck with that."

8

I'm a country music cliché ...

"What'd he say?"

Vanessa Duckworth, Duck to almost everyone, stood at the kitchen counter chopping onions for the hotdogs her wife was cooking on the grill.

"He said he couldn't help me."

"Do you trust him? Do you believe him, that he didn't send the package?"

"I don't trust anyone."

Duck laughed loudly. "Ha, ha, ha. That's my girl."

I met Duck in prison. I was eighteen and in for five long years at the North Carolina Correctional Institution for Women in Raleigh. Duck was doing the last ten of a fifteen-year sentence for manslaughter. She was a general contractor with her own crew when things went south on a job site. Duck killed a man. She struck him in the head with a hammer when she caught him raping one of her female crewmembers.

She would tell anyone who asked, "I did fifteen years for hitting a man in the head when I found him raping my friend, and I'd do it again. If I were a man, they'd have given me a slap on the back and sent me home, job well done. Lesbians don't rate that kind of understanding when a man's privileged dick is involved."

That might be why she did the whole fifteen. Duck never showed remorse. I didn't either. So, we did the time deemed appropriate for our respective crimes. I suppose that's why she took me under her wing like a little duckling. Duck was my prison mother. Five feet ten inches of solid muscle compared to me at one-twenty-five on a heavy day and five feet three inches tall, having Duck on my side seemed a good choice.

We hit the weights together and stayed out of trouble. Duck kept me focused on the prize—my life on the outside. I got a college degree and a body built by the endless hours of boredom in the pen. When I got out, Duck set me up with an old lawyer pal of hers, and that led to my career as a—you know, I really need to come up with a title. Anyway, when Duck was released, my Dad had become ill and needed help. Duck needed an income and a place to live. She moved in as my father's caregiver in 1990 and stayed even after his death in 2000.

"Hey, hand me that jar of relish," Duck said, before she asked, "So, what next?"

"I figure I'll go on down to the pub and make my presence known. I assume from the subterfuge that someone in this county knows what happened that night, but is too afraid to speak up."

Duck slapped a spoonful of pickled relish into a tub of potato salad in the making and commented, "Or you're giving a fucking nutless coward way too much credit."

"You'd never know she had a college degree," Claudette Washington said, as she entered the kitchen through the sliding back doors. "And, by the way, that's very sexist. Implying balls have more courage than vaginas is quite laughable. They shrink up at the least little thing."

"You are quite right, my love," Duck said, and then kissed her wife on the cheek as she passed. "Besides, it could be a woman."

Claudette always had a pair of reading glasses atop her head. I had watched her hair go from brunette to white when she and Duck would visit me as I hopped around the states. She still wore colorful stretchy headbands to hold back her shoulder-length flipped bob, worn in the same fashion displayed in the pictures of her from the sixties in the memory books on the coffee table. An architectural historian, Claudette carried an air of studiousness wrapped in a classic wardrobe not changed in a half century. Audrey Hepburn-like in dress and manner, prone to wear black turtlenecks and contouring slacks, Claudette thrived as the femme to Duck's butch carpenter vibe. The typecasting was not lost on me.

"We should consider that the person who sent the package knew you'd come," Claudette said, while she dug around in the refrigerator. She emerged holding a second package of turkey wienies. "The whole point could be to lure you out in the open."

I smiled at my friends' protectiveness. "I don't live underground. I have a social security number, credit, possessions, a home address. I could have been found if someone meant me harm. They sent me a package, so why go to the trouble of bringing me here? Are they expecting a showdown at the OK Corral?"

Duck pointed a potato salad covered spoon at me. "But here in Doe's Ferry, discrediting you could be easier, considering your past. Drugs, violence, sexual deviancy—my God, this little village is a media goldmine of white trash southern stereotypes."

I laughed and added, "Throw in my no account momma and the prison stint, and I'm a country music cliché."

"Or the main character in a Disney movie. Do any of them have both parents living?" Claudette asked.

Duck laughed. "Jane is definitely Bambi. That's what we called her when she showed up at the prison. Those big brown eyes were stuck wide open, like a scared animal."

"I felt like prey in a forest of predators."

"You were," Duck said, before addressing Claudette, who was on her way back to the deck. "Why are you cooking sixteen hot dogs? Do you know something I do not?"

Claudette smiled over her shoulder, "My darling, I know very many things you do not."

Duck gave her a cocked head expression, amused but still making a serious inquiry.

Claudette gave into the look. "I just got off the phone with the last of the household members. They will be joining us to welcome Jane to her restored home. That's seven for dinner, and I'm taking the leftovers over to the hospice house."

In addition to Duck and Claudette, the Doe House was home to four other women. Two of them, Sophia Masters and Gloria Diaz, were participating in internships with Duck and Claudette, learning the restoration business from grant writing to how to straighten a two-hundred-year-old wall. Tiffany Jefferson, an Air Force trained mechanic, ran the service station, which provided income for her and the household. Tiff's intern, Latisa Watson, was learning her way through a modern mechanic's manual. The interns earned a paycheck and self-reliance. They would pay it forward through the Doe House foundation when they could, either with financial donations or sweat equity on the properties.

The foundation was Claudette's brainchild. Her grant writing abilities made it a reality. All residents, with the exception of

Claudette, had done time for finally standing up to an abuser. No one outside of Duck was allowed to have a significant other in the house because she ran the place for me and this was her permanent home. No boyfriends or girlfriends sleeping over, no illegal substances, clean up after yourself, and no drama were the house rules. The women in this house were here to learn a trade that would support them comfortably and stockpile some earnings for a new beginning.

"I'll grab more buns from the freezer." Duck threw an onion at me. "You chop another one of these."

"Grab more chips, Duck, and don't forget to check the baked beans," Claudette called out and then went back out to tend the grill.

I found myself alone in the kitchen where, just hours old, I had been placed on the table in a soiled tee shirt. I imagined my grandmother at the old cast iron wood stove, which the restoration team saw fit to keep but had refitted for gas. She made the best biscuits, and though I grew up free range with an atypical bonding experience, my grandmother loved me. She died while I was in prison.

My grandfather spent so much of my childhood in his chair or bed; I have few memories of him otherwise. I do remember him at that same kitchen table crying with a telegram in his hand, one that said my father was missing in action. I recalled my grandmother sitting there, head in her hands, the day my grandfather finally passed away. I remember thinking that I didn't know she had loved him that much. The table held happy memories too—birthday cakes and science projects, breakfasts with my dad, board games on rainy days with my friends, the day the telegram came to say John Doe was coming home.

"Hey, where'd you go?" Duck was back with another package of hot dog buns. "Memories, huh?"

"I never saw any of this new. It was already old by the time I came along. The place looks so different, but the same still."

Duck smiled. "That's the point of restoration, not renovation."

"I guess so."

"Kid…"

I was fifty-eight years old, and she still called me by the name she gave me in prison.

"…what's your game plan? You do have a plan? You didn't just reappear in a place you swore you'd never set foot again without some kind of a plan, right?"

"I thought I'd just wait for whoever sent the package to show their hand. Whoever it is thought this through enough to summon me. Let's see what they have to say."

"These are powerful men, Jane. You've seen how past behaviors had no bearing on the recent confirmations across the board. And like it or not, these people will remain in power for a few more years. Don't get in their way."

"Duck, I vote. That's all the political content I got time to care about. You know what I do care about? I care about an innocent man who had his life taken away. These people killed one man and ruined another while suffering no consequences."

"You left out what they did to you."

An involuntary chuckle preceded my response. "Yeah, well, my wounds are minor compared to others who came through that courthouse. Lady Justice got sick with Spencer cancer and turned her back on Doe's Ferry long ago."

"I don't 'magine he was the first to bend the law to suit him and his friends," Duck said, as she finished wrapping the new package of buns in tin foil and threw them in the oven with the others already warming. "The old judge spent a lot of time with your father toward the end. Visited often those last few years."

"Ha!" I exclaimed so loudly Duck jumped. "I think he was looking for forgiveness, atoning for sins. He's afraid of dying. Evil people get worried toward the end, just in case any of that religious mumbo jumbo is true."

"I've spent time with the judge, Jane. He did a lot for people with AIDS in this area. He told me once he couldn't believe he didn't have it."

I was shocked. "Judge Carroll Spencer discussed his sexuality with you?"

"Honey, I called that old chicken hawk out the first time I saw him. We had an understanding about how I don't abide liars. He also agreed that dying men don't need mendacity served to them out of well-meaning kindness."

"Don't try to humanize him, Duck."

Duck walked by me with the potato salad to place it on the kitchen table.

She asked, "What if the judge is the one who sent you the package?" Before I could answer, she directed, "Hey, get some oven-mitts and put the baked beans on those two trivets at the end of the table."

I did as asked while answering her question with one of my own, "Why would he want his son taken down right at the pinnacle of their collective achievements?"

Claudette re-entered as I was speaking and joined the conversation with, "Maybe he knows exactly what kind of weasel his son is and is doing his patriotic duty. May I have one of those paper plates behind you, Duck?"

"I know who this man is, ladies. His good deeds cannot mitigate his evil-doing."

I passed Claudette with the hot baked beans held out in front of me. She smiled and made the "mmmm" sound.

"Those smell heavenly," she commented, before continuing our conversation about the judge. "It has been my experience that the evilest men do the kindest things."

I smiled at Claudette, not wanting the evening to turn too dark, not just yet. "They do it so they can point to those anomalies in their lives as examples of compassion when we all know better."

Claudette agreed with a nod. "In the end, it's all about the id and the immediate gratification of needs. Men like the judge have many needs, all more important than anyone else's."

Duck said, "I have a need to eat," and then asked, "Are the dogs ready?"

Claudette headed out the door with the paper plate, answering, "Yes, and the girls are on their way down."

Footsteps creaked on the stairs as one by one the other four occupants of Doe House appeared around the kitchen table. We all knew each other because I interviewed them in prison before they were let out. This was a second chance for them—like an attorney in Durham gave me thirty-five years ago.

There were hugs all around and then Duck passed out iced tea for a toast. With sweating glasses dripping over the food, we clinked them together, as Duck said, "Welcome home, Jane Doe, and thank you for sharing it with us."

#

Tiff raised her hand to quiet the others and make a point.

"Wait, wait, wait. So, I said, 'Ma'am, I appreciate that you prayed about it, but apparently God had more important things to do than change your oil.'"

The table erupted in laughter only to be interrupted by several horns blowing and voices shouting.

"Hey dykes, suck my dick!"

"Pussy lickers!"

73

There were other taunts too garbled to make out. I stood with the rest of the women to peer out the windows overlooking the ferry dock. Tires squealed, and a couple of lift kit enhanced four-wheel-drive pickup trucks followed a Dodge Challenger as it roared away.

"There goes Four, out with his minions for the evening," Duck observed.

"I only saw three," I commented.

The women chuckled among themselves, and then Latisa explained, "The one driving the black truck is called Four. He's the fourth—"

"Hains Lawton Forster, the fourth," I said. "He's the sheriff's son."

Gloria, with her Latin cadence, called it as she saw it, "Pizado. He is mommy's boy, do no wrong in her eyes. His papi can't win this fight with mommy and abuelo."

"Does this happen often?"

Tiff answered, "It used to be every now and then when the juvenile delinquents got enough alcohol in them to pay us a visit."

Latisa glared out the window at the ferry dock. "My boyfriend's crew would kick all their asses. Little punks."

Latisa's problems had begun at thirteen when an abusive stepfather joined her family. At age seventeen, she broke his skull with a tire iron while he was beating her unconscious mother with a pistol that had failed to fire when he pulled the trigger. She did eight years for manslaughter. The system was so fucked up.

I wanted to know these women were safe in Doe's Ferry. I had assumed they were. I'd heard nothing of these verbal assaults. I didn't know what sexuality the women who applied to Doe House were unless they told me. It didn't surprise me that a bunch of rednecks would assume a house full of women had to be lesbians. But even if these women were part of a sister-wives lesbian commune, how consenting adults chose to have sex wasn't grounds for ridicule or harassment. Unwarranted shame had done enough damage in Doe's Ferry.

I mumbled, "Bunch of evolutionally challenged Neanderthals."

Duck went on to explain further, "Since the ferry shut down and we started surveying for the architectural dig that will return the dock area to its eighteenth-century status, we discovered the dock on the south side, by the sheriff's house, is actually part of the original Doe tract. Hains took it in stride. Four and his mother did not, hence the taunting and occasional vandalism."

"Are you tearing down the wharf?"

Claudette answered, "Yes, but we will rebuild it as a much safer modern dock with public access. The plans are to replicate the fishing and warehouse docks as they stood in the late 1700s, about the same time the second foundation for the house was originally built. We were also miraculously granted permission to rebuild the offloading docks that used to be out in the deeper channel. We hope to demonstrate the waterman's way of life, but we'll need the Forster wharf for public viewing."

Duck chimed in. "Everything will be open to the public. Four believes he's losing his private dock, which he is, but it wasn't his to begin with."

"I know Hains's son is a piece of work from reading the news," I said.

"Oh, yeah, and that bull shit," Latisa shouted.

I looked at Duck and asked, "And Hains allows his son to hassle you?"

I had a hard time believing Hains would allow a son of his that much leeway. I could believe that Hains, like many who doled out the hazing in high school, could make excuses for how boys "locker room" talk and behavior could get out of hand. As disgusting as that sounds, when you're bussing tables while passing as a young dude in a men's only club, the insight into male dominance hierarchy is enlightening, to say the least. But white hats like Hains don't taunt women or allow others to do so.

"I don't think the sheriff likes his own kid," Sophia said.

Duck explained further, "Hains said as soon as his son steps on our property or makes a threat of physical harm he will arrest him. Four knows the line and where it's drawn, courtesy of his grandfather and uncle, the judges."

"The ferry dock land comes back to me as of Saturday," I said, and couldn't help the smile that enveloped my face. "I think this is all going to work out just fine."

9

Same old same old...

"I'll be damned. The rumors are true. How the hell are ya, Jane Doe?"

The bartender returning my credit card seemed familiar. I intended to use the card, making sure the locals had verified my identity. I wasn't anticipating it happening quite so fast.

"I'm all right. Are you little Tommy Lynne?"

"Yep, but not so little anymore, huh?"

Tommy Hunter died not long after my dad. He had a daughter eight years younger than me. I babysat Tommy Lynne a few times, and now she had taken her place at the helm of Hunter's Pub. Tommy Lynne had grown into a fifty-year-old that looked forty, with the same curly auburn hair. Blue eyes were rare for redheads, which made Tommy Lynne's even more alarmingly enchanting. She wore a Hunter's Pub tank top that allowed for a view of her deeply tanned and freckled cleavage when she leaned across the bar to hand me the beer I ordered. I may be closing in on sixty, but I'm not blind nor lacking a libido. And if I'm not mistaken, her smile meant she gave me the peek on purpose.

I couldn't help the grin when I replied, "No, not so little."

"I never thought I'd see you back here. Your dad used to keep me updated on your whereabouts. He was very proud of how you turned out."

"I wish we could have spent more time together, but he wouldn't live anywhere else and I sure as hell wasn't coming back here."

Tommy Lynne leaned in, so as not to have others overhear our conversation or because she liked showing me her tits. Either way, I looked and listened, while I sipped from the beer I ordered just to fit in and watched the room without appearing to do so. It's a skill.

"I was by his bed when he passed," Tommy Lynne said. "I know he told you not to come home when he was dying. He sure loved you an awful lot to tell you that. Most folks around here don't understand why you didn't come to his memorial, but I do."

The memory began closing my throat. My eyes started to burn. I held up my beer bottle.

"Thank you for being his friend. Here's to John Doe," I toasted. "Rest in peace."

Tommy Lynne picked up an unaccompanied beer from the bar and clinked the bottom against mine. I'm not sure it was hers.

"To John Doe."

We both took a swig and set the bottles down. I watched a sad memory cloud Tommy Lynne's face, but then she smiled and wiped the bar down in front of me. She had questions. I figured she was trying to decide how to ask them. A guy in a John Deer hat held up his empty mug for another draft, which pulled Tommy Lynne away from the interrogation I was about to receive.

I took the time to count the six men and two women in the pub and make mental notes about each one's appearance and choice of drink. The beer on the bar had no owner, not a visible one. Eight breathing bodies, and one unaccounted for. I could reach an exit before anyone could grab me—a good place to be when you're the stranger. There was an emergency exit I could not see from my vantage point, but it was not an entrance.

There could have been someone in the restrooms, maybe the owner of the lonely beer next to me, but I felt comfortable with my tactical assessment. In seconds, I had clocked the room and its occupants. It's just what I do. Details—who, what, when, and where— that was the business I dealt in. If my client wanted to know an alibi would hold up, I uncovered the details. If they wanted crumbs laid for the police, I'm their Hansel and Gretel rolled into one. I answer my clients' questions, no more, no less. I'm not a private investigator. Licenses are restrictive. I don't testify. I put myself in the room where the shit goes down.

My skill lies in being welcomed with my true motives undetected. I'm a spy without a country or a cause other than the scales of justice weighing out equally. I guess I'm a witness to truth. As I said earlier, I really don't have a job title, but it pays well. I catch liars for parties who pay good money to know things. I don't get involved in what is done with the information I uncover. I'm a dot connector. I put the dots on the map for others to follow. Details are my currency.

The pub had changed on Tommy Lynne's watch. The neon Schlitz sign had been switched out for a local craft beer logo. The place was lit up, not dank and dark as before. Flat screen televisions tuned to a variety of sports were scattered about the walls. The haze of cigarette smoke that had permeated every crevice of the space no longer hung in the air. Tommy Lynne had done an excellent job of keeping the place quaint and local-friendly but had raised the bar, so to speak.

When she returned, I commented, "The place looks great. How in the world did you remove years of nicotine and wood burning stove smoke stuck to everything?"

Tommy Lynne laughed. "I hired the Doe House Restoration Company."

"Good choice," I responded with a smile.

"We pulled what wasn't permanently attached to the building out of here. We cleaned for two solid weeks and re-stained the hardwoods. Duck helped a lot with keeping it old looking while making it new. Sometimes when it's sweltering, I can still smell the cigarette smoke leaching out of the old timbers."

I pointed at the wall of ales and booze lining the shelves behind the bar. "I see the number of taps has tripled. You know what your dad would say."

Tommy Lynne mimicked her dad perfectly, saying, "We got three beers. Want somethin' else? Go to the grocery store, buy it, take it home, and drink it on your couch."

"Yep, I heard him say that often."

We laughed together as I continued cataloging details and Tommy Lynne went to get change for a pool player. I was happy to see the pinball machines in the back corner appeared to be the same ones I'd tilted a time or two in my youth. A good pinball machine from back in the day was hard to find. The pool table was new. The old one had a hairline crack in the slate under the felt by one of the corner pockets. A stranger's money could vanish, and they'd never know why the locals avoided that hole and why his shots never went in when he shot at it.

After a few long minutes, Tommy Lynne returned and started her mission to acquire information. I admired her attempt to unearth my reasons for stepping a foot in this godforsaken county.

"I'm guessing since you're here the shit must be gettin' real at Doe House."

"What shit would that be?"

This is the mantra of my success: Never offer information. Make the person interrogating you give up what they know first. If you want answers, let the person you're probing ask the questions. When you see what they don't know, it's easier to manipulate targets into telling you what they do.

"I thought maybe Duck called you down here to deal with Four and his redneck band of merry men. Hains doesn't seem to want to do anything about it."

"Redneck band of merry men. Ha, that's funny. Do you know them too?"

Tommy Lynne was more than happy to inform on the rowdies.

"Let's see, there's the Pine boys and that Bartlett girl. The Walker kids get involved too, but at least Olin Jr. has tried to wrangle them."

I asked to be sure I heard the names correctly, "As in Johnny Bartlett and the Pine twins' kids?"

Tommy Lynne laughed. "No, but it's their grandkids."

"Damn, people around here got old," I said and tipped the beer to my lips.

"They all had babies in their teens," she explained. "Now those babies have teens."

I swallowed a tiny bit and let the rest wash back into the bottle. I preferred pot to alcohol for many reasons, but the most important was I remained in control. I discovered in my youth that I suffered from the same addictive genes as John Doe, so I decided to forego the whole alcoholic lifestyle and simply not drink. I acted like I drank in many situations, but when heads were turned my beer would disappear. I'd pour it out or switch it for an empty bottle on the bar. Tommy Lynne observed me, so I swallowed.

She noted, "Not much of a drinker, are you?"

"No, not really. Just never developed a taste for it."

"I hear ya. Being around it all my life, I've seen the damage done. I'm not much of a drinker either." She looked around before continuing. "I smoke me some herb when I can," Tommy Lynne whispered across the bar. "I take my vacations in recreational marijuana states now."

No alcohol, a steady job, and she wouldn't bitch about the pot I use to keep the wolves at bay. Tommy Lynne was looking better all the time. The wolves of which I speak were a genetic link to my father, our post-trauma reactions played havoc with our minds.

I chuckled and said, "You are quickly becoming the most interesting person still remaining in this county."

"You should come over. We can sit out on the deck and burn one."

I think she saw my hesitation, because she added, "I live alone with my animals and have no neighbors within eyesight."

"Do you still live at the end of Tuck's Bay road?"

Tommy Lynne smiled. "I can't believe you remember. Yes, I took down Mom and Dad's house a few years back. I built my dream home."

"That's awesome. Good for you."

Someone caught Tommy Lynne's attention behind me. A huge grin took hold of her face and lit it up with affection reserved for the ones we love the most.

"And here comes my man. I want you to meet him."

I turned on the barstool, following Tommy Lynne with my eyes as she stepped around the bar to introduce me to her 'man.' I felt the sting of dashed hopes, even as I really had none. I wasn't looking to hook up in Doe's Ferry.

"This is Tuck, the only man I'll ever love."

My gaze followed Tommy Lynne's to a black Labrador retriever with a muzzle white with age. His whole body wagged at seeing his girl.

"The mutual admiration is quite apparent. Hello, Tuck. You are a handsome lad."

Tuck let me pet him and then disappeared behind the bar.

"He stays back there while I'm working. He'll make a round about once an hour for rubs and snacks. I tell people not to give him junk food, but how do you resist that face? I have to keep the weight off him because of his arthritis."

"How old is he?"

The fear of losing him clouded her expression, when she answered, "Seventeen."

"He looks fantastic."

I wanted to take her mind from the knowledge that she was losing Tuck, no matter what she did. Death comes for us all. I brought the subject back to a more pleasant topic.

"Only man, huh?"

"Oh yeah, I mean, I thought you knew. Yep, Tommy Lynne, the resident lezzie. Every community should have at least one, out in the open anyway."

That drew a laugh from me. "We both know you are not alone."

Tommy Lynne followed Tuck behind the bar. "I'm currently without a steady date, which brings the curious housewives out of the woodwork. If you're available, I'm sure they'll want to take you for a ride too."

"My housewife phase ended years ago."

It had been a while, but I'm quite sure my bartender was hitting on me, when she said, "Speaking of phases, did you know I had a huge crush on you when you worked here. I used to volunteer to bring Dad's lunch and dinner just to see you. I was heartbroken when they took you away."

I ignored the darker mood of the last statement and focused on the part that made me smile. I nodded with my response, "I remember you seemed to be hanging around outside a lot when I'd be washing the bar mats or crating bottles on the weekends."

"You were this goddess-like teenager, and I wanted to be near you, but I had no idea why. I had that feeling explained to me a little later by a tourist down at the campground."

I burst out laughing. "Wow. I think we read the same script. I share a similar fond memory of a campground girl."

Tommy Lynne slid a glass of ice water in front of me. She garnished it with a lemon slice. Taking the still full and warming beer, she said, "You really should come by Sunday afternoon. I'll cook a steak, and I can tell you about the things your dad and I got into. I dearly loved John Doe."

When I started this journey into the past, I had no intentions of interacting with anyone other than my former playmates and the guilty men who ruined our lives. I planned to come and go as quickly as possible, putting Doe's Ferry in my rearview mirror by Sunday. I couldn't believe what I heard myself say.

"What time?"

"Let's make it four-ish. We can do dusk like me and your old man used to."

"Sounds great."

The door to the bar opened, and two wrinkled and worn, graying old men walked in. I began to wonder if I looked that old when Tommy Lynne addressed them.

"Speak of the devils themselves, Johnny Bartlett and Randy Pine, ladies and gentlemen."

"Eve'nin', Tommy Lynne," both men replied in unison.

This appeared to be a customary greeting and not one performed for my benefit. Tommy Lynne made eye contact with me as she grabbed two long neck beer bottles from the cooler behind the bar. She was waiting for me to make a move. I appreciated the fact she was willing to leave my assumed identity as a tourist intact, but it wasn't necessary. If I wanted the county to know I was here, these two represented an opportunity for an information dump into the Doe's Ferry social media hotline.

I spun on my bar stool to face my old acquaintances.

"When trailer park boys and courthouse kids get together, there's usually trouble."

Johnny took a second glance at me. I could tell my face sparked a memory. Randy had probably had too much alcohol over the years to locate my visage in his diluted memory banks. I gave them both a clue.

"Care to double or nothing that bet on who can get up the light poles at the field the fastest? I think I've probably still got a step or two on you both."

"Jane Doe. Well, I'll be damned."

"I seem to get that reaction a lot," I said, smiling broadly at one of my childhood white knights.

Johnny came toward me with his arms open. I stood and received a bear hug like I hadn't had in a while. When he let me go, I smiled up at him.

"It's good to see you, Johnny."

Randy wanted a hug too. We were never that close, and I don't recall hugging him at any other time in my life, but I relented and let him pretend I was a long lost pal.

After the hug, Randy held me at arm's length, which grew increasingly tiresome by the second, and said, as only Randy Pine could opine, "Seeing you in this county is like backin' over a deer. That shit don't happen 'less the deer's already dead."

I patted Randy's arm and said, "Not dead yet, but there's always tomorrow."

I used his fit of laughter to loose myself from his grip and take a step back, putting more distance between us. Randy wasn't scary. He just smelled like the inside of a beer can that had been used as an ashtray at a party and left under the couch for a month. Johnny had taken better care of himself and appeared sober at the moment.

The sparkle in Johnny's eyes reflected the genuineness of his next words, "I don't know why you're here, but I'm glad to see you. I've thought of you often, Jane. I always hoped you had a good life, somewhere else."

"I did, Johnny. I do, still," I assured him.

"Come, sit with me. Let's catch up."

I didn't want to sit with a drunk Randy Pine. I'd seen that act as a teenager. Johnny must have been an excellent friend to walk the alcoholic into the local bar so often the bartender had a routine for them. People can judge if they want, call Johnny an enabler, but if your friend is going to drink whether you are with them or not, then home safe is better than ditch drunk and dead. A lifelong drinker in Randy's condition probably wasn't driving a vehicle more substantial than a lawnmower anymore, anyway.

"Sure, I'll sit with you," I said. "Let me grab my drink."

My hand had just wrapped around my glass when the door to the bar opened again. In walked Supreme Court nominee short-lister Judge J. P. Spencer, accompanied by a video crew from the network that shall not be named and one of its blonde interchangeable talking heads.

"Let me handle this," JP said to some guy with too much gel in his hair, wearing a headset and carrying a clipboard.

Johnny, Randy, and I moved out of the way and found a table near the back of the room.

Johnny leaned over and spoke close to my ear, "That prick should have been the one behind bars."

I stared at JP, while I responded, "I believe in karma, Johnny. I wish no ill will to anyone, only that they reap what they have sown."

"Then this motherfucker here should be bursting into flames any minute," Randy drunk whispered, almost loud enough to be heard by the crowd at the bar.

Johnny and I both turned to look at Randy and erupted in laughter. Drunks say the darnedest things.

After a few minutes of conferring with Tommy Lynne, the cameraman set up, the bright lights came on, and the reporter put on her fake smile. JP lifted the mug of beer Tommy Lynne slid onto the bar and held it up for the camera. He smiled, and that's when I saw the scar was still on his chin. JP, of course, told everyone it was an old football injury. Cindy told me, when he ran for his first public office while we were still in high school, that JP thought it made him look rugged, like Harrison Ford. Otherwise, I'm sure a man as vain as JP would have covered it with plastic surgery by now.

I watched in disbelief as this loathsome creature held the beer mug up, smiled into the camera, and declared, as if it were the golden ticket to his desires, "I like beer, too."

"Jesus, this guy," Johnny said. "It amazes me how now being a total prick is something to brag about. Shit's comin' full circle. Dark times." He took a swig of his beer.

83

Even drunk, Randy had a way of truth-telling. "He ain't even got his own meme line. That other dude already claimed drunk frat boy privilege."

I raised my eyebrows at Randy's insight. Johnny chuckled.

"Randy's been listening to podcasts with me while we fish."

I shook my head and declared, "I try not to concentrate on the day-to-day. I vote when the time comes. I stand when the cause is worthy, but I can't be invested in this stink on the daily."

An icy voice, sharp as a razor, cut through the air, "Then why are you here, Jane?"

The abandoned beer on the bar—I'd forgotten the unaccounted for customer. Forty years had passed, but I knew the voice, the inflection, the condescension.

"Ah, here she is," JP said, coming toward my table.

He smiled, the white of the scar showed, he reached a hand out, and took his sister's arm.

"This is my little sister Cindy. She still lives here in Doe's Ferry."

The reporter asked, "Are you in the law profession, as well."

Cindy Spencer Forster, the first girl I ever kissed, and the first person to betray me, smiled for the camera.

"No, I chose a different field of public service. I'm an ER nurse, but my husband is the sheriff, and my son will be joining the military in the fall if that counts. We're just an all-American, law-abiding, happy family."

Randy blew through his lips. I think he tried to whistle, but only air came out. He followed the burst of air with, "lymphaticus—the word of the day—mad, loco, crazed, brainsick."

"Did you guys hang out with my dad?"

Johnny nodded. "Yeah, we did."

Randy grabbed my hand and started to weep. "I stayed sober for John Doe. He was a hell of a dude, man."

I let Randy mumble some story about his friendship with my dad while I watched Cindy. She stood on her tiptoes to whisper in JP's ear. He saw me and blanched white for a millisecond, before recovering his jovial, good ol' boy persona for the camera.

"Okay, then," JP said to the film crew, "I guess that does it for B-roll of Doe's Ferry. Shall we retire to my father's study for the rest of the interview?"

The blonde in the power suit and too much makeup agreed it was a great idea to move things along. I wished I could ask a few questions, but it was too late to be that person now. I had my chance and blew it.

The only way JP would ever pay for his arrogance and criminal behavior was if someone managed to get a confession out of him. I should know. I've been, for lack of a better term, stalking JP Spencer for forty years, looking for a way in and a chance to take him down.

The crowd with JP started filing out. Cindy took a swig of that hot beer on the bar, waved good-bye to Tommy Lynne, and then gave me a look that told me exactly what I needed to know. She still hated my guts, and I was the last person she wanted to see. The feeling wasn't far from mutual, although I wasn't investing as much energy in despising Cindy Spencer as she appeared to be in loathing me.

"Now that is what I call a 'kiss my ass' grin if I've ever seen one."

I realized Johnny was speaking to me and that I was nodding and grinning at Cindy, just like when we were kids, and she drew a line in the proverbial sand, just moments before I wiped it out of my way and forged ahead.

I raised my glass in a silent toast. Cindy strolled with purpose out the door. Tommy Lynne brought two more beers for the men at my table.

"Johnny, that'll be the last for Mr. Pine tonight."

"Yes, ma'am."

She turned to me. "After seeing that little display, I'd say you and Mrs. Forster have a complicated history."

Randy started laughing and, true to form, spoke the truth. "You have to have loved someone to hate them that much."

"We all loved her," I said, surprising the locals. "She was our Sandy from Grease."

Johnny nodded and smiled at me. "You remember that night she and Hains got in the fight and her drunk ass ended up in my car and all over my dick. You wouldn't let her go alone. You were a good friend."

"And you were a gentleman if I recall. Most guys would have tossed me out the door and enjoyed the spoils."

Johnny nodded. "Yeah, well, that kind of drunk has never appealed to me." Then he just laid it on the table, "None of us could ever figure why she did what she did. Rattin' out your best friend takes some serious disconnects."

"What makes you say she ratted me out? The feds took me out in a sting directed by US Attorney JP Spencer."

"You don't know, do you?"

"Don't know what, Johnny?"

"Cindy Spencer told them to use you for the buy that night. She told them you worked for Porky and took a cut. That's why they came for you, Jane. Cindy set you up."

"How do you know that and I don't," I wanted to know.

"It's in Porky's file. Mom had it at the trailer. I used to read through it for fun. He took a plea, or he wouldn't have had a chance of release. None of the stuff his lawyers dug up ever saw the light of day."

I had my own theories as to why that undercover agent targeted me to ask, "Hey, do you know where I can find Porky Newman?" That theory still held, with the addition of further conspirators. My interrupted life, it appeared, had been a family affair.

10

Ace of spades...

"Why would she do that?"

I chunked a rock out past where I could see and heard it splash despite the steady coastal breeze.

Splish!

"I was already fighting charges for drugs that were planted on me by her fuckin' brother. Did she hate me that much for telling her the truth? Why the hell did she do that?"

My question had been sent into the dark water beyond the ferry dock lights. I'd been repeating it since leaving the pub. I had listened as Johnny described the sting operation in detail, trying very hard not to show the emotion that now raged in my chest. I nearly lost it at the part where Cindy told the investigators I regularly dealt cocaine at the high school. She claimed it was how I managed a job, athletics, and good grades. I did handle all that without amphetamines, something Cindy would never have been capable of, not without a tutor, and a job was beneath her. I know this because I helped her through her first college math class while I was still in high school. Cindy leaned on me for emotional support, too. Then she went and made me out to be Porky's teenage crime partner.

"What a bitch."

Another rock flew.

Plop-sheee, it splashed into the water.

Of course, none of Cindy's accusations came up in my case because it just wasn't true. I had known of an anonymous informant, but never in a million years did I think it had been one of my best friends. As it turned out, she was the only eyewitness to my drug-dealing career. They couldn't find a single person to verify her version of events. From the conversation at the pub, I learned that Porky gave up a lot of people, but he refused to take me with him. He swore I was just an innocent kid who happened to know where his van was parked. I'd hug that woman-beating, child-abusing piece of shit if he hadn't died of a heart attack in prison.

"I appreciate your criminal code of ethics, Porky, you old bastard."

I let a palm-sized rock fly. I waited for the ploop-sploosh sound. I would have played softball in college, but for that prison sentence. Without Porky's testimony and no corroborating witnesses for Cindy's tales, what made a full on sting operation come at me so hard? I had only one theory. My demise was directly related to disfiguring JP Spencer. I also wouldn't shut up about his role and that of his father in what happened to Malachi.

Even with JP urging the prosecuting US Attorney to add trafficking to my charges, the ones that stuck were possession with intent to distribute an ounce I had never seen before and conspiracy to distribute with the trailer park drug king. I was charged for pointing at a van in the pub parking lot. I knew JP wanted me in prison so badly that he was the one who planted the ounce of pot on me. I didn't drink or do drugs when I was a teenager, other than the occasional joint I'd pilfer from my dad's stash. But they found an ounce and my fingerprints inside that cooler. Apparently, if the cops say it's yours, it's yours; at least that was the way in 1979.

It's like Duck whispered to me on that first dark night in prison, "There's a lot of people not guilty of what put them in here, but ain't nobody innocent, honey."

"Shit."

Splush!

Hell, I was the class Valedictorian up until I was arrested and Hains took my place. I knew JP hated me and he threatened that I should forget about Malachi. I had not known that Cindy betrayed me so thoroughly, without thought to the consequences to my life. Or had she known precisely what she was doing, ridding herself of the only person who held a mirror up to her underlying ugliness? I knew more than one dark truth that the Spencer family did not want to be seen in the light.

"Let's ruin a kid with a promising future to protect our sick as fuck family. Ahhhhh!"

I flung a smooth round stone into the wind. I barely heard the thin rock cut into the waves.

Splishhhh.

I flashed on the memory of my arrogant eighteen-year-old ass, without a lawyer and ignorant of the corruptible nature of the system, admitting to knowing Porky was a dealer and to pointing out his van. This later constituted an admission of guilt to the court. Claiming what went on in the parking lot wasn't any of my concern turned out to be a weak defense. Because of this experience, the people I know get a metal wallet card with instructions for safely and smartly interacting with the police. At baby showers, I slip them into the box with the gift and a note that says, "Teach your children well." My business cards say, "Shut up. Ask for a lawyer," on the back.

"Motherfuckers!" I yelled at the darkness in front of me.

"I've cried into the wind here, from time to time. She often sings, but never answers my questions."

My eyes closed and reopened, like a stage curtain coming down and up to reveal a new scene. The memory of that voice carried toxins with it. My brain struggled to handle the chemical dump the presence of the man behind that voice created. The ground shifted at my feet. I dipped my chin, closed my eyes, and took a cleansing breath, seeking a balance between fight or flight. I felt the childhood fear leave me, replaced by a mature loathing—the kind of hatred a mentally healthy person learns to shed in order to mend. I never mastered that part of healing. I'd say I'm moderately medicated and old enough to know my revenge is truth and it is best served cold with a side of overwhelming evidence.

Have I mentioned how much I dislike electric golf carts? They make no sound, especially with a stiff breeze blowing in off the water. I didn't hear the cart approach and chastised myself for being so preoccupied in self-pity. I leaned down, picked up another rock, and tossed it as far as I could. It whistled through the air before landing in the building waves with a sploosh. A storm was brewing offshore and on.

My silence prompted the golf cart driver to speak again. "They say it'll be noisy when this storm blows through."

"Yep," seemed the appropriate response, since the sky in the distance boiled with clouds backlit by flashes of lightning.

"I snuck away to have a cigar. Care to join me. I always bring an extra, in case I should stumble upon a friend out for a walk."

I turned to see Judge Carroll J. Spencer, now retired, sitting at the helm of a personalized golf cart. The front panel read, "Here come de…" in small script, with "JUDGE" painted beneath in flowing letters large enough to read from afar. I suppose the cultural appropriation of a phrase made famous by Flip Wilson and later Sammy Davis, Jr., which originated with cult black comic Pigmeat Markham, was lost on all involved in bestowing the honor on the judge's ride. This cluelessness, quite typical of the Spencer family, was absolutely on point with the white supremacists they indeed were.

I replied to his invitation, "I am not a smoker, nor am I your friend."

"I'm sorry. I thought you were."

"Then you have been mistaken, sir."

The judge remained distinguished in his last years, dapper even. He wore a red and black velvet smoking jacket, à la Hugh Hefner, which definitely set his apart from the rest of the neighbors' wardrobes. Dashingly elegant or not, the old judge's affect came off more as ancient queen than Ashley from Gone With the Wind, which is what I had assumed he was going for when we were both younger. The judge played well the role of effeminate, yet straight southern gentleman found in every town and village. I always thought it ironic that the vain and arrogant Judge Spencer was also so cliché. Some men like him lived their lives as heterosexual family men and were just that. Many failed at the façade. The judge only pulled his husband and father act off because his young lovers were technically of age and his wife numbed herself with cocktails and Bridge parties.

Duck had accused me of holding the judge to a different standard between bites of a hot dog earlier in the evening.

"You judge him because he chose to keep his homosexual activities cloaked in a heterosexual veneer, which we all did if we didn't want trouble," she had said.

Even with marriage equality now, it wasn't safe to openly love whom you love in many places. From the earlier interaction with Four and his cronies, I surmised Doe's Ferry lagged behind the social revolution.

I tried to explain to the women at the dinner table, "My problem wasn't with the judge's sexual activities or the May-December dynamic of his chosen relationships with men; it was his misuse of power. Judge Spencer could have sucked the dick of every consenting nineteen-year-old in the county, but what he couldn't do was use his position to intimidate young men into letting the old letch touch them."

And now he sat in his golf cart in front of me, the antagonist of my life's story.

"I have been mistaken often, as of late," the old man replied to my curtness with a chuckle. "I apologize. I'll leave you to your stone casting."

I couldn't stop the escaping snort of laughter. I couldn't ignore the irony of his alluding to casting stones. "I must be careful of my glass house, is that it?"

"I'm sorry? Did you say something? I'm afraid I've grown quite hard of hearing."

I shook my head. It wasn't worth repeating. It seemed pointless to actively despise and engage with this frail old man, who didn't seem to know to whom he was speaking.

"Hey, Papa. Escaped from Opal again?"

A young man walked up out of the shadows. I could tell by his stature and his square jaw that this was Hains the Fourth in the flesh.

"Ah, young Four. What brings you out to visit your old Papa on this stormy evening? Shouldn't you be chasing some girl about the county?"

"Oh, you know, Papa, I let them chase me. I saw your cart and thought I'd walk you back home. Lots of strangers running around with all that's going on with Uncle JP. You need to be more careful about wandering till this blows over."

Four had glared at me the entire time he spoke to his grandfather. He was the product of his genetic makeup, the spawn of good and evil. This teenager who did not know me simmered with his uncle's rage behind his father's eyes. This boy was a cocked hammer waiting for someone to pull his trigger. It wasn't going to be me.

I wasn't there to martyr myself. That would be a fruitless venture anyway. Why sacrifice what's left of my life to the cause? Hadn't I already risked the future that should have been because I wouldn't be silenced? The citizens of Doe's Ferry already didn't care that this shriveled up old man and his offspring had ruined so many lives. No one wanted history corrected. No one wanted the truth to come out.

I watched Four's eyes slice me to pieces with his disdain. He had to know my identity and what that meant to show so much contempt. He'd never seen me, to my knowledge, but he was fixated on me with the kind of focus a cat has on a mouse in the grass. No, I didn't want to die or go back to prison, but I did want justice for Malachi, and for Asa, and for me.

Intimidating looks be damned, I couldn't help myself when I said, "If I remember correctly, the old judge likes it when things blow. Oh, wait. I think it might have been the other way around?"

The judge looked at me and smiled. I couldn't believe it, until he said, "I really should wear my hearing aids out of the house. What did you say, dear?"

I spoke loudly and clearly, so he'd be sure to hear me, "I said you like to blow things."

"Shut your filthy mouth, dyke," Four growled.

I laughed, which is my go-to reaction when someone starts taunting me. I really don't give a damn what is said to me or about me. The only thing that concerns me when facing an aggressor is what weapons they bring to the fight and how to counteract them, hopefully without either of us bleeding.

"It's not the first time I called the judge there a cocksucker, isn't that right, old man?"

Four took a step toward me, as he shouted, "I'll kill you, bitch."

His grandfather grabbed his arm, stopping Four from advancing on me.

The judge said, "Four, be still," as he peered at me through his glasses, squinting my face into focus under the glow of the streetlight. "I'm not familiar with your case, but if you come by my office tomorrow, we'll find out what's going on and try to help you. You do that. You come on by. No need for name-calling. No, no need for that."

"Four, take your grandfather home, and see to it that Opal locks the doors and sets the alarm."

Four's glare switched from me to someone he loathed more, his father. Silently, he walked around the front of the judge's golf cart and sat down beside him.

He continued to glare at his father, when he said, "Come on, old man. Show me what you can do in this thing."

Judge Carroll Spencer forgot about me, smiled at his grandson, and said, "All right, young man. Let's go for a spin."

I watched the golf cart make a U-turn, reading the words on the back panel, "There go de JUDGE."

"Jesus," I said, shaking my head and laughing to myself.

"I know it's completely tone deaf. Cindy's idea," Hains said.

"Of course. The girl that wouldn't kiss the black boy would not have a clue how racist that is, would she?"

"No, none," Hains agreed, chuckling with me.

I watched the dim little LED lights of the golf cart bounce through the church lawn. Faint laughter found us between the gusts now coming steadily from the west.

"So, the judge has dementia."

Hains nodded and answered, "Yes, for about five years. It's a lot worse now, mostly at night. Seems to have gained speed in the last few months."

Hains wasn't wearing a uniform anymore. He had switched to soft worn jeans and leather boat shoes with no socks. The flannel shirt and fleece vest finished the men's catalog cool guy look.

He continued explaining the judge's state of mind, "It would be a waste of energy to confront Judge Spencer. He lives in a special space between reality and a world of pure imagination."

"Like Willy Wonka."

Hains laughed. "Yeah, pretty much."

"I'm curious, did his sexual proclivities follow him into la-la land."

"He's an old man who doesn't remember to put on pants sometimes, Jane. You can give it a rest. He's in a special hell now. His brain is dying. A little compassion might be in order."

I don't lose control. I don't let emotions make me do stupid things. My calm and rational behavior in the worst of circumstances was a source of personal pride. Yet here in Doe's Ferry none of those qualities rose to the surface.

"He's still breathing. My compassion is reserved for his victims."

"Victims?"

"You're kidding, right? Are you going to pretend Judge Spencer did not sit in judgment of this county, while at the same time preying on young, poor men?"

"I never knew of him messing around with anyone underage," Hains said, strangely protective of his father-in-law.

Knowing what I knew, this defensive bent was extremely strange indeed, but I was focused on the judge's behavior.

"He preferred his boys between seventeen and nineteen—old enough to be legal, but adolescent enough to pass as the young teens he really preferred. His type was always slick skinned, nearly hairless, late-blooming, pretty boys of legal age to consent."

Hains shrugged with his comment. "So, he had consent. What's your problem?"

"In addition to the pretense of married father and community moral leader, in my opinion, the judge's position of power made age and consent irrelevant."

Hains knew I was right. He kicked at a rock with the toe of his shoe.

"I've been throwing them. It's good therapy."

I let another rock fly. It was small, only rating a little plop. Hains picked up a few mid-size rocks. He threw the first one, a large round stone, and turned to me with a smile as the "Bloosh!" met our ears.

"Hains, the rot started somewhere. I don't know, maybe it was here all along, but the judge made it worse. He used Asa. He used Malachi. How many others don't we know about? How did those affairs end? I know how two of them concluded."

Hains tossed another rock. "Careful, Jane. Those kinds of accusations got you nowhere before."

I tossed a rock. "Actually, those accusations got me put in prison."

Hains chuckled. "You're impossible."

"Impossible, but right. The judge carried out those illicit affairs with implied permission of people like your dad who could have stopped him but chose to look the other way. I learned to detest them all, but especially Judge Carroll J. Spencer. For him, the raging hypocrite, I reserve my deepest scorn."

"Don't waste your time hating him now, Jane. It won't ever hurt him as much as it hurts you."

"I won't ever forgive him for what he did to Asa, never."

#

"You don't have to take his money," my dad had said.

I was digging in a pile of parts, looking for an old wiring harness we could use on a go-cart we were making. We had decided we needed lights. The pile I searched happened to be outside of the camper where Asa had been living since the incident with JP and his frat brothers. The windows were open so I could hear everything being said.

"I can't keep living off you, John," I need to make some extra money so I can get my car from Virginia.

"I'm paying you top dollar by the hour. You don't have any expenses."

"I know, but I can't make it fast enough."

"How about I go get your car with the wrecker and bring it down here. We can fix it. No charge."

Asa refused Dad's offer. "It's more complicated than that."

"I'll pay what you owe, Asa. Let me help you."

"I don't want to start out like this. I don't want money in the middle of this relationship."

I kicked over a pile of hubcaps, ending my covert listening activities.

"Shhh. Who's out there?"

"It's just me, Dad. I'm looking for something."

"Don't be spying on folks. It isn't polite," Asa said, smiling at me when he stuck his head out the window.

He looked better now. His face was almost healed. I thought he looked like a young Paul Newman in Cool Hand Luke. It was probably the devilish grin he seemed to always wear.

I answered him, "I'm not spying, but folks that don't want to be heard should shut their windows."

Asa's grin widened. "Fair enough."

"I need a wiring harness. Know where I can find one?"

"What's it for," my dad asked. He was out of the camper and had come around to the other side where I was digging in the smashed up front end of a Pinto.

"For the go-cart."

He wiped his hands on the faded pink shop rag, a habit he had even when his hands were clean.

"Look over on the other side of the garage, by the oil drums. There's a box of different ones under the window."

"Thanks, Dad."

I ran past him, as he called out, "Be careful. Look for snakes."

"See you later, Harriet the Spy," Asa called after me when I rounded the camper.

"Later, dude."

When I got to the front of the station, I saw JP Spencer getting back in his car. I slid to a stop. My low top canvas tennis shoes kicked up a cloud of dust.

He yelled out the passenger side window, "I put five bucks on the counter. Tell your dad it's a lousy way to run a business. I could have stolen the damn gas, and he'd never have known." JP rubbed his chin, the scar still pink and healing. "I'll catch you later, Jane Doe." He pointed his finger at me like a gun and pulled the imaginary trigger, then he blew away the smoke at the end of his finger barrel.

His Nova SS roared to life with his laughter, before he sped away, making sure to lay some rubber on the new road as he went.

"Asshole," I said under my breath.

My mission took priority over JP's message. I wasn't going to bother my dad with JP's criticism anyway. The judge's son had already forgotten he was supposed to be sorry he beat up Asa and blacked Doodie's eye. But then, I wasn't sorry I had hit him with that radio antenna either.

"Turd," I added before I continued my quest.

On my way to find the box, I met Doodie and Malachi coming around the other corner of the station.

"Hey, I thought you were pulling the old tires off," I said, confused about their sudden appearance.

Malachi said, "You were taking too long."

Doodie told the truth. "Hains and Cindy were kissing. It's gross. We came to help you."

I looked at Mali, who shrugged off his white lie. "He's right. It's gross."

"Okay, well, Dad said there are some harnesses behind the station. Come on. We have to watch for snakes, though."

Malachi started up right away, "Snakes! You white folks can go on and play with them snakes. I'll just wait out here by the phone, so I can call the ambulance when you get bit."

"Come on, Mali. I'll protect you," I teased.

"First you were going to tie me up and dunk me in the water last month, and now you're dragging me into snake-infested weeds. Do you secretly want me dead, Jane Doe?"

"Not today, buddy. Hey, Doodie, grab a couple of those long pipes over there. We'll poke around with one of them and use the other one for a weapon."

Malachi continued to complain, "Nothing is ever, like, let's just go get the wire from the store. We got to traipse through woods and fight off snakes."

Doodie the encyclopedia tried to allay Mali's fears. "Chances are if we find a snake it will be non-poisonous. Of the thirty-seven species of snakes found throughout North Carolina, only six are venomous."

"That doesn't make me feel better, man."

"Okay, you stay out here by the path. Doodie and I will go get the box."

"What if y'all scare the snakes out here to me?"

"Then run, you big baby," I said, growing tired of Mali's fit of cowardice.

Doodie went first. He claimed special snake finding powers because of his extensive knowledge. He did have a cool set of encyclopedias and read them regularly, so I let him take the lead. I would have sent him alone, but my mechanic skills outweighed his animal husbandry in this instance.

"Don't make any sudden movement," Doodie warned, as we crouched near the racks of sheet metal stored behind the garage. He continued talking in the hushed voice of Marlin Perkins from Wild

Kingdom, "If I was a snake, this is where I'd come for shade in this heat."

I don't know why I was so grumpy. I guess seeing JP had set my nerves on edge. I told Doodie, "Shut up, man. You're creeping me out."

I saw the box spilling over with wiring pulled from wrecked cars. It was under the boarded up back window like dad said. It may have looked like piles of junk to the uninformed, but John Doe knew what and where all of it was.

"Shh, I think I see something," Doodie said, wandering away from the direction we needed to go.

Tired of being cautious, I passed Doodie, who was engrossed in carefully parting the tall grass around the piles of sheet metal with his piece of lead pipe. I walked right up to the wooden slat-sided box and tapped the side with my pipe. Seeing no movement, I picked up the whole box of wire. We could sort through it in the shop, away from ticks and snakes. I started back toward the waiting Malachi. Doodie finally realized I had passed him and stood next to the path with a look of awe on his face.

"You just make noise, and they'll go on," I said as if I were now the snake expert.

Doodie's eyes widened. He covered his mouth to muffle his scream and pointed at the box. I looked down and saw nothing, but Doodie began to panic, so I knew something was definitely wrong. I looked down again. This time I saw the black head of a snake the size of my fist, followed by a large portion of its long body sticking out of one of the front slats of the box. The head bobbed and weaved, seeking the source of its distress.

Doodie's hand finally could not hold his scream in check. His loud cry and retreat caused my legs to follow him, but I couldn't let go of the box. It was frozen in my terror-stricken hands. Doodie looked back, saw me running at him with the snake leading the way, and screamed again.

"What the hell," Malachi said, as we came at him on a dead run.

Doodie looked back again, tripped and fell in front of me. I had no time to clear him and stumbled over his body. The box flew from my hands and landed at Malachi's feet, where it broke open and exposed a giant black snake tangled in a mass of wire and splintered wood.

The scream that came out of Malachi's mouth probably woke a few of the dead buried behind the church. The bottoms of his Converse fleeing the scene were the last parts of Mali we saw before he disappeared around the curve in the path.

"Are you hurt?" Dad asked me, as he came running around the corner.

"No, that wasn't me screaming. It was Doodie and Mali."

"Are they hurt?"

"No, but that snake there scared them both shitless."

"Hey, language," Dad said, but he was smiling.

Asa walked over to the exploded box, snatched the snake up near the back of its head and untangled it from the wood and wires. Doodie and I watched in amazement as Asa told us about the reptile he was rescuing.

"It's an Eastern Black Snake. These are good guys. You want them around to keep down the rodent population."

He pulled it free of the last wire, checked it for injuries, and then placed the snake in the shade near one of the big trees, where it slithered under the kudzu vines and disappeared.

"Hey there, John. Is everything all right back there?" Sheriff Forster stood out in the driveway.

"Oh, hey Sheriff. Yeah, the kids found a black snake. Pretty good sized one too."

Hains's father did not look happy. This wasn't a social call. I ran through my mind quickly, wondering what I had done now.

He eased my mind when he asked my dad, "Can I see you and Asa for a minute?

"Sure." Dad turned to me. "Clean up this mess and find something to put that wire in, since you smashed my box."

"Yes, sir," I said, but I knew as soon as he turned his back, Doodie and I would sneak to find out what the sheriff wanted.

We did just that. We inched our way to outside one of the garage bays where we could hear what was being said.

"Well, John. I don't know what to tell you. The tools were missing, and here they are. If you didn't take them, then Asa did. So, tell the truth, and maybe the judge will go easy on you."

"Fuck you, and fuck the judge," came Asa's reply. "I didn't take shit. I knew that cocksucker was setting me up. I knew it."

"It's okay, Asa," my dad said. "I'll get you a lawyer. Just keep your mouth shut."

"A lawyer won't matter. He wants me gone from here, so he planted this stuff on me."

"Who? The judge?" The Sheriff wasn't convinced. "Son, the judge has been in court all day. Those tools went missing after you left there this morning, according to JP."

I put two and two together pretty quick and shot out of my hiding place like I was fired from a cannon. "JP was here. He put those tools in the garage."

Dad asked, "Did you see JP here, today?"

"Yes, he said he put five bucks on the register and pumped his own gas. Go look. I didn't touch the money."

We moved as a group to the register. There was no money anywhere in sight.

The sheriff said, "Jane, I know you like Asa an awful lot, but lying isn't going to help him."

"I'm not lying. I saw JP. He put his finger to his head and pulled the trigger like a gun and then blew out the smoke. He said he'd catch me later."

"He's threatening my kid. What are you going to do about that, Sheriff?" My dad wanted to know.

"I'll speak to the judge. For now, if we can't find the five dollar bill, then it's just your word against JP's, Jane."

The sheriff moved to stand behind Asa.

"Why isn't that good enough?" I asked. "Why would you believe JP and not me?"

The sheriff didn't answer.

Asa smiled at me as the handcuffs went on behind his back. "It's just how it is, kid. Keep your nose clean. I'll see you around."

I couldn't stop myself. I ran forward and hugged Asa as tight as I could around his waist. He couldn't hug me, but he looked down at me and said, "Friends for life, Jane Doe. Take care of your dad. I'll be back."

As Asa was led away, I started to cry. I yelled after the sheriff. "I hate this place. When I grow up, I'm going to come back here and put every one of you cocksuckers in prison, where you belong."

My dad didn't tell me to watch my mouth. He stepped up beside me and hugged me to him. I looked up to see tears running down his cheeks.

#

The memory of Asa's arrest faded as I returned from the past to the ferry dock, where Hains waited for me to speak.

"Asa took a plea because he had no choice, Hains. The District Attorney threatened to prosecute my dad for having the tools on his property. Asa just quit fighting after they promised to leave Dad alone if he pled out. He didn't steal those tools. JP did. He hated Asa being around the judge and set him up to go to prison for five years for something he did not do. It would not be the last time, and you know it."

Hains smiled at me, reminding me of the young boy I used to love. "Yeah, but that backfired on JP, didn't it? Asa actually ended up being around all the time."

"Only a month. That's all it took for Asa to make the judge mad and that was the end of that."

"Didn't you get arrested that day, too?"

"Yep, my first time in handcuffs. I had a foot in mouth problem as a youth."

Hains laughed. "I have a hard time believing age cured that."

I laughed too. "Yeah, well, you're probably right."

Hains began to recollect my first arrest. "I went to the dentist that day. Do you remember?"

11

Like a rock to the bottom...

Asa came back to Doe's Ferry right before Labor Day. Judge Spencer made it possible for him to serve his sentence in the jail, where he was released daily to work on the county's vehicles in Dad's garage. Sometimes he had to go work at the judge's farm, but mostly he was around us all the time. We could almost pretend he wasn't a prisoner.

Working for the judge was a way to earn "good time" he told my dad. He hoped it would shorten his sentence. It was all up to judge cocksucker, so I was wary of making any mistake that could cost Asa. I hid one of Dad's bathing suits in the boathouse so Asa could keep his clothes dry when he went for a forbidden swim. The boys and I never told anyone, especially Cindy. Her inability to ignore a rule, unless it directly benefitted her, kept Miss Spencer out of the loop on some of our adventures. I was happy, Dad was more settled, and Asa seemed as content as a prisoner could be.

I thought my dad missed having his Marine buddies to look after. He was a different guy when Asa was around. Dad's drinking slowed. He and Asa spent hours with their heads down in an engine, side by side, laughing the day away. We hung out together in the evenings more. We fished some, put together giant jigsaw puzzles, and sometimes we read books on the back porch. I didn't hear him fighting in his jungle nightmares as often. John Doe had learned how to smile again.

Asa seemed happy too. He had access to the same area we kids were free to roam. Let out of the jail at sunup, he returned to be locked down at dusk. He had a clean, warm bed, got two hot meals and a brown bag lunch each day, and he wasn't in prison with a thousand other guys.

"Could be a lot worse," Asa would say and walk back toward the courthouse at sunset.

The one bothersome thing, he said, was the way people looked at him in the prison issue clothes he was forced to wear. That stripe down the outside pant leg tended to be universally recognizable for what it was from a mile away. Once the viewer grew closer, the numbers over his chest pocket verified the stripe's authenticity. Even with his Cool Hand Luke charm, people saw Asa as a criminal, and that hurt his pride. I had a plan to help with that.

"Sure is hot today," Malachi said that afternoon.

"Uh huh."

"Come on, let's go swimmin'," he urged me.

"Maybe in a little while," I answered, clutching a brown paper wrapped package to my chest.

"We won't have too many more good swimmin' days left. It'll be October soon."

"Yep."

"Maybe he isn't coming today, Jane."

"He's coming. He said he would be here after lunch."

The judge's big black car rolled up in front of the station. Asa got out of the passenger side.

Judge Spencer called after him, "We'll probably need to go back out and look at that pump again tomorrow."

Asa looked into the car, answering, "I think it's good for a while, Judge. I'll let you know when it needs another check."

The judge's lips formed that sneering smile I'd come to associate with Asa being very uncomfortable. "Don't make it too long, Mr. Speight. Regular maintenance prevents those long drawn out workdays you seem to detest more and more."

Mali and I stayed back in the shadows out of instinct. Hostility hung in the air.

"Maybe you should find someone else to work on your farm," Asa said. "Someone younger."

"Oh, but I like you so much, Asa. I'm not yet ready to let you go. For now, John Doe and I will simply share your services."

"John isn't using county funds for private interests."

"Watch how you speak to me, son. I control a lot of what happens to you daily. I think I've been quite indulgent, but that can change."

"Sometimes I think doing my time over in Maple prison would be better than knowing I'll have to see you every day. I am reminded with every passing minute that I'm in prison because of your son."

"You're in jail, Asa. Prison, I assure you, is much harder than you can imagine. And if you should go there, it will not be a minimum-security farm. I suggest you rethink your position and apologize to me this afternoon in my chambers."

Asa slammed the car door but stood still as the judge pulled away. He waved his middle finger at the rear window.

When he turned around, Mali and I were waiting for him.

I asked, "Is Judge Cocksucker being a pain in the butt again?"

I wasn't at all sure what being a cocksucker entailed. I knew it had to be more than the literal interpretation. Malachi tried to explain what two men did and why people freaked out about it. He only knew because he found some books with stories involving all kinds of sex acts in his dad's shed, but no pictures, just some pencil sketches. This book made Mali our go-to source for X-rated information. I was kind of glad there were no real pictures. I really didn't want to know that much about any type of sex. I was willing to wait. It all seemed so wet and sticky if watching Cindy and Hains kiss had anything to do with it.

The anger on Asa's face left, replaced with a grin. "Yeah, he's a real prick today. Where's your dad?"

"He isn't back from lunch. I told him I'd wait for you and watch the pumps."

I had planned this moment for several weeks. I'd worked for my dad and anyone else who would pay me. When I had enough money, I went down to Swann's to spend it on a gift for Asa. I clutched that package to my chest until the anticipation of handing it over felt like it would burst my heart.

"Here." I thrust the package at Asa's chest as soon as he was within arms reach.

"What's this?"

I felt my face turn scarlet. Now that I had given him the gift, I was overcome with embarrassment. Asa saw that and knelt down in front of me to open his package.

"Wow, this is cool," he said, as he lifted a pair of jeans and a bright white tee shirt from the paper wrapping.

"I hope they fit. Maybe you can wear them at the shop and then put the jail pants back on before you go home at night. I can wash 'em for ya."

"I'll thank you not to call that place home," Asa said of the jail, and then hugged me to him. "Thank you for the gift sweetheart. I'll go put them on."

Asa walked toward the office to get the key to the restroom. He smiled and winked at me as he disappeared around the corner of the building. I was eleven, but I understood what a crush was. I sure had one on Asa Speight.

"Okay, can we go now? The trailer park boys are supposed to be down at the ferry dock this afternoon. When the ferry goes to the mainland for the last time, Johnny is going to jump off the dock. I don't want to miss that."

"You go ahead, Mali. I have to wait for my dad to come back."

It was a lie. I could go now that Asa had returned. I just didn't want to.

"Okay, but you might miss me swimmin' the channel today. I feel like I can do it now. I'm ready to try."

"Malachi, the only swimming you'll do is like a rock to the bottom."

"I've been practicing with Asa," Mali smiled and backed away. "You'll see. I know I can do it."

"Where's Hains and Doodie?"

"Hains had to go to the dentist. He'll be back soon, I guess. Doodie is mowing his grass."

The smile faded from my face. "Don't go in the deep water without one of us. Wait until one of us gets there. Those other boys won't help you if you get in trouble. They aren't your friends, Mali."

"They're all right, Jane. Jeremy told me to come."

"Promise me you won't go in over your head until I get there, okay."

"I promise, but hurry up. I really think I can do it today."

"Be careful, Malachi."

On his way back from the restroom, Asa asked, "Be careful doing what?"

Malachi skipped past him "I'm going to swim today, man. I'm going to do it."

"Don't go by yourself, Mali," Asa warned.

"I'm not. There's a bunch of us guys going."

Malachi disappeared around the corner of the building, taking the path toward the church and on to the ferry dock. I was forced to stop thinking about Mali because I was overwhelmed with the best-looking thing I'd ever seen. Everything slowed to a crawl, like a slow-motion movie segment, including Asa flipping his long blonde bangs back, and the cigarette dangling from that careless grin. I'd never seen a movie star up close, but I thought Asa Speight could have been one. Wearing his new jeans and the sparkling clean white tee shirt, he was a sight to behold. I imagined seeing James Dean in person kind of felt like standing in the beam of Asa's smile.

He turned in front of me and asked, "How do they fit?"

I managed to say, "They look nice," without gushing too much.

"Nice? Is that all you can say?"

"How about bitchin'? They look bitchin'." I'd heard some older kid say that at the football game last Friday night.

Asa's head fell back with a long laugh. "Bitchin'. Yeah, that'll work," he said, as he looked over his shoulder at his reflection in the service station's plate-glass windows. He was paying close attention to how the jeans fit his ass, which I wondered about.

"Cindy does that, staring at her rear-end to see what it looks like. She acts like her butt is the most important thing about her." I stood next to him, looking at the reflection of my backside beside his in the big window. "Is it really that important, Asa?"

"How old are you again?"

"I'll be twelve in November."

"Then it isn't that important yet."

"What are you two doing?" My dad had just come around the corner, returning from his lunch break.

Asa and I turned around to see that he was smiling at us.

"Jane wanted to know if how your jeans fit on your ass is really important," Asa explained.

Dad looked down at me. "It will be, but not for a few years yet, honey."

"Good," I said. "Because mine is flat as a board."

Dad and Asa were laughing at me when Doodie came skidding around the corner, out of breath, and trying to speak words that sounded more like grunts. Doodie packed a few extra pounds on the large frame he hadn't quite grown into. He was like a big puppy with giant paws and legs going in all directions. If he ever grew into those feet, he was going to be massive. Strength was his asset, running his nemesis. Even Malachi's baby sister could outrun our big friend.

"What's going on, Doodie?" Dad asked.

All Doodie could do was gasp for air.

"Calm down and breathe a sec so we can understand you."

Doodie doubled over, trying to catch his breath. "Jane…Mali…help" was all he could get out.

Already moving toward the path, I asked, "Is Mali okay?"

Doodie stood up straight and gushed out, "Trailer park boys gonna throw Mali off dock." He heaved a breath in and finished with, "Mali say get Jane. Help." He continued to gasp and mumble, "Too many of 'em. Couldn't stop 'em."

My lungs were on fire, and my legs felt like spaghetti by the time I rounded the church steps with fifty yards to go. I could see a crowd of boys running around the restrooms and picnic tables chasing Mali all over the ferry dock. The ferry itself was way offshore with another twenty minutes left on this leg of its last round trip to the mainland. The boys would scatter when the ferry got closer, or the cops showed up. The deputies regularly slowed to yell out the window, "Get the hell out of there," but nobody ever got in trouble for playing at the dock. I hoped one would drive by now.

"Hey! Hey!" I yelled, but the mob couldn't hear me.

I heard footsteps behind me, and the sound of a runner sucking air like a sprinter at full throttle. Asa went by me so fast I felt the wind he created. I looked back to see my dad was coming too, but his hobbling gait was much slower than mine and certainly not at Asa's pace. Doodie staggered behind him, spent but determined to be part of the rescue party.

Asa was yelling, "Knock it off. Knock it off," but the boys on the dock didn't hear him.

He'd been working with Malachi, trying to talk the fear of water out of him. Malachi could swim. I'd seen him do it. The second he thought about how his feet were not on the bottom, he panicked, went stiff, and sank. He fell out of Hains's boat and nearly drowned until he stood up and realized the water was little more than waist deep. Mali wouldn't ride in the boat after that.

I could hear a bunch of jumbled threats, a few "queer" taunts with an occasional "Ferry dock fairy" drifted past my ear.

"Dammit!" I dug down deep for every ounce of speed I had.

Malachi was too pretty for his own good. He was sweet and kind, never seeing the danger others posed to him. Mali just assumed people would like him. What wasn't likable about a good-looking kid who smiled constantly and brought joy into the room? Apparently, being a nice guy offended some people. It usually only took one jackass to egg the others on.

106

I thought that the song "Vincent" was written about a guy a lot like Mali. This world was not meant for people with our sweet boy's spirit. He was the angel everyone loved. His universal appeal to young and old, male and female, and an ability to move between ethnic groups caused an occasional bully to call him out for some perceived slight. Mostly, the boys our age honed in on Mali's lack of testosterone-fueled aggression. Hains, Doodie, and I had been watching Malachi's back since the cradle. I should never have let him go to the dock alone.

In the seconds it took Asa to close the distance, the trailer park boys had Malachi in hand, swinging his body out over the water and back, taunting him with a watery demise.

I screamed, "Nooooo!"

Asa yelled, "Drop him!"

The boys let go. Malachi seemed to hang in the air and then drop out of sight, like the coyote in the Road Runner cartoons. Asa never broke stride and dove in behind him. The sheriff pulled up with Hains running behind his car. I had not slowed down.

I ran through the trailer park boys, yelling in Jeremy's face as I passed, "You asshole," before stopping at the edge of the ferry dock to look for Asa and Malachi.

"I got him," Asa shouted up to me.

He had a wild-eyed, but very much alive Mali gripped tightly to his chest and was using a sidestroke to bring them both to the shore. I turned to face the boys on the dock.

"He can't swim you jerks."

"Yes, he can," Jeremy said. "I just saw him swim the channel not ten minutes ago."

"He sinks when he's scared. You could have drowned him. And what's with calling him names. You all like Mali. What the hell is wrong with you assholes?"

"Jane Doe, watch your mouth," Sheriff Forster demanded.

"You're worried about her mouth when these boys could have killed Malachi? Come on, Forster. Get your priorities straight. I'll discipline my child. You do your job."

"Careful, John," the sheriff warned.

Asa and Malachi approached from the bank, climbing the hill to the dock where the rest of us stared at the sheriff and my dad. Dad had gone quiet. He had a hand on my shoulder. I looked up at him, watching his jaw muscle twitch. His eyes were dark and empty like I'd seen in the woods when he took on JP and his friends.

I touched the hand that now clamped down hard on my shoulder and said, "It's okay, Dad. Let's see if Mali and Asa are all right."

Dad's grip loosened. He stopped glaring at the sheriff, and we moved to where Asa and Malachi stood dripping and shivering. The clouds had drifted to block the sun and dropped the temperature a few degrees. A deputy appeared with a blanket, which Asa wrapped around himself and pulled Malachi into his arms to warm him faster. I thought Mali was trembling more from fear than cold, but he didn't resist being folded into the blanket with Asa.

The commotion at the docks must have drawn attention from the courthouse, as another deputy and a few other adults came rushing our way. The judge came trotting up with them, still in his robe.

He asked, "Is everyone okay?"

Malachi nodded because he was in shock and not speaking.

The judge came over to Mali and Asa. "What happened here?"

I answered, even though I wasn't asked, "These jackasses threw Mali off the dock."

"Is that so?" The judge commented, still looking at Asa and Mali. He turned away and walked to the deputy that served as his bailiff. They spoke in hushed tones. Then the judge waved to everyone and took his leave. "The sheriff seems to have this under control. You boys be careful with your pranks. Someone could get hurt."

"That's it? Someone could get hurt? They could have killed him," I complained.

The bailiff mumbled something to a deputy who in turn whispered behind his hand to the sheriff. Hains's father turned and walked toward Asa and Malachi. He pulled the blanket back and looked closely at the two.

"Arrest him," the sheriff said.

The other deputy over by the trailer park boys asked, "Which one?"

Sheriff Forster beckoned, "Malachi, come with me. I'll take you to your momma."

Asa wrapped the blanket around Malachi's shoulders. The deputy that had done the whispering smiled and walked toward him.

"Asa Speight, you are under arrest for attempted escape."

My dad said, "What? He wasn't escaping. He came to save the boy."

The sheriff held tightly to Malachi's shoulder and said to my dad, "The prisoner is not in his prison-issue uniform. That constitutes an escape attempt. The judge ordered him arrested."

"That's bullshit!" My dad stepped in front of Asa.

"If he interferes, arrest him too," Sheriff Forster said, pointing at my dad.

"You're letting that old letch tell you what to do Law?"

My dad called the sheriff by his real name. Law was short for Lawton. Nobody called Hains's dad Law. He was always just Sheriff Forster, or Sheriff. His wife called him Sheriff. Dad wasn't done insulting the huge man. "I always figured you were above his reach, but I see that ain't so."

The sheriff glared at Dad and told his deputy, "Arrest him."

"On what charge?" Dad asked.

"You gave him the jeans. That's abetting."

I stepped in front of my dad. "I bought the jeans from Swann's. Ask Mr. Sam. Dad didn't know anything about it. I just gave them to Asa a few minutes ago. He was trying them on when Doodie came to get us."

"It doesn't matter, Jane. Asa knows the rules."

The deputy pointed at my dad. "So do I arrest him or not?"

"Let him be, but go ahead and process the prisoner for transport back to the prison. He can't stay here now."

"He saved Malachi," I screamed at the sheriff. "What's wrong with you fucking people?"

"Arrest her for abetting an escape attempt and for having a foul mouth," Sheriff Foster said and walked back to his car with the still silent Malachi. He got in and drove away, as the deputy slapped the cold steel around my wrists for the first time in my life. My grandmother had been right. I really needed to change my ways.

My dad came at the deputy cuffing me, but the bailiff stopped him with a hand in his chest and a warning, "Easy, John Doe."

Asa said, "Calm down, John. Jane will be home by dinnertime. He's just proving a point."

"And what would that be?" Dad asked.

"The sheriff? He's just teaching Jane about authority and rebellion. The judge, well, he is asserting his control over my balls."

"Shut your mouth, faggot," the deputy with Asa growled while at the same time punching his handcuffed prisoner in the gut.

"Stop! Don't hurt him," I yelled.

Asa smiled at me through his pain as he was dragged away. "I'll be back, Jane Doe. You ain't seen the last of me."

#

"I couldn't believe you yelled at my dad like that and all he did was lock you in the holding cell for a few hours," Hains said with a chuckle.

"I was cuffed but not charged. Your dad cooled off, and everything went on as the judge planned. It was the beginning of the end."

"We had seven good years in between, didn't we?"

Hains question indicated just how much he wished to pretend his Ozzy and Harriet existence extended to the rest of us.

"While Asa was gone, it wasn't so good for my dad or me. But after he came back, those high school years, we did have some fun—until we didn't."

Hains threw another rock. This one went so far I didn't hear it enter the water. I heard him sigh, before turning back to me.

"My dad wasn't involved in you being sent to prison, Jane."

"I know. It was a federal investigation."

"But he knew JP sent them after you. I found a folder he kept on the crap JP pulled all the way back to when he was twelve and beat that kid down at the beach."

"The press would love to have that."

"Yeah, well, I burned it a long time ago, long before any of this Justice talk started."

"Too bad. So, your dad could have warned me. He could have stopped the whole thing by arresting JP for any one of the things he'd done before he came after me."

"If the evidence existed, Dad would have done something. There just wasn't any. No one else saw what you saw that night, Jane. By then, JP was a US Attorney."

"It all came down to my word against JP's, like it always did, and he made sure no one would ever believe me."

"Your story didn't fit the facts. His story matched the investigation's findings. JP was not there when Malachi died."

"He didn't die, Hains. He was killed, and Asa had nothing to do with it. He was not having sex with Malachi."

"Everybody has secrets, Jane. You kept the campground girl to yourself, didn't you?"

"Yeah, but you knew. You said so."

"But you never told me about it."

"I told Malachi."

Hains smiled down at me. "We all told Mali things. He was the keeper of our secrets."

"And I was the keeper of his."

110

Hains's eyebrows rose a bit before he cloaked his intrigue. What did I know? He was curious but afraid to know the answer to his question.

"It was forty years this past April," he said. "I have looked out my bedroom window nearly every one of those forty years of sunrises to see this ferry dock and remember."

"Until it is set right," I said, "we are never going to be able to forget."

I left Hains with the thoughts swirling in his mind and went to the boathouse to deal with the memories he had stirred in mine.

12

It started that afternoon...

The boathouse had been repaired with new supports sunk to replace the old rotting pilings. It was a clean and functioning space, as opposed to its former life as a kid's playhouse and general catch-all for things no longer wanted. I poked around on the shelves. Duck had saved a few boxes of items she said I should look through. Now was as good a time as any, since I was there and had no plan to return in the future. I ate another edible and prayed I had enough to get me back home.

I poked around in the first box only seconds when my laughter echoed in the cavernous space. No boats hung over the water to absorb some of the sounds. I picked up the red light I used to summon my playmates. It was still wired and had a plug.

"The bat signal," I said aloud and chuckled at my idea of an emergency at eleven years old. As I reached toward the receptacle, I mumbled, "This could be a really dumb thing to do."

I squinted and put one hand in front of my face as if that would stop electrocution. When the plug slid in without arcing or exploding, I opened my eyes fully to the interior of the boathouse glowing red. I immediately removed the plug and returned the room to the amber glow from the new low voltage LED light bulbs installed by Duck.

"Wouldn't want to summon anyone by mistake."

I pulled a stack of magazines and papers from the bottom of the box where the red light had been stored. There were a couple of Life Magazines, some old newspaper clippings chronicling our lives, what appeared to be a year's worth of Women's Sport magazines, and a collection of travel brochures. A pamphlet from the Biltmore Estate in Asheville fell out of the stack and fluttered onto the floor.

I remembered picking that pamphlet out of a roadside rest stop's local attractions display in the early seventies when I crisscrossed this state with my father for five years. Asa served that time in Old Craggy up in the mountains on the other side of North Carolina. Dad and I visited as often as we could, but it took two days just to get there and back, more than eight hours each way. We made side trips and explored old blacktop roads, sleeping at rest stops and eating service station junk food for breakfast.

We lived in the longest state east of the Mississippi, five hundred and ten miles from Manteo to Murphy. I've seen nearly every stretch of road from the coast to the mountains because Judge Spencer seemed to think that if Asa were far away, we'd forget about him. Total dick move, if you had asked me, but no one did. I don't know what he expected to teach the three of us, but what the judge taught me was that my dad was as loyal as they come and "leave no man behind" was not just a saying, it was a way of life.

We never had a new car. Dad would throw his tools and some extra parts in the back of his latest muscle car rebuild, and off we'd go on an adventure. We always made it. Dad was a mechanical genius. I never doubted him for a second. Those trips were the longest continuous moments I spent with a father I barely knew. I learned a lot about who John Doe was on a two-lane blacktop. There was still so much I would never understand.

As a child, I thought my dad went to see Asa sometimes without telling me. He'd be gone for a weekend and not say where he had been when he came back. I don't think Dad wanted to lie to me. Instead, he was often vague or wouldn't answer the questions. I learned not to ask. When I was older, I understood where he went to silence the demons. Kid me had no clue.

During those five years, Dad stopped drinking himself to death every day. He still drank, and he still got drunk, but the time lengthened between incidences of complete madness when he'd be lost in some waking jungle terror. After a bad episode, Dad would check into a veterans' hospital in Washington, DC for a little while. He'd return without a word about what had happened, and we'd go on until the next time the wheels fell off his wagon.

Before Asa was let out of prison in 1977, we asked him if he'd like to live with us, even if it was in Judge Spencer's backyard. I think he

113

was secretly happy to rub his freedom in the old cocksucker's face. I'd taken to calling the judge a cocksucker long before I actually knew what I was saying. At my age now, I have many friends who enjoy fellatio with their male partners—I'll take a pass on that one—and who also agree the use of the word cocksucker is all about inflection. There aren't too many ways to coo "cocksucker" in a loving way.

Dad and I built a small apartment on the back of the service station. Asa came home to a full-time job and a place to call his own at the beginning of my junior year of high school. By that time, I already considered Asa family. We lived happily like that for one year and seven months, until Sunday, April 29, 1979.

It began as a sunny spring day with prom and graduation looming ahead of us, our childhood about to be left behind. Hains was king of the high school, a star athlete in three sports, and headed to play quarterback at State on a full-ride athletic scholarship. Doodie also excelled in athletics, particularly football, but had chosen to join the Army. He said he could pay for college with service and see the world. He would leave for boot camp right after graduation. Cindy was finishing up her first year of nursing school. To keep Hains under surveillance, she went to the local junior college while we finished our senior year of high school.

I was also headed to State on an academic scholarship, with an additional small stipend awarded to play softball. I was first in our class, Hains second, and Doodie was in the top ten. Malachi focused on just getting out of high school. He was capable of making much better grades but said he'd leave the over-achieving to us three.

Mali was the first to point out the discrepancy in grading and pretty much everything else. I helped him write a paper because he had started giving up even trying. When we got our papers back, I had an A, and he had a C.

"They will grade me as they expect me to be, black and unable to compete at the same level as the white kids."

I was livid and reproached our sophomore English teacher.

Mali had smiled at me on the way out of the principal's office that day—because evidently if one calls a teacher incompetent and racist one ends up in the principal's office—and said, "Go on, keep fightin' the man, white girl, but don't fight him for me. I'm gonna chill, and when the time comes, I'll peace out and leave this backwater in the rearview. Feel me?"

We both ended up with zeros on the paper for cheating. Thankfully, the incompetent racist dropped the lowest grade at the end of the semester. Mali didn't' care about his grade. He passed. Good enough. He had plans to be a fashion model and a designer. He had no idea how to make that happen, but he was sure it wouldn't if he stayed in Doe's Ferry. I couldn't imagine leaving him behind.

I told him, "Come live with me. I don't have to play ball. We can get jobs and rent an apartment."

"Girl, I'm going to be famous. Don't you worry about me." He flashed that million-dollar smile. "You can come to visit me in my penthouse in New York City."

Honestly, I believed him. Malachi was the kind of pretty that made everyone stare. He was also smart and very creative. He won a contest for photography and sang solos in the school choir. Malachi was going to be whatever he wanted to be, but it would be far from me. For the first time in our lives, the four of us—Hains, Doodie, Mali, and me—would be split up. We were like quadruplets from different mothers, and the thought of them not at my side gave me nausea. For weeks, coming up on graduation, I felt impending doom. If I had been honest, I would have told the boys I was afraid to be alone without them. Instead, I grew sullen and cantankerous with everyone. Every day since I have wished I could go back and tell them all how much I loved them.

The sun shined as brightly as our futures on that day. By sundown, the life we had planned was over, but it all started that warm coastal Carolina afternoon.

#

"Jane."

"Jane!"

Cindy knocked the elbow I was leaning on out from under me to get my attention.

"What?" I demanded, grouchy at being disturbed so rudely.

"What are you reading? You haven't heard a word I said."

"A Cat on a Hot Tin Roof."

"Didn't we see that movie? Paul Newman and Elizabeth Taylor, right?"

I rolled over on my towel and sat up. "Yes, that's the one."

"Then why are you reading it?"

Cindy saw no need to read anything that had been made into a film she could watch. Since her family installed a videotape player, I thought she quit reading altogether.

115

"I'm reading it because movies don't follow the original text most of the time. What if I quoted the movie in my paper on Tennessee Williams and it wasn't in the play I was supposed to have read?"

"You worry too much, Jane. Old lady Braum won't even read your paper. You're the Valedictorian. She'll slap an A on it and never crack the first page."

"Is that what you told Hains about his paper, or are you trying to lower my GPA so he can be at the top of the class?"

Cindy stuck her tongue out at me and blew a raspberry. "Neither of you is any fun. If you both aren't playing in a ballgame somewhere or practicing to play in one, your heads are face down in books."

"I would think your first year in nursing school would require some book time of your own."

Cindy defended herself. "I do my homework before Hains comes home from practice."

"Your dedication is admirable, if not a little terrifying."

"Oh, shut up," Cindy said, punching my leg. "What do you care? You're too busy to hang out with me."

"With school, ball, and work, it makes for a long day. I'm tired by the time you're done being up Hains's butt."

"You go to bed with the sun. You're like an old maid."

"You try going to work at four o'clock in the morning. You'd be in bed early too."

"I can't believe you clean the pub before you go to school. Just keep your dad off the bar stools and save the cash for college."

"This job is perfect. I can still play ball after school. I would have had to quit to take any other jobs."

"Jane, you have a scholarship to State, and you're going to play softball. They'll feed and house you. You don't need money."

I shook my head at her. "You have no idea what it takes to live on your own. Grandma isn't well, and Granddaddy dying left Dad with all those medical bills. He doesn't need the extra pressure of continuing to support me too."

"Is that why your phone was disconnected when I called this morning?"

"No. Dad just forgot to pay the bill. He and Asa drove over and paid it Friday, but they can't get it back on until Monday. Dad isn't broke, but Grandma is sick, and he's distracted. He'll need money to pay her expenses. I don't want to be an extra burden. That's all."

"He could stop supporting Asa."

"What's that supposed to mean? Dad couldn't fix all those vehicles by himself. Asa works hard. He earns anything he gets from my dad."

"I'll bet he does," Cindy said, with a smirk.

I turned to glare at her. I thought sometimes we were only friends due to the circumstances that threw us together.

"Hey," I said, "Do you really want to open that can of worms? You do remember how Asa got here in the first place, right?"

"That old rumor. I swear people can turn a good deed into something dirty in the blink of an eye. My father is married with children—proof the rumors are untrue."

"With that logic, how can you say those things about my dad?"

Cindy's mind perplexed me at times. Her answer was one of those times. "Your father never married."

I laughed. "But you will concede that John Doe had sex with a woman at least once, right? So, following your reasoning that's proof your innuendo about my dad and Asa is based on nothing but conjecture."

"You're going to be a brilliant lawyer, Jane Doe," Cindy replied.

I decided not to insist she stop the charade her entire family had taken up regarding the judge's proclivities. The judge wasn't interested in Asa anymore. He had no use for a grown man. Besides, the judge had a different young man around, mowing his grass and working out on the farm. Judge Spencer said his new yardman was a down on his luck distant cousin from up in Virginia. I doubted anyone believed that story.

Even with a bird in hand, the judge was still poking around in the bushes. The old cocksucker had come after Malachi with an intense desire much stronger than that he had shown for Asa seven years before. Mali said he thought it was funny to tease the old coot, and made it his mission to take the judge for anything he could get.

The judge liked to dress Malachi up and take him to community meetings. Judge Spencer claimed to be mentoring my beautiful young friend. Mali had only grown more gorgeous as he aged. He said if people wanted to pay to look at him, he did not have a problem with that. Anyone could see the lust in the judge's eyes when he leered at Malachi. No matter what the judge did or said, though, Mali would never let that old man touch him. It drove the judge nuts and gave us a sense of satisfaction to see him want something his power and money couldn't provide.

I let Cindy's naïve defense of her lecherous father go unchallenged and picked up my book. I thought she'd take the hint that I'd rather not talk, but that didn't stop her chattering. We were lying out on the old deep-water docks, about five hundred yards offshore. It was the one place we could drop our bathing suit straps and reduce our tan lines. This was more important to Cindy than me, but she didn't want to go alone. We borrowed Hains's skiff and went out to tan after lunch.

"I hope there are a few more afternoons like this before the prom. You are so lucky. You stay tan all year long."

"I don't have much choice. I was born that way."

"You don't wear makeup. You don't even have to try."

"Yeah, well, gentlemen prefer blondes," I answered, pointing at her hair and not taking my eyes from the page.

"I need a good tan to set off the color of my dress. Have you decided on a new dress?"

I gave up reading again and answered, "No. I'm thinking about wearing the one I wore last year. Mali said we could dye it black and drop one shoulder, pin the flower on the other side, and pretend it is new. Besides, nobody will remember what I wore last year. It's not like I'm you or one of the other cheerleaders they all lust over."

"You can't wear the same dress, Jane. It just isn't done."

"It isn't done by rich people. Poor people have been wearing altered pre-worn dresses to the prom for generations if they went at all."

"You aren't poor, Jane. I heard my dad say the land John Doe inherited from his dad is worth a fortune."

"It's only worth money if it's sold. Dad won't ever sell it. He'll scrape to pay the property taxes until his last breath, but he'll never part with the only piece of the original land grant left. He made me promise not to sell it when it's mine."

"You aren't going to live here after college, are you?"

"No way," I said. "Come August, I'm outta here."

Cindy smiled and put her hand up for a high five, saying, "Amen to that." I slapped her hand, and she went on. "If you aren't going to stay here, I imagine you'll sell it, and we'll never see you again."

"I thought you weren't going to be here either."

"Oh, I won't. Hains is going to play for the Los Angeles Rams, and we're going to live in Hollywood."

"You don't know that," I said, laughing at her fantasy.

"If I keep saying it, it will come true. I kept saying I wanted him to go to State and that's who he signed with."

"That's not much of a leap. Hains has wanted to go there since he could walk. He has State sheets on his bed, for Christ sake."

"Don't use the Lord's name in vain, and how do you know what his sheets look like?"

"Retract the claws, kitty cat. I can see the Forster clothesline from my house. Besides, Hains is my brother. You know that."

"I'm sorry. I do know that. It's just, well, I think—oh, I don't know, I think Hains is messing around with Becky behind my back."

I really didn't want to answer her implied question. Cindy wanted reassurance that Hains wasn't cheating on her again. Hains had always been unfaithful, since sixth grade, and most of the time with more than one girl. Who could blame him? He was a stud in the prime of his life and Cindy wouldn't leave him alone no matter what he did or with whom.

Cindy Spencer would tolerate any behavior from Hains, as long as she was the one who wound up with the ring, be it his class ring or the family heirloom diamond intended for his betrothed. Hains only had to weather the storms when social norms demanded Cindy make a scene to re-establish her place as alpha female. It had been harder to remain queen of the high school to her king when Cindy had graduated a year ahead of us. The day-to-day maintenance of that position was harder from afar.

"Becky will be gone in two months. Her parents are moving to Florida as soon as she graduates. She's going to college down there. You'll never see her again."

"But until then, I'm supposed to ignore their constant flirting that they think I don't see."

"Tell him you see it. It's only fun if he's getting away with something. The excitement of illicit affairs is what makes them appealing. In the light of day, the attraction vanishes."

"Maybe you're right," Cindy conceded with a smile.

I probably should have dropped it there, but I said one thing too many.

"Cindy, are you prepared to spend the rest of your life with a man who will fuck anything willing to stand still long enough?"

"That's a horrible thing to say about someone you call a friend."

"I love Hains. He is family, but he is a total dick to you, and you take it."

"He loves me. He says so. He just likes to flirt and mess around, but he always comes back to me."

"You do know that college quarterbacks get their fair share of offers from women a lot more sophisticated than the girl back home."

"I'm not going to be back home. They have married housing, you know. He'll calm down once we're living together in Raleigh."

"Cindy, come down from the clouds. Hains isn't going to marry you before he finishes college."

"You don't know that, Jane. You're his friend. I'm his future wife. I know things you do not."

"Whatever, Cindy. Waste your life over a man that treats you like shit and will probably leave you for a runway model the minute he makes it big. No man will ever do me the way Hains Forster, does you. Nothing is worth that humiliation."

I should have stopped. I didn't, and it hurt her. Good ol' Cindy could always be counted on to lash out with a vengeance once provoked.

"You're just saying that because you're queer like your daddy."

I was stunned silent, unable to move momentarily, as thoughts raced through my brain. I didn't date a lot, but I did. I even had a boyfriend from time to time. But unlike most of my female classmates, high school love matches were hardly my focus. Awkward fumblings in the backseats of cars weren't my idea of a good time. I did meet a guy at 4-H camp two summers ago. I really liked him, and we enjoyed a two-week sophomore fling.

However, my immediate concern was that Cindy somehow found out about my short but intense affair the previous summer with Maria from the campground. She had come back from a semester as an exchange student in France and had a few itches to scratch in this desolate county. She found me a willing participant in her sexual exploration. It took me months to recover from her sudden departure. I was sure her parents had discovered our liaison wasn't really French tutoring, but Maria said her grandmother was ill. I was crushed and told no one.

I didn't care what Cindy called my dad. He was a grown man. He could take care of himself, which is what he said the first time I shared my concerns over the rumors about his relationship with Asa. I knew Asa made my dad happy. That's all I cared to know. But if anyone found out about my sexual fluidity, my scholarship and athletic future would be in jeopardy. Not to mention the public shaming if word got out in Doe's Ferry.

"You start a rumor like that, and it could cost me my future," I said, glaring at her.

"It's not a rumor if it's true."

"What are you talking about?"

I took the chance that Cindy knew nothing about Maria. She didn't. She was lashing out because she was scared her fantasy wasn't going to come true.

Her non sequitur answer made no sense. She declared, "Hains is going to marry me," as if saying it made it so.

"Fine, he's going to marry you. I hope you're both very happy. That doesn't make me queer, so don't say that again."

I rolled over and leaned on my elbows, holding my book up so I could go back to reading and ignore Miss Spencer.

"He has to marry me," Cindy said, this time with the desperation of "Maggie the cat" from the play I was reading. She was most definitely hanging on by her claws.

"I'm sure he will," I mumbled, while I tried to find my place on the page I had been reading.

"No, Jane. He has to marry me. I'm pregnant."

I shot up onto my knees. "I thought you were on birth control pills."

"I forgot to take them a few times, I guess."

"Forgot? You forgot? How do you forget to take a pill and then go fuck your boyfriend? Did you tell him?"

"That I'm pregnant?"

"No, that you were trapping him by getting pregnant. You knew there was a chance when you missed the pills. You should have told him. I wouldn't be surprised to find out you didn't take them on purpose."

Cindy flushed red. "I did not intentionally trap Hains. It takes two to tango, anyway."

"Yeah, well only one of you was given all the facts before the dance started."

"It doesn't change anything. We were going to get married anyway. We're just doing it sooner than we planned."

I started grabbing my stuff, shoving it into the canvas bag I brought with me.

Cindy asked, "What are you doing?"

"I'm ready to go. I've had enough of 'girl' time for the day. I need to write this paper. It's due tomorrow."

"Why are you so mad, Jane? Hains isn't mad about the baby."

"Because he's an idiot. He should be mad as hell. You did this on purpose. You knew he'd do the right thing. You knew he'd marry you. That's who he is. But it will never make him faithful to you, Cindy. He'll always wish you were somebody else."

I was close to revealing a secret I had promised to conceal on my life. I stopped short of pushing the dagger all the way in. I had wounded her. I didn't need to make it a mortal blow. Cindy stood and started gathering her things. She shoved them into her bag, all the while yelling at me.

"Fuck you, Jane Doe. That was a horrible thing to say."

"Truth hurts," I snapped.

"You're just jealous. You've always been in love with Hains. He picked me, Jane. Get over it."

"Oh, Jesus. First, you say I'm queer, and now I'm in love with a guy I call my brother. You are a real piece of work, Cindy Spencer. I guess I shouldn't be surprised, considering you come from a family of lying assholes."

"At least I do not have to peel my dad off a bar stool every night."

"At least I don't have to peel mine off the yard-boy's dick."

"That is a lie, and really rich coming from you. Your dad has his faggot lover living at the station."

"Oh, now you sound exactly like your asshole brother. Is JP so anti-gay because he knows your dad is, or because he hates himself for having the same desires? Asa said the worst beatings of his life were from men who really wanted to fuck him. He still has scars from JP's beating."

"The men in my family are not queers."

"Oh, yeah? Then why don't you ask your father what his real intentions are with Mali? Your dad is a sick old pervert."

"He's helping the underprivileged," Cindy offered as her dad's excuse.

"That's what he says. Ever wonder why your dad insists on watching Mali try on all the new clothes he buys him at the men's store?"

"Because he doesn't want his protégé to look like a bumpkin."

"Mali could wear a potato sack and look like a runway model. Besides, he studies GQ like it's a bible. Malachi can dress himself."

"Daddy just wants to make sure he's getting what he's paying for, that's all."

I laughed. Tennessee Williams may have played a part in my desire to pull back the curtain on our lives. Suddenly, the lies we told each other needed purging. I couldn't take one more pretense, one more ounce of mendacity. We lived lies every day, all of us. I burst forth from that moment determined to lay bare the whole fucking mess.

"Ironically, though I know you're talking about paying for the clothes, your father has also offered Mali money to let him touch his body."

"You are lying," Cindy spat.

"Mali said when he gets up to a thousand dollars, he'll probably let the judge suck his dick."

"I hate you, Jane Doe," Cindy screamed.

"Good, because now I can tell you what I really think. You're a manipulative bitch and always have been. I hope Hains wises up before you ruin his life."

Cindy threw her bag into Hains's skiff and climbed down the ladder into the bow. Our chests heaved with anger, but we went silent. I assumed we both were afraid of what we might say next. Our friendship had always teetered on the razor's edge of how much shit I was willing to take from her, and how many times Hains had patched things up between us. This time, I doubted there would be reconciliation.

I stayed on the dock with the small cooler, waiting to hand it down to Cindy. She didn't take it. Instead, she went to the back of the boat, primed the gas line, and then pulled the crank handle. The engine fired up on the first pull. I knew she was furious because I usually had to start the motor. I was genuinely shocked when Cindy untied the bow, stepped back to the engine, and engaged the propeller. She pulled away, stranding me offshore surrounded by fifty-eight-degree water.

I yelled after her, "Fuck you, Cindy Spencer."

She raised her middle finger in salute and never looked back.

"Dammit!"

I looked at my watch. It was only two o'clock. It wouldn't start cooling off for a few more hours. By then, Hains would have realized what Cindy had done. I was sure that's where she had gone to report my behavior. I sat down, opened my bag and pulled out a plastic tampon holder from the bottom. Inside, I had hidden a joint I took from my dad's stash and a lighter. I fired it up, opened the play to the page I had been reading, and tried to forget all about Cindy Spencer.

I read aloud, "What is the victory of a cat on a hot tin roof? I wish I knew—Just staying on it, I guess, as long as she can."

I took a long toke and blew out the smoke. I looked over my shoulder at Cindy, who was now tying up the skiff to the Forster wharf and repeated Maggie's line, "Just staying on it, I guess, as long as she can."

123

13

And then he was gone...

The note said, "Refresh your memory."

I heard a pebble hit the boathouse window, which interrupted my reflection on the afternoon that had set the dominoes in motion. I went to the door and opened it. A large manila envelope had been placed on the doorstep, with a rock on top to keep it from blowing away.

On the front of the envelope, written in black marker, was the phrase, "Refresh your memory."

I stepped back into the boathouse, out of view of the person who left the package. Obviously, I was being watched.

"Hum, curiouser and curiouser," I said, examining the envelope before opening it.

It looked okay and felt like it contained paper. I opened the clasp on the back and peeked inside. It was a stack of typing paper. Not expecting to find a domestic terrorist depositing poisoned documents on my doorstep, I pulled out the contents and read the cover sheet aloud.

"Transcript of the taped interview with Jane Doe conducted by Sheriff Law Forster on April 29, 1979."

My body remembered. The reflexive shiver came as my mind's eye revealed eighteen-year-old me in a small room with cold brick and fake wood paneled walls. Wrapped in a blanket, holding a hot cup of coffee to my chest for warmth—maybe it wasn't warmth I sought, perhaps I just wanted to feel anything—I remembered a kind of stinging numbness, like mishitting a softball with an aluminum bat on a cold day. My whole body vibrated, and I hadn't yet felt the full extent of the suffering. I knew instinctively, even at that age, when the loss began to hurt, it would be for always. I didn't need the words on the page to recall every second of that night. I had replayed those moments each time I closed my eyes to sleep for the last forty years.

#

The sheriff asked, "Are you feeling better, young lady?"

I nodded, though I couldn't stop shivering.

"Let's start at the part where you woke up on the deep water dock," he said, as he slid the recorder a little closer to me. "What time did you wake up? Do you know?"

"Yes, sir. The sun was just above the horizon. I looked at my watch. It was five-thirty."

"That's about the time the clouds rolled in. Went from really nice to cold and windy pretty quick, as I recall."

"Yes, sir. I could hear rumbling in the distance."

"Water's still pretty cold this time of year."

"Yes, sir."

"I don't imagine you were happy about having to swim in after Cindy left you."

"No, sir. I was not. But I could see the lightning behind the clouds. I couldn't stay on the only thing sticking up out of the sound for miles."

Sheriff Forster smiled. "No, I don't guess you could."

"I knew Cindy didn't tell Hains what she'd done. He wouldn't have left me out there. She had to know a storm was coming." I paused and added, "What a bitch," under my breath.

The sheriff cleared his throat. He hated it when I cursed. He'd been on me about it since I said my first "shit" upon banging my thumb with Hains's wooden hammer at age two.

"You mentioned a cooler earlier, one that washed away? Why did you bring it? You could have gotten to shore a lot faster without it," he said.

"I knew it would float if things got bad, plus I needed some way to get my things home. I dumped it out and stuffed my bag inside to keep my wallet and the school book dry. I still had a paper to write when I got home."

"We'll find it. I'm sure Mrs. Braum will understand if we don't."

"I don't care about the paper, Sheriff," I said, confused at his distraction from the reason we were there.

He shifted in his chair. I had always made Law Forster uncomfortable. I was too untamed for a man like him.

125

"So, you made the decision to start swimming. You could have become hypothermic."

I remembered standing on the deep water dock squinting at the shoreline, focusing intently on first Hains's house, then mine and Malachi's, and finally Doodie's. I couldn't see a soul stirring. Sunday supper was being served before everyone sat down to watch "60 Minutes." As usual, no one was looking for me.

I answered the sheriff. "I didn't have a choice."

After plunging into the frigid water, I had pushed the cooler out in front of me and kicked toward shore. I knew as long as I kept moving, my core temperature would be okay for about thirty minutes in mid-fifty degree water. Besides, I'd be able to walk for nearly the entire second half of the swim in. I would have been out in less than ten minutes without the damn cooler to lug along. Obstacles appeared to be my curse in life because nothing was ever easy.

"As usual," I added to the sheriff, "my path had to be the hard way."

Law Forster smiled. He'd known me since birth and helped raise me right along with his son. He acknowledged my road had a lot of obstacles with a nod. He moved on from my decision to purposely expose myself to hypothermia, and asked, "When did you first see Malachi?"

I closed my eyes. I could almost feel the waves lapping at the back of my neck again. I had tried to stay on top of the swell and ride the storm current in. I didn't look up at the shoreline again until I was halfway there.

"I stood up in chest-deep water about halfway in. My legs and lungs were on fire, and I had to rest. The whitecaps started pounding me."

"Is that when you saw him?"

"Yes. When I focused on the ferry dock, I could see Malachi. I could tell it was him, more from his shape than actually seeing his face. I yelled at him, but he couldn't hear me. That was right when the heavy rain started."

Sheriff Forster folded his arms over his broad chest. He reiterated, "You couldn't see Malachi's face. You identified him from his shape."

"Yes, sir. You know I've known Mali all my life. I know what his silhouette looks like. You can't miss that mop of curls on his head."

"Okay, go on."

"I was starting to shake really bad. The cold was getting to me. I knew I had to get out of the water. I was about to start swimming again when I saw a guy walk up behind Malachi."

"How did Malachi react to this person?"

"He jumped back when he saw him, and then they stepped away to where I couldn't see them anymore. His body language projected fear."

"Could you tell who it was?"

"Not for sure, it was too dark. But I thought it was JP Spencer, and then I saw the other one."

"You saw another man?"

"Yes, he followed Mali and JP into the shadows. He was moving faster, almost running."

"Let's just say 'the first guy' and leave JP out of this discussion until we know for sure it was him on the ferry dock. Do you know who the second guy was?"

"No, it happened too fast. I could tell it was a man. He wasn't big like you and Hains. He was more my dad's build. It could have been the judge. They're about the same size."

"Was it your dad?"

"No."

"You said this person was the same build as your dad."

"I said he was the same build as the judge too."

"How can you be sure it wasn't your dad?"

"I just know, okay?"

"All right. What happened next?"

"I put my head down and kicked as hard as I could for as long as I could before I looked up again. I was about seventy-five yards offshore when I stopped to catch my breath. And then...and then—"

I paused there and couldn't go on with the story. I wanted the world to rewind. I sat the coffee mug down and dropped my forehead onto my folded arms on the table. I couldn't cry. I couldn't feel, but it hurt. The numbness wasn't painless. I'd been dazed pretty good once by a bare wire in the ceiling of the boathouse. The feeling was similar, but the current shock to my system was far worse than being thrown off that ladder. A faint ache drummed against my chest. I knew if I let go, the wall of agony I held back would wash over me. I thought I would drown in my sorrow. I never had, in my young life, faced a loss so great. I was sure I would not survive.

"Jane," Law Forster said softly. He touched my arm, more father figure than sheriff at the moment. "Jane, you have to tell me what you saw. Then we'll get you home where Doc can give you something to help you rest. You'll feel better once you've had some sleep."

I didn't raise my head, when I said, "I'm never going to feel better."

"Yes, you will. It takes time."

My head popped up. "The only time that will make me feel better is the amount JP Spencer is going to do."

"Hold up now. Don't get ahead of yourself. You were swimming into shore. What did you see next?"

"I saw them push Mali off the dock," I said, glaring across the table at the sheriff.

"Who did you see?"

"JP and someone else."

"You can swear you saw JP Spencer."

"Who else could it have been?"

"So you're saying you didn't see JP. You just think it was him."

"When I first saw that person, the one Mali was afraid of, I am almost positive that was JP Spencer. When I saw Mali go off the dock, it was raining hard. I could only tell that two shapes were looking down in the water where he fell. I had raised my head to look at the dock just as Mali hit the water. I saw him struggling to swim."

"So, you didn't actually see him pushed. He could have slipped."

"He was naked, Sheriff. I don't think he voluntarily went for a skinny dip. He couldn't swim that well. He panicked and sank in water over his head. We all knew that."

"I just need to know, did you see him pushed?"

I glared across the table and gave my answer, "No."

"What did you do then?"

"I let go of that stupid cooler and started swimming as fast as I could. I watched him go under. I dove a couple of times before I found him. He was unconscious, but he couldn't have been under more than a minute."

"And that's when you pulled him to shore."

"Yes. He wasn't breathing. His lip was bleeding." I looked down at the pink stains on my wet tee shirt. "This is his blo—" The floodgates opened, and the tears came. "Oh god, Mali. Why did they do that? Why?"

I had screamed at him, begged him to breathe. He was so pale, his lips blue. In my panic, the muscle memory of the CPR training I had undergone to be a lifeguard had kicked in. I cleared his airway and breathed for him a few times, before slamming my fist into his chest and screaming, "Don't you die on me. Don't you die on me!"

I pumped his chest, counting under my ragged breaths. I breathed air into his mouth again, screamed at him, "Live goddammit" and then he coughed. First a little cough, but then he threw up. I turned him on his side so he wouldn't aspirate. He coughed a few more times and took a few shallow and weak breaths.

"Mali! Mali! You're okay, buddy. Come on, breathe. Mali?"

He wouldn't open his eyes. I needed help. I screamed again, "Help! Help! Somebody help us."

No one came.

The sheriff's voice brought me back into the room. He tried to refocus me. "He wasn't breathing, but you got him back. He was breathing when you left him."

I wiped the tears from my cheeks and answered, "Barely, but he didn't open his eyes."

"So you ran to get help. Where did you go?"

"I went to Bertie's house."

"You were in your backyard. Wasn't your dad home? Why didn't you ask him to help you? Why didn't you go in the house to use your phone?"

"The phone got cut off Friday. I thought dad was still at the station. I didn't see him."

"Then how do you know it was not your dad and Asa on the dock earlier."

"I know my own dad, okay," I said, slapping my hand on the table. "It wasn't him."

It wasn't him. I knew because I ran to the boathouse after I pulled Mali from the water. The lights were on, so I figured Asa and Dad were in there smoking cigarettes out of the rain. I burst through the door and found them together, but they weren't smoking. Knowing your parents have sex and seeing it is uncomfortable. Finding my dad fucking Asa was too much to process considering the circumstances of that discovery. I slammed the door and ran toward Bertie's house. There was no way I was telling the Sheriff anything about what I saw in the boathouse.

The sheriff accepted my adamant answer and moved on. "Okay, we'll leave that for now. So, you went to Bertie's house. Then what?"

"She ran back with me." I broke down crying when I said, "I told her he was alive. I can't get that scream out of my head."

At that point, I had nothing else to say; or rather I couldn't speak another word without losing any composure I still clung to. I listened as Hains's father explained that Mali had succumbed to a head wound. A wound that I did not see, supposedly because it was deep in the back of his head under his wet hair. Sheriff Foster said Mali had to have hit his head on the dock when he went over the edge. While I was gone to get help, Mali ended up back in the water. The sheriff surmised that my unconscious friend must have come to and in his confusion walked into the sound. I had my doubts about all of it.

Hains entered the sheriff's version of events because he was on his porch during the storm and thought he heard screaming. Then he heard my dad and Asa calling for me and came to find out what was going on. Instead of me, Hains found Mali facedown in the water. This time, he could not be revived.

"We'll have to wait for the medical examiner's report to be sure," the sheriff said. "You did all you could, Jane. With a head injury like that, I'm surprised you were able to revive him at all."

"If he walked in the water by himself, where is his necklace. That's all he had on when I pulled him on shore. I saw the mark on his neck where it was yanked off. Who did that?"

"Hains could have done that when he found him, honey. It's no one's fault, I think, and I'm just as sorry as I can be."

I could only respond, "I shouldn't have left him alone."

"About that," Sheriff Forster said, "when you left him, you say you went to Bertie's, but Hains heard your dad calling you. That's why he came looking to help find you."

"Maybe dad heard me yelling for help."

"But you said he wasn't home."

Unintentionally, I paused just long enough to let a lawman like Law Forster know I was lying, when I replied, "I didn't think he was."

The sheriff chose that moment to drop his bombshell. "What if I told you I have a witness that puts Asa and Malachi in a romantic relationship?"

I rose up on the edge of my chair. "I'd say they're a damn liar."

He tried to persuade me. "Maybe Malachi didn't tell you everything. He could have kept it a secret."

I glared at him and spoke extremely succinctly in a low and controlled voice. "Malachi was not having an affair with Asa. He was involved in a romantic relationship, but it was not with Asa."

"Who was it with?"

"With all due respect Sheriff, I don't have to tell you that. It has nothing to do with my friend, who is dead now, and who I intend to see buried with his dignity intact. He was thrown off the ferry dock, or chased off, by someone he was afraid of, not someone he loved."

"All right then, I guess that's enough for this evening," the sheriff said, patting my hand. "I know Malachi was special to you. Remember the good things, Jane. He'd want you to."

I jumped up from the chair and shouted through my tears, "He'd want to be going to the prom next month and graduating in June. He won't be doing either of those things because JP Spencer is a monster no one in this courthouse seems willing to stop."

"JP isn't a rogue teenager anymore, Jane. He's a US Attorney with a lot more power than his local judge father. Be careful what you say and who you accuse. You said yourself that you cannot positively identify the two people on the dock."

"What happened to justice, Sheriff?"

"She's still holding the scales, but she can't weigh in on tragic accidents. We all loved Mali."

I said, "Somebody didn't," and then stomped to the door without asking permission to leave. With my hand on the knob, I turned back to say, "I won't be quiet, Sheriff."

He smiled at me, and I saw Hains in his expression. "No, Jane Doe, I don't imagine that you will."

#

I threw the transcript on the worktable that ran along one side of the boathouse. There was a fish cleaning station at the end farthest from the door. The screaming in my head sounded like the claws of a cat sliding off a steep tin roof in the rain. Tennessee Williams references aside, I was losing my grip. The sound could have been the long branches of the old willow tree lashing the top of the boathouse as the wind made her dance. Either way, I felt the stress migraine coming. My eyes went to the corner where the filet knives used to hang over the open hole, where the fish guts would be swept after cleaning the day's catch.

The boathouse had been repaired, but parts looked just as I last saw it in 1979. I walked over to the corner and removed the one last knife hanging on the wall. It was rusted and pitted. I'm sure it had not moved for nearly half a century. The board where the nail held the knife looked a little warped on the edges, and to the uninitiated appeared to be just a weathered gray piece of trim. I knew better.

131

I reached under the worktable and pulled a hidden pin. The right side of the board popped up and with a little push opened on the hinges attached to the left side. A familiar small plastic container with a lid snapped tightly closed remained inside, exactly where my dad would have left it. The plastic had clouded with age, but inside, I found a pack of Marlboro reds and a Zippo lighter. The lighter was too dry to work. The cigarette pack held no tobacco, but it did contain two perfectly rolled joints in yellowed papers.

"That's my boy," I said to the ever-present aura of John Doe.

I'd do nearly anything to keep a migraine from gaining its footing on my brain, including smoking pot in a state where I could easily go back to prison for a second charge of possession. I had better lawyers now. It was worth the risk.

"I wonder what twenty-year-old homegrown tastes like."

"That's not homegrown."

I turned to see Duck just peeking in the boathouse door. She smiled and pointed at the joint in my hand.

"It's prime medical grass cultivated by Uncle Sam. May I join you?"

"Of course," I said, glad for the company, after being alone with my thoughts for too long.

"Your dad showed me the secret stash spot shortly after I moved in. Funny thing, he used to say the same government that put his daughter away for trafficking marijuana prescribed and prepared for him the finest in medicinal pot products federal taxpayer money could provide. We drove up to Virginia to pick up tins of it. They gave him THC pills when he couldn't smoke anymore. Used to make him laugh at the irony—and sad too."

I chuckled. "I met some old acquaintances down at the pub this evening. They said Dad used to sit in the front yard and blow pot smoke toward the judge's house. Is that true?"

"The judge would come to fetch the evening paper from the box at the end of his driveway at the same time each night. John would set up a lawn chair on this side of the road and fire up his evening dose. That's how they started talking to each other."

"Who crossed the road first?" I asked, but knew the answer.

"Carroll, uh, Judge Spencer made the first move."

I gave Duck the pause she deserved for the new wrinkle in the story, before I said, "On a first name basis with the neighbors, are we?"

"Been here a good while now, kid. Part of that was alone with a dying man. Folks around here were good to your dad, and they have

132

been kind to me. They welcomed my wife into the community. This is our home. If an old man wants to be called Carroll, then I can oblige without it coloring my character in your eyes, can't I?"

The whole time she talked I looked for a lighter, matches, anything to light one of the old joints.

"Need one of these," Duck asked while holding up a lighter.

"Yes," I said and snatched it from her hand.

"Careful, that shit is so dry it may burst into flames. Tell you the truth, I forgot it was out here, or it would have been gone a long time ago. These girls just coming out don't need to go back in over some old dried up weed, you know."

I lit the joint and took a few deep tokes, coughed, took a few more, coughed till I gagged, and then took one more hit.

"Trying to fry your lungs or your mind, kid?"

Duck waited while I gathered myself and finally took a really good breath.

"Damn, that's harsh," I said. "How old is this shit?"

"At least a couple of decades."

"Jesus, do you think it will still work?"

"I guess we'll see. It was grown at some college in Mississippi. Came in tins of three hundred cigarettes at a time. It was good quality too."

"I know Dad was relieved not to worry about going to jail for taking a harmless drug that let him sleep at night."

"It helped with his pain, so he didn't have to stay so heavily medicated with narcotics. And it helped him eat when the other drugs made that difficult. Bush senior's administration shut down the Compassionate Use Marijuana program in the early nineties when applications surged due to the AIDS epidemic."

I sipped a bit more smoke into my lungs and talked in the breath-holding manner known to stoners. "How very fucking compassionate of them."

"Your father was grandfathered in, so they had to keep sending it. I think the last can he got was in ninety-eight, maybe. Hard to remember. He had switched to the Marinol pills by then but got the tins to share with folks who came by to visit. Guaranteed a steady stream of visitors. I think it really burned the FDA that he lived so long."

I blew out a cloud of smoke. Coughing ensued.

"You're going at it like you're trying to smoke it up before the cops come."

I coughed one last time and held the joint out to Duck. "That's the idea. I feel a migraine coming."

"Oh," Duck said and took the joint from me. She toked on it a few times, while I talked.

"I brought edibles, but I'm running low. I'm gonna hit that," I pointed at the joint, "until I feel the click. If I don't, I'm gonna smoke this other one too. If that doesn't work, I'll need a dark room and a couple of days."

Duck passed the joint back, as she said, "Could be worse. You could be in prison."

She said that about everything because nothing in Duck's mind could be as bad as experiencing it while in prison. I had my first migraine in a cell, four feet wide, nine feet tall, and twelve feet deep. Duck nursed me through it in the brightly lit, deafening, unforgiving atmosphere of a women's prison. She was right. It could always be worse.

"Here's to not being in prison," I said, toasting with the quickly shrinking joint sandwiched between my index finger and thumb.

I took another toke and coughed some more.

"You need to chill the fuck out."

"I'm trying, but I saw JP tonight. I also encountered both the judge and his grandson." I pointed at the envelope and transcript I had tossed on the counter. "Then someone dropped this off a few minutes ago. Apparently, I've drawn the attention I was looking for."

I tried to continue the rotation, but Duck held up her hand.

"No more for me. Go ahead."

Duck flipped through the interview transcript, while I coughed and toked. I hardly ever smoked marijuana, but I did medicate through other means to keep things in balance. I inherited a mind incapable of processing trauma in a healthy way; thus the regimen to achieve my version of normal—lots of exercise and a healthy diet, supplemented by CBD and THC infused oils, teas, lotions, and edibles, all legally obtained with a medical marijuana license. I knew what worked for me and moved to a state where it was legal to do it. Unfortunately, the license did not travel from state to state and offered no protection from arrest for possession outside the borders in which the products containing THC were obtained. I took work mostly in green states now.

"What's the end game for this person, Jane? Why are they involving you? If they have evidence that until now has remained hidden, why do they need you to bring it to light?"

"I'm the bait," I said.

I began feeling the effects of the THC on the fledgling migraine. I took one more toke just to make sure, before snuffing out the roach and dropping it into the cigarette pack with the un-smoked joint. I tossed the pack on the worktable and reached for the envelope the transcript came in. There was one piece of paper left inside. I pulled it out. The edges were scorched. I noticed the back of the transcript Duck held was also browned as if it had been saved from a fire.

"What's that?" Duck pointed at the charred page in my hands.

"It looks like Law Forster's notes about Malachi's death."

"Anything you didn't already know?"

I read through the former sheriff's handwritten notes—one page, that's all Mali rated. "Cause of death: head trauma, bleeding in the brain. There was water in his lungs, blunt force trauma to the face, most likely a fist. Anal scarring, indicating old and recent sexual activity. A head wound caused by a long cylindrical object, like a tire iron."

I pointed at "tire iron" on the page.

"Look, he crossed it out and wrote, 'Hit head on ramp when he jumped.' Malachi's head was not bashed in when I found him, Duck. Someone did that while I was trying to find help."

"What did they finally rule happened?"

"According to the official story, Malachi took his own life because queer boys do that sort of thing."

"And your version of what happened? They just ignored all that?"

"We, Asa, my dad, and me, we didn't believe that line of crap and said so. That's when they came for us."

"Small town justice can be unfathomable to those who have not lived it," Duck commented. "I haven't seen Asa since the last time I took your father up. It always made John so sad, but he went anyway. How's Asa doing?"

"The same. He'll never change. Every day will be the same for him for the remainder of his life."

"Do you want him out? Will you care for him?"

"His doctors seem to think he's better off with his current routine. He's not in a horrible place. Asa is happy. He's Peter Pan in a world where he never has to grow up."

"Then why are you doing this?"

"Because people still think Asa was a child molester and I want him cleared of that stain. I want to know what really happened to him in custody. That was no self-inflicted head trauma. I want to know the source of the anonymous molestation charge that got him locked up in the first place and why the file was sealed. I also appear to no longer be the only one that wants to see justice for Malachi."

"They tried to tie Asa and John up in Malachi's death too, right?"

"They had witnesses, JP, and the judge, who claimed to have seen Asa and my dad chasing Malachi. I knew it wasn't my father or Asa on that dock. They were in this boathouse having sex. I couldn't out my dad and tell the truth back then. I lied and said they were at the station. Of course, they weren't, which made my lie look worse when dad told the truth and said he was in the boathouse with Asa. The sheriff had reason not to believe a word I said, that and the ounce of pot someone planted in that damn little cooler."

"Oh, yeah, they came hard for you."

"Yep. The Spencer family did a professional job of shutting up the disgruntled voices. They got Asa, they threatened my dad with a murder charge and planted drugs on me. I discovered tonight that Cindy told the feds I was the high school coke dealer, just in case the possession charge didn't stick. Meanwhile, I was still naïve enough to expect people to believe me because I was telling the truth."

Duck laughed loudly. "That truth thing. It'll get ya every time."

"One week after Malachi was murdered, I pointed out the local 'anything you want' dealer—someone even the cops knew was always holding at least one illegal substance—to an undercover DEA agent, who, by the way, used to live down the road when he was still in high school and asked for said drug dealer by name. Yeah, I was toast. Possession and distributing—see ya later, Jane Doe."

"Okay, I see why you hate that family so much," Duck said. "But, I still don't see that anything has changed in the evidence department. It's still your convicted drug trafficker word against a man about to be nominated to the Supreme Court."

"Someone pulled these papers out of a fire and wanted me to see them. I think the bread crumbs are going to lead us exactly where the evidence we need is hidden."

We both jumped at the knock on the door. My heart started pounding against my chest wall when I saw the badge through the windowpane.

Duck must have seen the panic on my face. She laughed and said, "Relax. It's just Deputy Duty."

14

I've been here before...

"Deputy Brian Duty, I believe you know my friend," Duck gestured with both hands towards me, inviting a cop into a place I had just smoked pot and where I was still in possession of a two decades old joint.

Duck didn't seem worried. And yes, Doodie had been my blood brother, but he also vanished when I got arrested. The last I'd seen him, he was headed to church that Sunday morning with a tape recorder. He had started recording the service for his invalid grandmother, my grandmother too, but the Smiths never claimed me. He didn't come to see me in jail before I got shipped off to Raleigh. I had no idea what he thought of me, or how he was going to react to the weed smell.

A giant man, he filled up the doorway. Doodie spent a lot of time at the gym it appeared. Even with all the unknowns and a badge sparkling in front of me, I couldn't help my reaction.

"Damn, Doodie, you did grow into those feet."

"Jane Doe, I heard, but didn't dare believe."

Doodie smiled and came toward me, where he lifted me into a bear hug and squeezed me too tight.

"Did the Army turn you into a hulk?" I asked, patting his back as he put me back down on the plank floor.

"No, I got into weight training after I got home a few years back. I got married. She lifts too. She's actually the one that got me into it. You look great. Wow. Jane Doe. I never thought I'd see you again."

He was almost breathless. His ears were bright red. Some tells never go away. He sniffed the air.

"Smells like you found some of John Doe's stash. He seems to have left joints like Easter eggs around our old stomping grounds. I've found a few. Not bad weed. Nothing like what's out there now. I'll be glad when North Carolina gets on board. Great investment opportunities coming for economically challenged places like Doe's Ferry. Solar and pot, that's the future."

"Still a reader, huh, Doodie," I said, chuckling at his breathless delivery of random facts.

"Yep, still learning something new every day. Man, it sure is great to see you, Jane. I hope we can catch up some while you are here."

"That would be great, Doodie."

"I'm sorry to have to tell you this," he said, pausing long enough to make me think he was going to give me a ticket or arrest me for the pot. Then he continued, "Someone has vandalized the ferry dock restrooms. I understand the property comes into your hands at midnight. Should I file a report for the state, or are you interested in filing a report yourself."

"After I go back home, Duck and the foundation board will let you know where to direct things like this, but as I'm here, let's go take a look."

"Not planning on staying, I guess," Doodie said, sounding disappointed.

"I never planned on staying, Doodie. You know that. If I remember, none of us had dreams that would have kept us in Doe's Ferry."

"I was gone for thirty years. Retired in 2009 and came home to take care of momma before cancer took her, met my wife—or I should say, met her again—got married and settled down right over there where I grew up. New house though. You should come over. Etta would love to see you."

"Etta Blount? You married Malachi's little sister?"

"I sure did. She was all grown up when I got back, divorced with a kid. Things just fell into place, and we got hitched. I adopted her son. Can't wait for you to meet him."

Duck chuckled. "They are so cute together. All lovey-dovey. And that kid, he's just amazing. Love that boy."

"And now you're back at Hains's side. Must feel surreal."

With his ears glowing red Doodie said, "It does, in a way. I've been all around the world, and here I am again."

"And a cop. Hains, I figured him for a badge. But you? I thought you would end up at NASA or IBM."

"Me too, really, but I took a different route. I did a little military police work while I was in service, mostly tactical, so the hire made sense for Hains. I'm just part-time. Signed on to keep busy and to help out when they're shorthanded and on the weekends during the tourist season. Tonight, I covered for a guy with sick kids and his wife is down too, all got the same bug."

The big goofy guy act was just that, an act. Tactical military police are the opposite of the persona Doodie was portraying. He tried being lovably Tim Tebow-ish to disarm the people his size may intimidate. I could use Doodie's need to put others at ease to my advantage.

"Well, Deputy Doodie, shall we go see what the neighborhood delinquents have done this evening?"

Doodie still had the same smile, higher on one side than the other. He showed it to me as he said, "Forty years ago Law Forster was probably putting on his hat and saying the same thing."

We started out with Duck following. She seemed content to let Doodie and me catch up.

I corrected him. "We never tore up people's shit."

"Oh, didn't we?" Doodie asked, holding the door open until Duck and I had passed.

"What are you talking about? When did we—" I stopped talking and bowed my head. I looked up at him sideways and pursed my lips, before I continued, "Yeah, there was that one thing."

Duck could stay silent no more. "I have to know all about this one thing. Rat her out, Doodie. What did the most innocent prisoner on D block do prior to doing time?"

We climbed the hill to the ferry dock; Duck huffing and puffing, me showing the effects of living in my worst nightmare for the last twenty-four hours, and Doodie jogging up the embankment like a twenty-year-old. Supplements, he had to be on supplements.

He waited at the top, using the time to tell Duck, "She talked me into helping her draw a large penis on the judge's lawn with diesel fuel two days before the garden club tour. Only nothing showed up, so she did it again with twice as much fuel. The next day, some tour guest flicked a cigarette into the grass and Fwwwwwuuuuummmpphhhh! Up the yard went in flames, burning a perfectly erect penis with matching set of balls into the judge's prize-winning yard."

"Did you get caught?" Duck wanted to know.

I was quick to answer, "Hell no. I never told a soul, did you Doodie?"

139

"Nope, not even Hains. That was just between us," Doodie said, offering his hand to Duck for the last step up. "We had a few of those missions."

"Where were the others?"

I chuckled. "Hains wouldn't do something like that and Malachi couldn't carry the fuel can. Doodie was last man standing."

"I thought it was because we were cousins and couldn't rat each other out," Doodie said, with a big grin.

"That is what I told you, isn't it?"

"Those little fuckers," Duck exclaimed.

I looked to see what she had seen that caused her reaction.

"Now that it's your property, you can file charges," Doodie said.

I tilted my head from side to side, trying to make out all these kids wanted us to know. The lighting wasn't the best, and Doodie's flashlight washed out the detail. The young people of this county seriously needed to get out and see the world. This was primal bullshit—attack that which is different—the product of un-evolved gene pools, dipped in by the same bloodlines one time too often.

"We all know who did this," Duck said.

"It's okay," I told her. "I'll take care of this, and there isn't going to be any more trouble. I promise."

"How can you say that? You're leaving in a few days. I'm stuck here with Four and his gang of lost boys."

"I heard there were girls too. Let's not be sexist," I said, trying to ease what I knew was a worrisome situation for Duck.

She was responsible for the women in Doe House. As felons lived there, no firearms were allowed in the home, not even for protection. There were a lot of softball bats in that house and women who could wield them. Thick doors, deadbolts, and alarms had been installed commiserate with the type of man who would come looking for one of these women. I had argued against historical accuracy and insisted on safety measures likely to deter someone intent on entering without permission. I could still understand Duck's concerns.

"What are you going to do, Doodie? Nothing, as usual." Duck glared up at the giant man. "Take another report and tell his daddy. That's what you all do."

"Duck, we have to catch him—" Doodie started to say.

"We did catch him," I said, still trying to make out the spray-painted images on the restroom's exterior walls. "Can someone tell me what that is supposed to be? I can make out the dick and the balls, but what in the hell is that?"

"I think it's a woman's lady parts. Not sure though," Doodie said.

"What's sad is I don't think they know either," I commented on the artists' anatomy knowledge.

Doodie laughed. "No, I'm going to bet they haven't a clue beyond knowledge gleaned from the pages of Hustler or Playboy."

"I don't know what is more disgusting, the 'go home pussy licker' or the 'Trump '20' bumper sticker." Duck yanked the sticker off the building, wadded it up, and threw it away.

"That was evidence," Doodie said.

"Yeah, like you're going to look into it." She laughed. "And what do you mean, 'we did catch him'? You can't just say that and start talking about vagina art."

I turned around and faced the side of Doe House. "Do you see the second window from the front? That's by the desk in the room I'm staying in. Do you see the little red light? That's a camera. After the local welcome wagon came by earlier this evening, I aimed a camera with a wide-angle lens at this area. It's a good camera attached to great software. There's also a microphone picking up every word we say, even through the rain earlier. Whoever did this will be easy to identify."

Duck hugged me. "I love you, Jane Doe. You are a slimy motherfucker, and I love you for it." She turned to Doodie. "Can we go drag that little shit out of his bed right now?"

"We need the video and a warra—"

"Whoa, hold up," I interrupted the plans to haul Hains's son into jail. "I might need this information for leverage."

Footsteps pounded up behind us. I heard the voice before I turned around.

"What's up, Doodie?"

I froze when I saw the source of the question.

I breathed out in a whisper, "My God."

Doodie smiled at me and then spoke to the young man. "Where's your mother? I thought she was running with you."

"I'm right here," a woman said, as she ran up out of the shadows.

I recognized her brother in her smile. This was Etta. I now saw the reason for Doodie's vigor. She went straight to him and stood on her tiptoes to kiss his cheek. He tried to hug her, but she backed away.

"Stop, I'm sweaty." She looked at the teenager and said, "Malachi is going to need a faster running partner. I can't keep up, and I'm slowing him down."

"You named him Malachi," I said, still in shock.

Very much like his namesake, this Malachi cut to the chase. He demanded to know, "Who are you?"

His mother answered for me, "This is an old friend of your uncle. She was his best friend, actually. Jane Doe, meet Malachi Duty."

The kid laughed. "Jane Doe, really?"

"Yes, really," I said for the millionth time, but I laughed because this kid's smile was so familiar.

He held out his hand, and I shook it. "Nice to meet you," he said.

"It's a pleasure to meet you, too," I replied, not sure what to say and unable to stop staring at my Mali's doppelganger.

"You go on and take your shower and go to bed," Etta said to her Malachi. "Brian can walk me home."

"It was nice to meet you," young Malachi said to me. "Good night, mom," he said, kissing her cheek. "Later, Doodie."

"Later," Doodie answered back, as they bumped fists and smiled at each other.

We watched him jog away.

Etta explained without being asked, "I work the late shift. This is our time together. We've been running like this since he was in a stroller. That's how I ran into Brian, literally, out for a jog."

"I had to run after the night nurse came, so we fell into a routine," Doodie filled in.

Duck laughed loudly. "It was like watching two teenagers find each other. I think we all knew before they did."

The light bulb moment should have lit up the ferry dock. "It was you. You sent Malachi's necklace to me."

Doodie and Etta looked at each other before glancing at Duck and back to me.

I eased their minds. "Duck is aware of everything. She knows all that I know about Malachi's death and subsequent cover-up."

Doodie spoke for them both. "Jane, we don't know what you're talking about."

"We sent it."

Malachi Duty reappeared with two friends, a male, and a female. The girl stepped forward to introduce herself.

"My name is Susie Swann, and this is John Smith."

Doodie pointed at the teens. "This is the modern version of the courthouse kids."

"What have you done, Malachi?" His mother asked him.

"Die rationem," the three teens said in unison.

"Day of reckoning," Doodie and I translated together.

Malachi held up a tattered Latin dictionary.

"This book belonged to your father. He wrote something in the front to you."

I took the old brain stained dictionary, missing its front cover and probably a few pages. I flipped through the pages to find my father's handwritten note to me.

> *Jane,*
> *"Truth is truth to the end of reckoning."— Shakespeare.*
> *If you're reading this, nail their balls to the wall.*
> *Love,*
> *Dad"*

15

Take me to church...

"When were you planning on telling your parents about all this?" Etta said to her son.

We stood around the Duty's kitchen table and tried to take in what these kids had done. Doodie's shift had ended, so he changed out of his uniform. He re-entered, pulling an Army sweatshirt over his head, and had questions of his own.

"Can you explain what all this is and where you got it?"

Susie Swann spoke for the teens. "Remember when we helped Malachi clean out Grandma Bertie's house last fall?"

"Yes, but I know this stuff was not in my mother's house. Brian and I combed it, for that tape specifically." Etta pointed at a cassette tape on the table.

"That," Malachi said, "was in a box of cassettes under grandma's side table. I took the box when we moved her to the nursing home."

"Just in there in that old tattered box, out in the open with a bunch of gospel tapes?" Etta seemed incredulous.

"It was in a Vickie Winans case, but it was labeled on the cassette 'Church 4/29/1979.' I lost that label somewhere. I think it's in my room. John Doe's Latin dictionary was in that box too."

Doodie asked, "Did you listen to the tape?"

John Smith said, "Yes, sir. Well, we tried to listen to it. We were looking for some fresh samples. Old school mix tapes sometimes contain that gold, know what I'm sayin'?

I must have looked like I had no clue what he was saying.

Etta explained, "These two are budding DJs."

Malachi added, "We're trying to break into the game with old school beats droppin' in behind the new tracks we write. Found some cool stuff in Grandma's box."

Susie, seemingly as sharp as the ancestor whose name she bore, stayed laser-focused, "At first, it was hard to tell what was happening on the tape. We thought it was a TV show, but then we recognized names. When we found the papers later, it started to make sense."

"Where did you find them?" I asked, flipping through a stack of scorched typing paper and pages torn from legal pads.

Susie answered, "That old wing-back chair Grandma Bertie always sat in had a hidden compartment in the seat. I think it was designed to hold magazines or something. Anyway, when we picked it up, the bottom fell out with all these papers."

Doodie laughed as he said, "I would ask Bertie when we were going to do something. She'd say, 'I'm sittin' on it a spell. I'll let you know.' I guess she was sitting on it, literally."

"Hains told me he burned a file his father had kept on JP Spencer from when he was a teenager. I'm pretty sure Law Forster knew JP pushed Malachi off that dock."

Every head in the room turned to look at me.

"Okay," I said, recognizing the look people have given me over the years. "I know I can't prove that, but it doesn't make it less true."

"But it isn't true," Etta said.

"I was there, Etta. I know what I saw."

Etta shook her head. "No, Jane. JP did attack my brother, but he didn't push Malachi off the dock."

I couldn't believe what she was saying. "But I saw —"

"Hear her out, Jane," Doodie said. "She was there."

Still not able to let go of my long-held belief that JP killed Malachi, I shot back, "So was I."

"I think we're going to need coffee," Duck said. "And I need to tell my wife where I wandered off to. I'll be right back."

Susie took Duck's exit as a chance to interject, "Before you debate who did what, let us tell you what we have and what we know."

Doodie, Etta, and I pulled out chairs and sat down at the table. Susie leaned over and picked up the tape. Whatever had been on it was probably lost forever. The little white plastic case bled tape in unruly streams, as Susie tried to wrangle it in.

"As you can see, the tape needed some love. Luckily, before it disintegrated, John got one digital copy of what was readable on both sides."

145

John eagerly explained. "I took the box of tapes home. Magnetic tape only lasts about thirty years, maybe a little more. Most of the stuff was just trashed, clicking and popping, dragging. Old tape starts to curl in on itself and will stick together. A lot of this tape was unusable, but I spliced the good pieces together. Sometimes you get bleed-through from the other side tape when it starts to break down. We had quite a bit of that here, but the simultaneous convos sounded so cool, I started sampling it."

"Then I walked into his room and heard my name on the sample he was working on," Malachi said. "Someone on that tape was talking about my uncle. I could tell from the date on the label it was the day he died."

"While they were cleaning up the tape, I was going through all these papers," Susie said.

I volunteered, "Bertie must have found the file after Hains tried to burn it. I wonder how long she had it."

"There was a church bulletin in there. It was printed for a ceremony they had when Judge Spencer became Judge Spencer. So, it had to have been burned after 1999."

"You mean JP Spencer, the younger judge," Doodie said.

"Yes, the one they want to make a Supreme Court Justice," Susie confirmed. "And that really shouldn't happen."

"Where did you get Mali's necklace, the one you sent to me?"

The boys exchanged looks. They'd be the easy marks if I wanted info. Their female counterpart was a tougher nut.

"Wait, you're getting ahead of the story," Susie said. "The papers, besides the transcript and notes we gave you tonight, those papers chronicle crimes and cover-ups going back years before the murder."

"You're saying murder, but Etta said JP didn't push him." I was bewildered.

Etta looked as perplexed. "He jumped. I saw him. Malachi was not pushed, physically. Emotionally, he may have reached a breaking point. But he did not hit his head like they said. That part of the official story was wrong. Didn't you say his head wasn't bleeding when you brought him to shore?"

I nodded and answered, "Yes. Only his lip was bleeding."

John started tapping his phone. A little cube speaker on the table came to life with the voice out of the past.

Sheriff Law Forster, said, "I can't cover up a murder, Carroll."

The cube might as well have sneered, because I saw Judge Carroll Spencer's condescending lip curl in my mind, when his voice said, "This community will believe what we tell them to believe."

"A boy is dead, Judge. We can't pretend it didn't happen."

"Do you want your own child ruined over this? That's what it will come to if you pursue this, Sheriff," said another voice, this one belonged to JP Spencer. "That boy jumped, hit his head, end of story. No one need know what happened on that dock tonight."

"What about Jane Doe? She saw you. She thinks you pushed him."

"She saw someone, but it wasn't me up there when he jumped." JP addressed the issue of my eyewitness testimony. "She didn't see what she thinks she saw, so that's easy enough to discredit."

"You were there. How do you explain that?"

"I went with my father to calm a distraught young man who came looking to the judge for help. We left him on the ferry dock, where he stripped his clothes and ran into the night. We returned home to retrieve weather gear and flashlights. When we got back, the young man was dead."

The sheriff commented, "You've thought this through, I see."

"So, no matter what that nosey bitch thinks she saw, it was not me who watched that piece of shit jump off the dock. You just need to get right with the story—he hit his head when he jumped on his own."

"But Jane saw he didn't have a head wound," Law argued.

"It was dark. She doesn't know what she saw," the judge said.

JP was more forceful in his statement, "I'll take care of Jane Doe. No one will believe a word that bitch says when I'm done with her. You worry about keeping Hains quiet."

"Hains isn't the one who killed Malachi," his father said but didn't sound confident of the assertion.

The judge spoke next. "If you don't play ball here, Law, guilty or not, Hains Forster never plays another down of football. We all have secrets of some sort, yes?"

"What about your secrets, Judge? Won't you have some questions to answer, considering your close relationship with the victim?"

The judge was flippant in his answer, "I counseled the boy, tried to direct him down the right path."

"The medical examiner is going to have questions," the sheriff said, sounding more defeated by the moment.

The judge tried to ease the sheriff's mind, "I'll speak to the medical examiner. There need not be any unwarranted revelations. Let his family put him to rest without community scorn."

147

Hains's father sounded panicked. "What if your yard-boy starts talking? What about Asa?"

The judge chuckled. "Young Wayne has been dispatched back to Tidewater. Asa will be leaving us shortly."

JP threatened, "A child molestation charge fabricated here, an ounce of pot planted there, I can be rid of anyone who asks too many questions about the death of that little nigger queer, including you Lawman, and including your son."

The old sheriff tried one more time to remain one of the good guys. He accused JP, "You planted that pot in Jane's cooler, didn't you? One kid is dead. Why destroy another one?"

The coldness of JP's tone gave me chills. I imagined him running his fingers along the scar on his chin, when he answered, "Revenge is a dish best served cold."

The phone began to hiss.

John Smith explained what we just heard. "That's the cleanest part of the conversations on the tapes. The rest is bits and pieces."

"Wait, there's more?" I said excitedly.

Malachi nodded his head. "Yes, but it isn't clear who is talking and what they are talking about. Too much bleed-through."

Doodie was looking at the tape guts Susie had lifted from the table. "It doesn't matter. The recording we just listened to is inadmissible. It's been processed too much."

John offered, "I kept all the pieces. You can send it to the FBI."

Doodie added, "We'd also have to prove the identities of those men on the tape. One is dead. One has dementia."

"And one is about to become a Supreme Court Justice," Susie said, still fixated on that fact, which I found refreshing in a young person.

Malachi said, "There are other people on the tape. Maybe they could testify."

"They can't," Doodie said. "They are dead too."

"You know what's on that tape, all of it, don't you," I prodded him. "That's why you didn't come to see me. You knew I would know if you lied."

Doodie stood up. "Jane, would you take a walk with me?"

Etta touched his hand. "Should I come too?"

"No, Jane and I are due this conversation." Doodie pointed at the table. "See if you can make sense of what they found while we're gone. We won't be long."

Etta looked at me as I stood to join my old friend. "Remember, Jane, we were all children, all of us. We did what we were told."

#

"Do you still have any of that pot left?"

We walked next door to the boathouse, just the two of us.

"Actually, I do." I reached for the old cigarette pack and pulled out the yellowed joint. I held it out to him and said, "Is this going to be that hard Doodie?"

"I gave up smoking and drinking in my twenties. Survival training will highlight every weakness. Mine was Marlboro reds and Budweiser binges to dull the ache. I have few options left that don't come in a pill bottle. I'd just rather not trade one addiction for another."

"So you exercise for the chemicals it produces to keep you balanced," I said.

He smiled at me. "On the old take your demons to the gym regimen yourself?"

"I am familiar with fighting off the darkness with diet and exercise." I pointed at his overdeveloped muscles. "I haven't gone to your extreme though. Maybe my demons don't weigh as much."

Doodie lit the joint with the lighter Duck left on the worktable. I watched him take a few hits—observed him seek that moment when he would feel his shoulders relax.

I asked, "The nights get dark sometimes, do they? Seen some things?"

I took the joint from his outstretched hand, took a hit, and passed it back, while he nodded an affirmative answer to my question. Since he wasn't talking yet, I began.

"I know it was you. You were Asa's accuser, the anonymous victim."

I suspected but hadn't known for sure until I saw his reaction to my declaration. Doodie leaned back against the wall and took another hit. He stared up into the cupola, I assumed waiting for what else I knew before he spoke.

"I know why Asa had to go. He knew too much. Had the investigation reached law enforcement outside of this county, they would have spoken to Asa eventually. Neither Judge Spencer, nor his son could allow that to happen."

"You are correct," Doodie said, holding the smoke in his lungs as long as he could.

"I know you Brian Smith Duty. I know the only way you would have told a lie like that would have been to protect someone else, someone weaker than you. You're a white hat at heart."

149

"If it makes me a better person in your eyes, I never gave any kind of statement against Asa. My mother did all the talking."

"Great, another Smith woman fucking up my life. By the way, that kid in there, John, who is he to us?"

"He's our second or third cousin. I never figured all that out. He's Uncle Thomas's grandson."

"Guess he got the smart genes from his mother's side of the family." I took one last hit, handed it back, and indicated I was done with a wave. Then I asked, "So, why did your mother lie about Asa?"

"Remember how I always had the newest toy, the best gadgets? I had the first pair of Nike shoes any of us had ever seen."

I nodded that I did remember.

"Well, as it turns out, both my mother and father were embezzling from the jail funds. Padding the grocery bill now and again, working another job off-site while being paid to watch the jail, just a little here and there, but it added up to a felony. The judge called in a favor, and the charges were dropped if there ever were any. I don't think anyone ever noticed any discrepancies. I believe the judge just guessed and hit pay dirt when my mom thought he knew more than he did and begged for mercy. He used it as leverage to force my parents to help rid him of one Asa Speight. My folks even kept their jobs. How corrupt is that?"

"Pretty damn corrupt. Did you make the tape?"

"Yes. I was in the church to retrieve my tape recorder and tape from the Sunday service. I had no idea what was happening at the ferry dock. I heard people in the vestibule. They sounded angry. I stepped behind the choir loft, because, if you'll remember, I was a nosey kid."

"Who was out there?"

"I don't know. I had been there a few minutes getting the tape ready to give to my grandmother. I always left her a message at the end of the service, so the recorder was running when I hid."

"You heard them talking about Malachi being killed, and you just hid?"

"Wait, I didn't hear. While I was hiding, I saw flashes of red lights in the church windows. I slipped out the back while the voices were still in the foyer. I came back to get the tape the next day."

"I don't remember seeing you that night."

"I found Hains first. I went with him to his house. He was inconsolable. I saw you, but the sheriff had you in his car. And then my mother told me what we had to do after I came home. I couldn't talk to you after that. I would have spilled everything, kinda like I'm doing now."

Doodie chuckled. He had picked up the habit from Hains.

He continued, "I took my exams early and left a month before I had planned. My parents were worried I'd be next on JP's hit list because I refused to lie about Asa. My dad had seen just how ruthless JP could be."

"Do you know what really happened at the jail?"

"Asa was handcuffed, and JP threw him into a cement block wall head first, several times. He wouldn't let my dad get help until he thought he was dead. He made my dad lie to the sheriff and old man Poyner backed him up."

"That asshole Poyner would have said anything to get out of the charges for exposing himself to those little kids. Funny how he just walked off that dock and drowned not long after making his statement about Asa's 'accident.'"

"Yeah, funny thing," Doodie said, snuffing out the joint on the worktable.

We both knew Poyner finally got what was coming to him. We didn't know who took care of that stain on humanity, but we didn't care either. The kids he'd molested over his lifetime had wished him dead for years, me included.

"I feel responsible for Asa's injuries," Doodie blurted out. "I refused to testify against Asa, which put the pressure on JP to find another way to silence him. I'd like to say it was because it was the right thing to do, but it wasn't. I was about to enter the Army. I wasn't going to tell people I'd been molested by a man. No way."

"It was the seventies, Doodie. There was no 'Me Too' movement. Victim shaming was an acceptable practice."

"I was seventeen. I said and did things I'm not proud of. I used to call Asa a fag when I was around the other guys, even though I really liked him. He was good to us kids."

"So did Hains. Remember we used to play a game called Smear the Queer."

Doodie shook his head. "Yeah, and the person with the ball was the queer, and we dog piled them if we could catch them."

"Yep, that's the one. I never wanted the ball. I wasn't fast enough to outrun anyone but you." We both laughed, then I said, "The seventies were not the best time to be an LGBTQ ally."

"First of all, we had a lot fewer letters to ally with." Doodie smiled down at me. "We've come a long way, baby. I'm glad to be your ally."

"We've come far enough that calling someone baby is politically incorrect. And why does everyone assume I'm gay?"

"Well, because of that girl in high school," Doodie answered.

"My god, does everyone know about that?"

"You were not exactly in stealth mode."

"Fine, I was a horny teenager with a girls' boarding school attendee willing to explain a few things to a sheltered country girl."

"So, you're not gay?"

"I'm whatever works in the moment, Doodie." I smiled up at him. "I try not to limit my options."

"Fair enough."

I got us back on topic. "I suppose JP's only choice after you refused to lie was to make it impossible for Asa to go to trial. I remember the prosecutor argued they couldn't let a child molester with a brain injury out to roam the streets."

Doodie nodded in agreement. "Not until he is deemed capable of mounting a defense, which will be never. Worse than a trial, if you ask me."

"Just like the tapes, no one can verify any of what you've told me. It's all hearsay."

"I'm sorry I couldn't be of more help at the time."

"I'm sorry we lost touch, Doodie. We'll have to remedy that and stay in contact from now on. You are pretty much all the family I have left, that claims me anyway."

"I came to visit mom in 2000. That's when she told me John Doe died and that you signed over the property we had always lived on to her. She said John never charged her a dime of rent on the land."

"No, he never did. Even when he needed the money, he never made any off your family or Malachi's."

"Etta said you gave her the deed to Bertie's property too."

"Bertie was family, and her children should have what was coming to them. And don't make me too altruistic. I'm not paying taxes on that land anymore either."

"Well, Mom thought it was so generous, she was miserable with guilt. She spilled her guts about what really happened to Asa. That's what is on the rest of the tape, my parents selling their souls. I'm truly sorry, Jane. You and I are family too, and I let you down."

"Your parents and the other adults involved did what they did, and that karma rests with them. I can't spend my life being mad at dead people. You can't spend yours apologizing for them."

We remained quiet for a minute. A minute is a long time when all you can hear is water lapping against pilings. I supposed we were processing what we had recently learned about our perceptions of past events.

I finally broke our mutual think-fest, when I asked, "How did Bertie end up with the tape?"

"I gave it to her. I forgot about it until the next weekend. I listened to the sheriff with JP and the judge. The kids say there's other stuff on there. I didn't listen to all of it. My parents were not in the mood to be accommodating, so I gave it to Bertie in the hope she would use it to get help. She was the only person that could have caused a stir. The rest of us were being blackmailed into silence or worse."

"Why didn't she use it? Didn't Etta say she saw what happened to Malachi? They could have corroborated parts of the tape with her testimony."

"Bertie told me to hush my mouth and never speak of that tape again. Her exact quote was, 'They done killed one black child. What makes you think they won't kill some more. They'll do away with you too.' She made Etta swear to never tell a soul what she saw."

"But when you got together, why didn't you do something then?"

"Because we couldn't get Bertie to give us the tape. She was worried about her other children and grandchildren."

"Etta said Mali jumped. Bertie said 'killed one black child.' Which is it? If what I saw didn't happen, then what did?"

"Mali did jump, Jane."

"Bull shit, Doodie. Malachi Blount had to be scared out of his mind to take the water as his only option. If he wanted to kill himself, which he did not, he wouldn't have picked his worst fear as the weapon."

"I didn't say he jumped voluntarily. From what Etta said, he was backing away from—She really should tell you that part."

"Was it Hains? Is that what would make his father, the lawman of all lawmen, take part in a cover-up?"

"Hains didn't kill Malachi. He loved him."

"We all loved him, Doodie."

"No, Hains loved Malachi more than we did."

"If you are talking about them having sex, I knew that. Mali told me, but he wasn't holding out hope that he and Hains had a life together."

"Hains had a lot of sex with a lot of people. It's just an act for him, like any other physical activity. But Jane, Hains loved Malachi. He was happy when you suggested Mali live with you in Raleigh."

153

"Is that what the judge had over Law Forster's head? The stud of the county turns out to be gay, and that's a reason to cover up his lover's murder?"

"I don't know why Law Forster did that. I know Hains was devastated that night. He just stared into space, not speaking, not moving. His dad told me to stay with him. I did, but he never said a word. He curled into a fetal position and cried himself to sleep."

"Hains had been weird for a while before that. I thought it was Cindy's excessive clinginess and managing so many women at once. He and Mali's down low relationship wasn't something I thought a lot about. To be honest, the testosterone fest that was y'all's entourage was revolting, and I was just trying to get the hell out of high school. Hains and I weren't spending much time together."

"Cindy was pregnant. Hains was scared and pissed because she tricked him—his words not mine. He was losing everything. In his fantasy, he would leave here, become a star quarterback, and pretend to be a playboy bachelor, with Mali as his best friend from home at his side. No one would be the wiser. He'd thought it through."

"He told you all this back then."

"Oh, hell no. He told me when I came back. He'd been in therapy for a while and felt the need to unburden himself of 'past lies of omission.' His description, not mine."

"If it wasn't JP and it wasn't Hains, who scared Mali enough that he would jump off that dock?"

16

Say a word and you're dead...

"Our father threatened Malachi. He was a mean drunk. Thank goodness he drove a truck and was gone most of the time."

"Start at the beginning, Etta. I'm going to take the kids over to Doe House to start on the preparations. It's going to be a long night," Doodie said, and then he looked at me. "These kids remind me of some others I used to know."

"They have great ideas," I said. "Listen to them."

Alone finally, Etta eyed me over a steaming cup of coffee provided by Duck, who led the parade back to Doe House, excited to finally be doing something about the tormenting teenagers. Etta took a sip from her cup, swallowed hard, and commenced her tale.

"We were all at home that Sunday night. Daddy had been drinking all day out on the sound, fishing. He was surly, and Momma was trying to feed him so he'd go on to sleep, but Malachi wasn't home. Momma sent me looking for him. Daddy insisted we all be at the table for supper when he was home."

"Your daddy did not like me."

Etta laughed. "My daddy didn't like white people in general."

"I had that impression. Like you, I was glad he wasn't around very often."

Etta nodded and continued her story. "I found Malachi on the ferry dock, but I didn't have time to say anything because just as I found him, so did JP. I remember hearing JP call Malachi a nigger and a faggot. I know I wondered what faggot meant. I sure as hell knew what nigger meant, and I wasn't going to hang around and wait for that angry white man to find me. I ducked into those high bushes around your house and listened out of sight."

#

"Come here you little nigger faggot," JP Spencer growled at Malachi.

"What do you want, man? I ain't done nothin' to you," Malachi said, as he struggled to break free of JP's grasp.

JP was much bigger than Malachi and overpowered him quickly. He smashed the young teen up against the big cypress tree that shaded the ferry dock.

Hidden in the shadows from the view of passersby, JP drove Malachi's face into the bark of the tree. The state's attorney could not contain his rage. The words left his mouth in demanding clipped bursts.

"You think it's funny. You and that little Doe bitch—running your mouths. You want a thousand dollars to suck your dick. How about I cut it off for free?"

"Let the boy go, JP," the judge rushed into the shadows.

"Shut up. I'm ending this since you seem incapable. I sent that yard-boy running back to Virginia, and now I'm gonna shut this piece of shit up for good."

"Leave him alone, JP. Malachi has done nothing improper," the judge pleaded.

JP snarled at his father. "This kid is laughing at you. He and that Doe girl are sitting around laughing at the stupid old pervert. How much have you promised just to touch him? I hear his going rate to let you suck him off is a cold thousand."

His face still smashed to the tree and blood trickling from his lip, Malachi Blount did not bend or break. He spit blood as he said, "Now it's two thousand."

The same snarling visage on the son suddenly appeared on the father. "You ungrateful little queer," the judge said, closing in on Malachi. "Take off those clothes, shoes and socks, too."

Malachi struggled against JP. "What the hell, man? I ain't done nothin'."

"Take them off, or I'll have JP assist you."

"All right, man. Get him off me," Malachi said as tried to break free again.

JP eased up just enough to let Malachi slip from his grasp.

"Take it off, all of it," the judge demanded.

156

When Malachi was stripped to his underwear, the judge ran his tongue over his top lip and said, "those too," pointing at the expensive Armani boxer-briefs the nearly naked young man wore.

JP, who had been gathering the clothing items, turned to his father and shoved the bundle into his arms. "You're enjoying this too much, you sick fuck. Don't let your perversion interfere with my life or I'll see you dead." He turned back to the now naked Malachi. "Don't come near him or my family again or they'll find your swollen rotten corpse floating in the sound one day."

"Malachi!" Hains Forster called out in the now driving rain. "Malachi, where are you?"

"Say a word and you're dead," JP warned.

JP and the judge ducked down and using the shadows disappeared down the side of the Doe house, heading toward their own home.

Hains appeared on the hill above the big tree wearing a rain slicker. He called into the darkness, "Mali, are you down there? I didn't know it was going to rain like this when I called you."

Coming down the hill, Malachi finally came into Hains's view, naked and shivering.

"What the hell? Mali, where are your clothes?"

"JP and the judge took them. I hate this fucking place. Take me away from here, Hains. I'll move to Raleigh, anywhere. I gotta get out of here."

Hains removed his rain slicker and put it over Malachi's shoulders, and then he kissed him. Hains Forster held Malachi to him and kissed him like it would be the last time. He pulled away, his tears mixing with the rainwater, and said, "Cindy is pregnant."

"Oh, my God," Cindy Spencer's voice jarred both young men. "Oh, my God," she repeated.

Hains let go of Malachi and ran toward Cindy. "It's not what it looks like."

Malachi took off the raincoat and threw it at Hains. He stood there naked, his arms outstretched like Jesus on the cross in all his magnificence.

He smiled at Cindy and said, "It's exactly what it looks like. Your dad wants to suck my dick, and the father of your baby likes to fuck me in my black ass."

Cindy took off running.

Hains ran after her, calling back over his shoulder at Malachi, "You asshole."

Malachi stood there in the rain for a moment, and then seemed to change his mind. He ran up the hill after Hains. The storm was really rolling in now. A figure approached in a rain slicker. It wasn't until he was close enough to strike that Malachi realized who it was.

William Malachi Blount, Sr. swung his meaty hand, palm open, into his son's cheek hard enough to lift him off the ground.

"You proud of taking dick in the ass, boy. I'll make you wish you weren't born, nigga."

Malachi backed toward the edge of the dock. With nowhere to go but into the water, he looked out over the sound and back at his approaching, drunk, abusive father and smiled—just before he jumped.

#

"I ran up onto the dock, just as Malachi disappeared over the side. That's why you saw two people," Etta said to me, taking a sip of coffee before finishing her account of what happened on that ferry dock in the pouring rain.

"I screamed at you. I saw you swimming toward Malachi. Daddy turned on me and started running after me. He was out of his mind. Vietnam made him crazy, Momma said. As you know, most PTSD sufferers back then self-medicated and raged in silence. My dad's rage usually exploded in violence once or twice a year, and always aimed at his family. That night, he chased me all the way to Swann's store, hell bent on killing me. I don't think he even knew who I was. By the time I circled back, Malachi was dead. I don't know who bashed him in the head, but he didn't hit his head on the dock. That I do know."

Etta stopped talking and looked at me. She put her hand over mine on the table.

"Jane, you're crying."

I was. I felt hot tears slowly falling from my full lids.

"I caused all of it."

"What? You weren't there. You at least tried to save him," Etta assured me.

"I fought with Cindy that afternoon. I wanted to hurt her, and I did. I told her the truth she ignored about her father's obsession with Mali, and about Mali saying his price was a thousand dollars. Cindy told JP. She had to have. That's what set the attack on Mali in motion."

"Why is it we tend to blame ourselves when bad people do bad things?"

Etta waited for me to answer her question. When I didn't, she continued.

"I work at the nursing home. I'm a palliative care nurse. I deal with people at their most vulnerable moments. What I have learned from my patients is that we spend too much time apologizing for being human. Self-blame is due to our desire to believe that we can be faultless. We are human and far from perfect. We say and do stupid things. Forgive yourself for being human, Jane." She handed me a napkin from the holder on the table and smiled. "They also say, 'Fuck the past. It's over.' "

"I'm a felon. The past is never over. But I agree with the 'fuck it' part."

Welcomed cathartic laughter followed.

When the room was once again silent, I said to Etta what I never got the chance to tell her mother.

"I'm sorry I didn't stay with him. I was impatient. Help was coming. Hains came back. He would have found us. I've replayed every mistake I made that day. I would have fought for Mali. I've fought a shadowy man wielding a piece of rebar in my dreams for years."

Etta leaned back and sipped from her coffee cup, before she said, "I hope these kids are right. That's a big spotlight they are about to put on Doe's Ferry."

"They are making art, not accusations. It will only disturb the guilty. I think it's brilliant."

"They're young. They're fearless. They don't yet understand the risks of speaking truth to power."

"When a politician can stand behind a microphone and tell one self-serving falsehood after another without redress, all we have left are these truth speaking kids."

#

"Hey, can you tell me what's happening here?"

A cameraman from one of the cable news networks approached me on the ferry dock with his giant bag of professional tools draped over one shoulder. We'd been hard at work most of the night and started again at sunrise. Signs of other life stirring on this spring morning had begun, and we were drawing the attention the kids wanted. Honestly, I had no plan, and theirs appeared to be the best option we had: psychological warfare.

"The retired ferry dock is going to revert back to a historically accurate community fishing wharf, and we're breaking ground today,"

I answered, while in the process of spraying a shovel I found in the garden shed with metallic gold paint.

"The graffiti I saw last night on my run, it was the most interesting thing I've seen in this place. I told our producer, and she sent me to get some shots of it. I thought the tarps were there to cover it up, but apparently, there is an art installation going on behind them."

"Yeah, well, we couldn't let that negative energy grow wings and fly around the country on your cable news networks. Wouldn't want the world to think the probable next Supreme Court Justice nominee comes from a place filled with racist homophobes, now would we?"

The cameraman looked disappointed. "I've shot so much wholesome local flavor, I regret to say I was hoping for some controversy. It's the only way this trip would be worth it."

He paused, grinned at me, and stuck out his hand.

"Hello, my name is Paul. I've been here a week, and I'm bored to tears. If my producer doesn't dig up some dirt on this guy soon, she may start eating the crew. We've never seen her after midnight. We think she feeds until dawn."

I laughed. This guy was funny.

"Well, now. We can't have you eaten. I'm sure if you hang out, have a hot dog and some sweet tea, someone will appear with a story or two about ol' JP. You know how us southerners love to spin a tale."

Paul looked to be mid-forties with a bit of gray in his temples. He put his bag down and rubbed his shoulder.

"What's your story, besides shovel painting expert? Do you have a name?"

I made another pass down and up the back of the spade with the spray paint. If this guy was hitting on me, he indeed had been here far too long. I don't give off a come hither vibe. I'm more likely to have an "I'll call ya" kind of interaction, then go home and do a background check on you before we have another.

I told him my name, "Jane Doe," expecting the typical reaction and got it.

"Come on, you can tell me your name. I'm not a bad guy."

"Really, it's Jane Doe."

"For real?"

"Where are you?" I asked.

I saw the light bulb come on.

"Ah, Doe's Ferry, Jane Doe, got it. Parents have a sense of humor?"

"Something like that."

"Hey, maybe you're the story. The village namesake, Jane Doe. What do you know about Judge JP Spencer?"

"Why don't you go ask that young man over there what he's painting on the sides of the restrooms? That's a great human-interest story. Besides, that flat-screen by the building is playing the security footage from last night. I'm pretty sure the people on the video will show up sooner or later to demand we turn it off. That might be a good Jerry Springer moment."

Paul picked up his bag and shouldered it with a grunt. "I have a feeling you are the story, Jane Doe."

I shook my head, "I'm not interesting, but those two kids setting up the DJ equipment are. They'll be doing original stuff. You might like it. And that young woman with the clipboard, supervising the banner hanging, she's pretty sharp. Stick around a couple of hours. They could be the story you're looking for."

"What kind of story?" Paul asked, walking away toward the restrooms.

"They were instrumental in the decision to dedicate the new park to a young man who died at this dock forty years ago because he was gay. It's nice to see young people engaged, don't you think?"

He nodded and said, "Yes, I do. Very progressive for such a conservative-leaning county."

"What are you gonna do about those gosh darn meddlin' kids," I said, smiling and playing my part as the jovial landowner.

Paul wandered over to the painters. The dock was a swarm of activity. Duck and most of the Doe House women were busy setting up saw horses topped with plywood sheets to serve as tables to hold the food and drinks. They had even managed to find some bunting. Claudette and Gloria would be arriving soon with supplies. They cut out at dawn with a shopping list. Doodie had borrowed a large cooker from Susie's dad and was in the process of firing it up. Duck had opened her supply shed for the young artist painting the mural on the outside of the restroom. Etta, covered in various colors of paint, was his assistant. Enough people had driven by now to cause a phone-tree reaction through the county.

"We'll have a crowd by noon," Susie said when she had handed me a cup of coffee just after sunrise.

Susie exuded the energy only a fourteen-year-old can have after very little sleep. Her prediction came true. People parked down at the courthouse and over at the church, curious to see the happenings at the

161

old ferry dock. Or, they had heard I was in town and had come for the expected show.

The banner hung properly, we stepped back to see it.

"Welcome to William Malachi Blount, Jr. Memorial Park"

While clapping rippled through the attendees, I looked over my shoulder at the judge's residence, where the younger Judge Spencer was holed up waiting to accept his nomination to the Supreme Court. He had calculated this to be the best place to launch his career as a homespun judge of impeccable standing. I doubted things were going to go as he planned. The bait had been set in the trap. It wouldn't be long now.

#

Just after noon, a woman's voice behind me asked, "Are you Jane Doe?"

I didn't answer until I had turned to make sure the inquirer wasn't carrying a weapon. Paranoia based on the odds that someone might actually want me dead seemed in order. A middle-aged woman in Rachel Maddow style glasses holding only a phone stood before me. I quickly applied my fake smile and calculated southern charm.

"Yes, ma'am. I'm Jane Doe. How can I help you?"

The woman extended her hand for me to shake, "Hi, my name is Presley Morgan. I'm a producer with NCN. My cameraman tells me there's a story here and you are at the center of it. Care to talk about the accusations you made in 1979 concerning the death of your friend Malachi Blount?"

Paul appeared behind Ms. Morgan.

"Ah, Paul's producer. He did mention you were eager to find a more compelling story than watching the sunrise over Doe's Ferry."

Paul grimaced, afraid I might repeat his comments about his boss.

"The people of Doe's Ferry seem to think you're here to, let me see," she looked down at her phone, "to expose Judge Spencer for the racist homophobe he is."

The kids had a plan so simple no one thought it would work, but it was brilliant. Being social media babies, they were very familiar with a viral event online. Susie proposed we create one at the ferry dock. The reactive nature of a viral environment might be just the thing to draw out an inadvertent confession. If nothing else, Susie suggested, the kind of scrutiny this would place the Spencer judges under might be enough to derail JP's nomination. That was our goal. If a murderer popped up, that would be a cherry on the top.

I played my role and said my lines to the producer. "I'm here to honor my friend, a young man who was forced off this dock by hate. Most of the last words he heard were racial and homophobic slurs. It really doesn't matter who said them, who overheard them, and who covered them up. The important thing is that we make a stand against hate speech of any kind and we do it here in Malachi's honor, at Mali's Place, a public park where all will be welcomed."

"But it does matter if Judge Spencer was a part of the cover-up."

"Ms. Morgan, if you want to know what role he played, you'll have to ask Judge Spencer, both of them."

"You mean the judge's father is also involved?"

It was a gorgeous day. The grill smoked with a steady stream of hot dogs being handed off to eager hands. Tea and water flowed. Laughter and goodwill permeated the air. Young Malachi and John Smith had been spinning tunes for a couple of hours. I don't know what one would call their style—instrumental, kind of techno beat crossed with spoken word poetry—but I enjoyed it. I signaled the DJs with a nod. They were prepared.

A new song began.

A hip-hop style performer's voice said, "Yeah. Uh."

The repetitive bass thumping started heads bobbing.

The voice said:

"This is what love looks like."

Alternating with another voice that said:

"No hate."

Music thumped beneath the words.

I leaned closer to Ms. Morgan so she could hear me, when I said, "Aren't these kids doing a great job with the music? It's all original."

With perfect timing, another voice that had been playing under the music, barely audible and on a loop, grew louder. The words clipped in time with the beat. Hardly noticeable at first, the phrase rolled in and faded again, making it difficult to quite catch the whole thing. It made the audience listen harder until heads started to turn and jaws began to drop.

Under the thumping rhythm and the alternating "No hate," and "This is what love looks like," a male voice clearly said, "I can't cover up a murder, Carroll."

People old enough to remember Law Forster knew precisely whose voice it was and began whispering to those who didn't.

163

Ms. Morgan asked Paul, her photographer, "Is that saying what I think it is?"

The tone of the music darkened. The hip-hop singers' words did too. Now they said, "This is what hate looks like," and "No love," intertwined with lines from the church tape. This wasn't a "Michael Row The Boat Ashore" style round. This was meant to make people uncomfortable, overpowering them with words of hate and the bitter truth, staggered, stacked, stabbing, pulsing into the hearts of those listening. The volume soared, and the voices fought to be heard. Alternating between beats, the sound built to a cacophony the Doe's Ferry residents and national media present could not ignore.

"I can't cover up a murder, Carroll."
"This is what hate looks like."
"No Love."
"This community will believe what we tell them to believe."
"This is what hate looks like."
"No Love."
"A boy is dead, Judge."
"This is what hate looks like."
"No Love."
"This community will believe what we tell them to believe."
"This is what hate looks like."
"No Love."

As suddenly as it overwhelmed the audience, the volume dropped out altogether. Silence fell over the dock. Seconds ticked by, one, two, three, and then the music boomed back.

"No hate."
"This is what love looks like"
"Bringing justice for a brother."
"No hate."
"This is what love looks like"
"Bringing justice to a mother."
"No hate."
"This is what love looks like"
"Bringing justice to this place."
"No hate."

The music stopped abruptly.

When they came out of the speakers this time, JP Spencer and Law Forster's voices were unmistakable to anyone who had known either man.

"A charge fabricated here, an ounce of pot planted there. I can be rid of anyone who asks too many questions about the death of that little nigger queer..."
"You planted that pot in Jane's cooler, didn't you?"

Although JP's final words had been spoken forty years ago, they were prophetic:

"Revenge is a dish best served cold."

On the word cold, the tarps erected to hide the mural were ripped away. The formerly drab gray cinderblock building had been transformed. The artist had painted two giant mirrored images that wrapped around all four sides. This kid was fantastic with a paint sprayer and a detail brush. The shadowing made a beaming Mali appear to leap out of the block walls. A person standing in front of the Spencer home or entering the new park would see Mali's image gazing back at them, with the words "THIS IS WHAT LOVE LOOKS LIKE," stenciled over and over around the middle of the entire building. The exact same image faced the courthouse and Hains's home on the opposite side.

The stunned crowd fell silent, before the younger among them and a few older persons like myself, erupted in applause and were joined by the remaining observers.

Ms. Morgan smiled at me. "Paul said you were the story. Can we get a copy of that tape and someone to verify its authenticity?"

Acting surprised at the insinuation, I said, "My story is I'm here to dedicate a park to my friend, and I think you can buy a copy of the original mix from the DJs. All the proceeds are going toward a park bench where people can sit and watch the sunset."

"Jane, I need to talk to you," Hains said, appearing at my shoulder.

"Howdy, Sheriff. Have you met Ms. Presley Morgan of NCN?"

Hains answered, "No, I haven't," while he glared down at me. "We've had some noise complaints."

I laughed and included Ms. Morgan in the joke. "Goodness, well we know who called that in. The Swanns are deaf, and everyone else within shouting distance not named Spencer is here."

Presley was on top of things and knew the players in our game of cat and mouse. She went right at Hains.

165

"Sheriff, I'm told that one of the vandals in the video is your son, who is also Judge JP Spencer's nephew. Care to comment on that? And what do you know about the taped voices we just heard?"

Hains grabbed me by the elbow and escorted me away from the reporter, calling over his shoulder, "No comment."

17

I told you I was going to be famous...

When we were out of earshot, Hains whispered through gritted teeth, "What in the hell are you trying to pull here, Jane?"

"I am not pulling anything. As the owner of the land, I am here to break ground on Mali's Place, a park to honor our friend. Your grandson is quite the artist. It's abstract, yet it looks like Mali could just walk right out of that painting. It took my breath there for a sec."

"Complimenting my grandson won't stop me from being pissed at you, and yes, Bart is an amazing artist."

"Why are you pissed at me? I was minding my own business in another part of the country when someone invited me here. Might those people be the ones responsible for all this?"

I spread my arms wide, indicating the mass of people now assembled on the old ferry dock. The haves and the have-nots of Doe's Ferry mingled together, whispering among themselves, wondering what would happen next, as they surreptitiously watched Hains and me out of the corner of their collective eyes. We turned our backs and spoke into the wind coming off the water.

"The video of my son and his idiot friends should have been handed over to my office for investigation, not put on display to insight vigilante justice."

"The modern-day courthouse kids wanted to show what hate looks like, and I think that's a perfect example. Isn't that what the sign says above the TV monitor?"

"Courthouse kids? That bunch that hangs out with Doodie's kid?"

When I replied, "His name is Malachi," pain creased Hains's brow and it infuriated me. "You can't even say his name. How fucked up is that, Hains?"

He acted as if I had said nothing.

"You know damn well that surveillance tape should have come to me first," Hains insisted, "before it was made public. And that song—where did they get those recordings?"

I made sure to repeat his name.

"Malachi and his friends, John and Susie, found the voice recording in Bertie's house and have compiled quite the file on Mali's case."

"Why didn't they ask me for help, Jane? If they have evidence, why not bring it to me? I'm not the bad guy."

"Doe's Ferry has taught her children well. So well, they sought outside help from me to assist in their quest to solve a forty-year-old mystery."

"It's only a mystery if they believe your story. Recordings can be altered or created whole cloth out of thin air—"

I interrupted him, "Doodie made that tape. He gave it to Bertie, who was afraid more of us would die if she came to your dad with it. The kids found it after she died. Bertie also had your dad's file, the one you said you burned." The memory of Malachi's mother rocking in that chair caused a smile to curl my lips. "Bertie sat on what she knew the rest of her life out of fear. Her descendants don't share her reservations about disclosure."

"Bertie was smart, Jane. That's exactly the reason the adults involved might have served these kids better by advising them to turn over evidence to law enforcement."

"The adults only found out a few hours ago, and it's not a bad plan. Susie says the power of viral info is in its quick dissemination. Look around, it appears to be working."

"Public conjecture isn't evidence."

I grinned at him, more for the benefit of the people watching than his.

"That video of your son isn't conjecture. It's my understanding that the women of Doe House did come to you about their concerns. You offered little assistance. I installed a camera to document the vandalism and to help identify the culprits. Everyone in Doe's Ferry knows exactly who that is in the video. But it doesn't appear anyone cares enough to do anything about the racism and homophobia. Forty years later and it feels like nothing has changed."

"I care, Jane. It's complicated."

I had known Hains as a child. I had no idea who he was as a man, but I knew who I was, and it wasn't far from the idealist I was at eighteen. I still fought for the underdog. I still cursed like a sailor. I still asked forgiveness rather than permission. When I looked into Hains Forster's eyes, I saw the conflicted boy I used to know always trying and failing at the perfection he demanded of himself.

"What do they have on you? What public humiliation are you unwilling to undergo that allows them to manipulate you like this?"

"Who? What are you talking about?"

"Your kid has taken his battle with you to the streets. Daddy's being called out, and baby boy is getting no reaction. What's that about? The Hains I knew would never allow his kid to behave like yours without consequences, but then something happened to that guy on a rainy night in April of 1979. He turned out to be a coward."

"I'm a coward because I wouldn't back up your crazy story about JP killing Malachi. Jane, it did not happen like that."

"Then what happened? Tell me the truth. Who hit Malachi in the head with that piece of pipe, and don't give me the 'he hit his head routine.' I've seen the original ME's report and the pictures. He was still lying on his side, just like I left him, unconscious. Someone stood over him and swung a piece of rebar or pipe and smashed his skull. Who did that, Hains? Who murdered Malachi?"

"I don't know," Hains said, much too flatly to be true.

"Come on, are you really going to try to lie to me, Hains? I've heard the rest of the tape the kids used in that song. Your dad covered up Malachi's murder to save your reputation. Was it worth it, all the lying, pretending to be this man you display for the public when you would rather be anywhere but here?"

Hains gritted his teeth. I could see his jaw muscles tightening. He wasn't angry. I was familiar with this mannerism, as well. Hains Forster was trying to decide something.

"Hains, I don't know what all is going on with you, but you can trust me. You always could have. I knew about you and Malachi. I know you loved him."

The loud mufflers and shouts behind us suddenly broke through our sharp focus on each other. We turned at the same time. I recognized some of the vehicles from yesterday. Four and his minions had arrived. There were a few additions to the cronies. More testosterone raging eighteen and nineteen-year-olds piled out of less impressive older model trucks and headed for the dock. Many in red baseball caps that read "Make Albemarle Great Again," offering Charlottesville-esque newsworthy photocopy sans the torches—but it was still early.

The radio on Hains's hip crackled to life. "Sheriff, do you want me to call in some back-up?"

I spotted a young deputy by the road with his radio up to his mouth. He appeared unnerved by the fifteen or so teenagers heading straight for the freshly repainted restroom building and the TV monitor.

I heard Hains at my side, saying into his radio, "No, I'll handle this."

When he strode away, I saw a glimpse of the man I thought he would be when we grew up. Smiling, I followed after Hains as Doodie closed in on my left. We fell in behind Hains, step for step, much like old times.

"It's over here, just like I said." A bubba in a football jersey led Four and his entourage to the flat screen.

Both sides converged outside the restroom with Mali's face exploding out of the block wall behind us. One of the bubbas had brought along a baseball bat, which he raised above his head, ready to strike the TV screen as if destroying it would eliminate the recording. When Hains called the bat wielder by name, I almost laughed aloud.

"Now, Lump," Hains began.

The nickname seemed apt. The guy with the bat was a large lump of pale pink flesh—his cheeks so full they forced his eyes into a squint. Four led the six others from the security video to stand next to Lump and across from his father. The deputy paced nervously on the outer edges of the crowd. Professional cameramen joined the amateurs holding up phones to document the occasion. Reporters slipped into the center of the action, sticking microphones into angry red faces. Satellite trucks inched into every available space on the roadside, as scandal-starved news crews hustled to go live from Doe's Ferry.

Hains, now entirely in the persona of Sheriff Forster, continued speaking to Lump, "I don't advise that you add further problems to the vandalism charge you're about to be arrested for."

Someone in the crowd yelled, "You gonna arrest your son, Sheriff?"

Hains paused, apparently considering the expressions on the faces of his constituents gathered on the dock. I'm pretty sure Doodie and I were both occupied with evaluating our defensive position because we simultaneously stepped to put the building at our back. Doodie smiled down at me, and we gave each other a nod to say, "I got you," without saying a word.

More voices called from the crowd.

"What about it, Sheriff? We all saw the video."

"We heard them voices on that song too."

"We sure 'nough did."

There was some victim-blaming, as if the women living in Doe House provoked the attack by existing. A few shouts of "Dyke House" came from the outlying extreme homophobic representatives.

"If that was my boy, he'd be in jail already."

Others answered back, "That's 'cause your boy's on them pills right steady."

"Them gals is criminals. Ain't no tellin' what they do up in that house."

"They painted over the writin'. Ain't no evidence now."

The arguing began as a low rumble and exploded into full-on shouting. A little more than half the crowd wanted the vandals arrested as a start, with an inquiry into the Law Forster recording to follow. The minority was louder and willing to dismiss Four and his friends' behavior as boys will be boys. Calls of "Fake news" rang out, even with video proof of the incident playing in a loop before them. Some wanted the past forgotten, others wanted the guilty of past decades to pay. Old wounds opened from one end of the county to the other.

There were quite a few men in the crowd who had once jumped at Hains's commands on the playing field. They were the first to go quiet when their quarterback raised his hand and asked for everyone's attention.

Former linemen and tailbacks stood a little taller, as Hains's barked, "Listen up. Hey, listen up!"

I recognized the wide receiver that hooked up with Hains for the yardage that garnered them both scholarships. Alan Powell wore a golf shirt, and I had heard somewhere he was back home playing gentleman real estate developer.

Alan backed Hains, echoing, "Listen up."

More previous studs of the county encouraged the crowd to settle down.

When the din quieted, Hains said, "The hate speech painted on this building last night is not how the world should view us. Those responsible will be charged accordingly," he paused to meet his son's glare and emphasized, "all of them."

171

Four's chest puffed out further than it already had. Every boy picks a day to challenge the old man. That day had come for Four.

"Some of us aren't as happy to have these dykes in our county as you are, Sheriff. Why is that?"

Most of Four's cronies faded back into the crowd when Hains mentioned some of them were about to be arrested. Five stalwart red hats remained firmly grounded behind their leader, shouting words of encouragement.

A few enthusiastically chanted, "Dyke House must go."

The rest of the county residents in attendance seemed to be watching, unsure which side would prevail. During elections, many voters don't decide where to cast their vote until sure of the likely winner. No one wants to back the loser. Four had been triumphant enough times that many in the crowd thought him a formidable opponent for Hains Forster, the winning-est guy they had ever known.

Hains ignored his son's question. He pointed at the TV monitor and said, "There isn't any denying what you did, so, if those of you on the video would head on over to the courthouse, I'd appreciate it. We'll process your arrest and have you home in time for Sunday supper if you cooperate."

Four really wanted a showdown. He poked at the bear some more, when he said, "And what if we don't cooperate?"

Again, Hains looked past his son to the others. "You're facing a misdemeanor right now. Don't make it worse by falling to peer pressure from the same idiots that dragged you into this mess to start with."

Four was definitely the idiot Hains referred to.

He answered his father's generous offer with, "Idiots are the ones turning themselves in for a justifiable statement of disgust at these abominations living among us. You'll have to arrest me, but I'm not going to be ashamed of my beliefs. I have a right to free speech."

"Do your beliefs include an understanding of the law that says you can't paint your free speech on someone else's private property?" Hains asked.

Four hissed, "Fuck you."

Hains chuckled. "Well, son, then I reckon Doodie here is going to put you in handcuffs and escort you to the jail, where you'll sit until your bail hearing. By then, I imagine your momma will be involved and come bail your ass out of jail like she always has. Then your Uncle JP will make a few calls, and the charges will be dropped to nothing more than a speeding ticket like he always does. You've never had to take responsibility for one thing in your entire life, so I don't expect it will start now."

One of the reporters shouted out, "Are you saying Judge JP Spencer has illegally interfered on behalf of his nephew in court proceedings?"

Among the crowd, voices could be heard answering the reporter's question.

"Hell yeah, he did."

"The old judge covered up JP's crap too."

"Remember when JP nearly beat that gay boy, Asa, to death and nothin' happened to him?"

"Yeah, he tried to kill him right there in the jail."

"That's what I'm talking about—ran that boy's head into a solid block wall."

"You heard them on the tape, covering up one thing after another."

"They killed that black boy painted on that building. That's what's always been said, anyway."

"Jane Doe was right all them years ago."

"Yep, and they set her up to get rid of her."

I couldn't help the smile I tried desperately to suppress. I was drawing attention to myself just standing there behind Hains, which I never liked to do. I had hoped the kids would be the focus of the reporters, but it looked like Hains and his son had volunteered for the spotlight. Susie's viral moment was happening. I glanced around the dock looking for the courthouse kids. I saw them standing at the DJ table, just before the loudspeakers erupted with JP Spencer's voice.

"No one will ever know. I'm going to fix this."

The recording was muffled and scratchy, the clarity fading in and out, but the people on the dock could understand what was being said once the crowd quieted to listen.

A female voice a few of us recognized spoke through choking tears, "He's dead, JP. Malachi is dead."

"Dad and I already talked to Law. You came home after you and Hains fought, got it? Now go get that blood off of you. Everything is going to be fine."

The tearful female asked, "What about Jane and Hains?"

"They only know what you tell them. Besides, Jane isn't going to be a problem much longer, and Hains's secret will keep him quiet."

"I don't know what happened. I saw that pipe and..."

JP's tone changed. "Shut up! Shut up! Never open your mouth again about this, you hear me. Stick to the story I gave you."

173

We all heard the fear in the female's reply. "Stop. You're hurting me."

JP's voice growled out of the loudspeakers, "I'm tired of cleaning up after this fucking family. I'll tell you what I told the old man, I'll see you dead, sister, before you ruin my life. Now, go clean up and get rid of those damn clothes."

Pardon the cliché, but you really could have heard a pin drop when the recording stopped playing. People exchanged glances, but no one spoke for a good ten seconds. Count it out. That's a long pause for a collective breath. Once they began, the comments came forth like a wave, swelling to a crescendo, with the crowd rowdily debating whether they had known all along or if this revelation was a complete shock. But no one disputed whether it was the truth. That seemed to be an accepted fact many had held close to the vest for years.

But not me—I had never imagined that Cindy swung a pipe into Mali's head. Forgetting about the conflict with his son, Hains turned to look at me, tears of long-held pain welling in his lower lids.

He said, "Mali was dead when I found him, Jane. We had a fight on the dock, and I ran away. I always thought he jumped because of the way I reacted. That's why I felt guilty. I wasn't there to save him."

I didn't care who heard my reply. The time for secrets had run out.

"You ran away because Cindy saw you kiss Mali and you were afraid of what she was going to say to everyone else."

Hains was taken aback by my knowledge.

He asked, "How do you know that?"

Etta had come to stand with Doodie and spoke up, "I saw you with Malachi that night. Cindy did too. Then she ran away, and you went after her. My dad saw the whole thing. He confronted Mali and scared him off that dock. He did jump, but I knew Mali did not hit his head on the way down. I've always known someone murdered my brother. My mother did too."

I glared at Hains. "All those years Bertie cleaned up after your father and the judge and then you. She knew they helped cover up her son's murder, and she knew you tried to burn the evidence."

The reporters started shouting questions and received some credible answers from the throng mixed with lots of hearsay. I didn't care what was said. The fact people were talking openly about a hushed up forty-year-old crime was all I could have hoped for until she made her appearance.

The crowd parted, as Cindy Spencer Forster approached her son and husband. She was not alone. Cheerleaders in high school always

174

ran in packs. Apparently, ex-cheerleaders did too. I recognized a few faces under the wrinkles and graying hair. Cindy still looked like the queen bee she was, just a little prettier than the others, a bit more put together than her peers. A hush fell over the assembled throng. I could only imagine this was the most excitement Doe's Ferry had seen since I left.

The queen bee glared at me but turned her focus to her husband.

"Hains, this is a misdemeanor at best. Write the boys a ticket and remove this video. Jane is just trying to start trouble like she always did."

Never able to take an insult from Cindy Spencer, I went with the first thing that came to mind.

"Enjoy the last seconds of your perfect life. It's about to end in five, four, three, two, one."

Cindy had not heard her taped confession, nor, apparently, had her brother. His entry in the old judge's golf cart could not have been better timed. The Spencer family's arrival seemed as if they had discussed the scheduling. I was sure that was precisely what happened. I looked over at Paul, the cameraman, who was busy trying to decide which part of the excitement he wanted to film.

I called out to him, "Be sure to get the front and back of that cart. You'll thank me later."

He smiled and gave me a thumbs-up as the press rushed JP. The golf cart came to a halt with Four and Cindy on one side, and Hains, Doodie, and me on the other, JP stepped out of the cart with his back turned to us, as the news media crowded in.

"Judge Spencer, what do you have to say to the accusations that you covered up the murder of Malachi Blount in 1979?"

"I was certain when I learned that Ms. Doe had returned to Doe's Ferry, that she would repeat these unfounded accusations. She turned the tragic accidental death of a remarkable young man into a personal campaign against my family. I'm afraid her years in the penitentiary, and her documented drug use have contributed to her mental decline. I hope she gets the professional help she needs."

"That ain't what you said forty years ago, JP," an anonymous voice called out.

"On that tape, you admitted to planting them drugs on her," shouted another.

"Sounded like you was covering for your sister."

"More like covering for his old man. Old Judge Spencer was a pervert. I can testify to that."

175

"John Doe said you set her up. I come more near to believin' a veteran than a snake in the grass like you," an older farmer in a Seed & Feed baseball cap said, as he held JP in his sun-wrinkled stare. He pointed at old Judge Spencer. "The apple didn't fall too far from the poisoned tree, I'd say."

It was happening. People who could not or would not speak in 1979 felt empowered. Sadly, many didn't care what really happened. If the election of 2016 proved anything, it showed us our ugly, racist, homophobic, xenophobic American underbelly. A few in attendance felt the need to assure the news media knew the deplorables were represented in Doe's Ferry.

"John Doe was a faggot—died of AIDS."

"Don't pay any attention to them JP. We know that tape was faked."

"Jane Doe's behind this charade."

I was impressed with the vocabulary choice, if less enthused with the follow-up chant.

"Lock her up. Lock her up."

I started laughing. I couldn't help it. This was all so absurd. Reality no longer existed. We were caught somewhere between a bad sitcom and an alt-right political rally. I came to the conclusion that this must be what America looked like to the rest of the world—a minority of crazed, ignorant, heavily armed, easily influenced, arrogant pricks shouting, "Lock them up," at the majority who stand dazed, unable to fathom where these people hid for fifty years before the current administration let them out.

With impeccable timing, John Smith hit a button on the mixer. The amplified voices echoed off the courthouse and rocketed over the sound waters. The words were layered, ebbing and flowing sentences, with words accented into one thought.

"He's dead, JP. MALACHI is DEAD."

"I can't COVER UP a MURDER, Carroll."

"I can be rid of anyone who asks too many QUESTIONS about the DEATH of that little NIGGER QUEER…"

"This community will BELIEVE what we TELL THEM to BELIEVE."

The Spencer siblings went pale, but not the old man. He was so far gone, Judge Carroll Spencer believed the hubbub was all for him. He waved and smiled at the crowd, which was beginning to point and exclaim about his family's guilt. The news media people went into a frenzy to be the first on the air with the breaking news. The young courthouse kids approached with triumphant grins, enjoying the chaos they had created.

I leaned over to Etta and said, "Someone might want to check the old judge's hearing-aid battery. He thinks he's on a float in a parade."

Etta nodded toward my right, "Heads up. I think Cindy may be heading your way."

I looked back toward the Spencers. While their father waved, JP looked as if he was going to throw up and Cindy glowered at me. Facing Malachi's murderer had run through my mind quite often, but it was never Cindy I saw at the reckoning. Hains and Four appeared to be in shock, Four more so than his father. I assumed Hains had guessed at Cindy's guilt and had not wanted to believe it. Apparently, Law Forster never told his son the truth of what he knew.

When Cindy took her first step toward me, I heard Mali's voice in my head say, "You know how she is," as he had so many times.

I had the most un-atheist thoughts about my role in the eternal rest of my friend. Malachi never left me. I carried his soul in my head and heart for forty years. He experienced life with me, always there, waiting for me to know the truth. I had accepted that I would never rest as long as his murderer remained free. He had only one question, now that we knew to whom it should be addressed.

Hains stepped between his wife and me at the last second; coming out of his haze to assume the arbitrator role he had always played between the two of us. I felt Doodie start to move and put a hand out to stop him.

"I got this," I said, giving him a reassuring smile, and then said to Hains, "Get out of her way. We're adults. I'd like to hear what she has to say."

People around us quieted down. The show they had come to see was about to begin. A ripple of murmuring carried through to the rest of those in attendance. Soon most eyes were on the old courthouse kids. Some of the media noticed too. Paul now had his camera focused on me. His smile indicated self-satisfaction for having been right—I was in the middle of the story.

Cindy pushed past her husband and waved a finger in my face, while she spat out, "Why couldn't you just stay gone?"

"Because Malachi's nephew and his friends wanted to know who hit his uncle in the head with that pipe and now they know. I just want to know why? Hains chose you. You didn't have to kill Mali, Cindy. You had already won."

177

Cindy's eyes fell on Doodie's adopted son and the necklace he was wearing. She demanded to know, "Where did you get that? Hains, arrest him. He broke into our house."

The artist grandson spoke up. "No, Grandma. I found it in your desk drawer and gave it to Malachi because it had his name on it."

JP awoke from his self-pity, as he watched his dreams melt away, in time to interject, "Cindy, as an attorney, I recommend you stop talking."

Cindy wasn't a girl JP could push around anymore. She was a full-grown bitch, with a white-hot temper and a mean streak to match it.

She wheeled on her brother and barked, "You brought this on us with your cover-up plan. Daddy was right. What jury in 1979 would have convicted a white girl of killing a naked black boy?"

JP's mouth fell open. Cameras filmed it all. Cindy returned her attention to me, her eyes ablaze with anger. Rage had taken over any rational thought, giving the former "I'm going to be a famous actress" fantasist a tunnel vision focus so sharp she completely forgot about the audience for which she performed. I, for one, enjoyed the show.

"I don't know where you got that tape," she began, weaving her tale for the jury, "but it doesn't tell how Malachi Blount attacked me, and I defended myself."

I replied with not much inflection, "Bullshit. Mali was unconscious, lying on his side. You smashed a pipe into his skull and then dragged his body back into the water."

"He was awake and tried to rape me," Cindy countered.

"Mali was gay," I said, chuckling at her desperation.

Cindy refuted my assertion, proclaiming, "Mali was bi-sexual."

The conviction with which she said it let me know at once what it meant.

"You slept with Mali. My god, were you all sleeping with him?"

Doodie shrugged and said, "I wasn't."

Hains moved so he could see Cindy's face when he asked, "Did you? Did you sleep with Mali?"

"I would have thought "Did you kill Mali?" would have been the first question, but of course who was fucking who is more important. This is how Mali got murdered in the first place."

Cindy shouted as if being louder would make it true, "He tried to rape me."

I smiled, knowing it used to make her so angry when I laughed at her temper tantrums, and pointed out to her, "The angle of the wound indicates either he was still on the ground or the person who swung that pipe was over ten feet tall. Forensic facts cannot be manipulated to match your narrative. You killed him because no one would ever love you like we loved Malachi, especially not the man you trapped into being your husband."

Cindy dove at me, hands going for my throat. Doodie stepped in front of me, which I allowed this time. I didn't come to Doe's Ferry to catfight for the folks down on the ferry dock. My huge friend blocked Cindy's path, slowing her down long enough for Hains to grab one of her wrists and pull it behind her back. I heard the handcuff ratcheting down on that wrist, while he reached for the other.

"Cindy Spencer Forster, you are under arrest for the murder of William Malachi Blount, Jr. You have a right to remain silent. I'll read you the rest of your rights when we get to the courthouse. I strongly suggest you exercise that first one and shut your damn mouth for once."

Four came to the defense of his mother, yelling, "Hey, cocksucker. Get your hands off my mom."

I had never seen Doodie move so quickly or with such purpose. Deputy Duty had Four on his stomach with a knee in his back and a cuff on his wrist in a flash. Four thought about resisting, but gave in and relinquished the other wrist to be cuffed.

The other deputy who had drifted about the periphery of the crowd appeared after the action had subsided. He passed Hains pushing the cuffed Cindy ahead of him.

The young, fresh-faced deputy asked, "Sheriff, can I do anything?"

Hains stopped and looked back at me. He then gave his deputy an order.

"Arrest Judges JP and Carroll Spencer for criminal conspiracy in the frame-ups of Jane Doe and Asa Speight, conspiracy to cover up a murder, and," he paused, "call the Feds. JP Spencer caused great bodily harm to a prisoner in custody when he was a US attorney. He should answer for that."

"Sir, I only have one pair of cuffs."

"Cuff them together, Deputy Twyne. They can come as a family."

The Spencers gave the deputy no trouble and allowed themselves to be cuffed together. Etta and the courthouse kids followed behind the escorted arrestees, along with most of the people on the ferry dock. I waved off reporters and found my way to the boathouse, where I closed the door and finally wept for my friends, for me, and for what we lost that night.

I closed my eyes and saw him standing there, my Mali, the most beautiful boy I've ever seen. He smiled at me and said, "Don't worry about me, Jane Doe. I told you I was going to be famous."

18

Blood brothers...

"You and Tommy Lynne seem to be getting along all right. Happened to see your car down at her house last night."

"Doodie, you did not just happen to see my car. You had to be looking to see down that lane, you nosey fucker," I said, laughing with a lightness not felt since before Mali died.

Feeling at peace was something I was still getting used to.

Doodie smiled over at me, taking his eyes from the road for a second. "Okay, you got me. I just wanted to make sure you made it down from the airport safely."

"My text wasn't good enough?"

"I follow the trust but verify rule."

I looked out the windshield at vast fields of tobacco, deep green and ready for harvest.

"Why are we taking the old by-pass? Nostalgia, or some other nefarious motive?"

"Remember that barbecue place by the river?"

"Is Stump's Place still there?"

"Yep, same family still smokin' meat in the same pit."

My mouth watered at the thought. "Two tiny paper straws in a coke bottle and a barbecue sandwich wrapped in wax paper. I've actually had dreams about eating at those picnic tables with you guys. Funny what sticks from childhood."

"I thought we'd stop and have lunch a little early. We'll take Asa a few sandwiches. He liked that place too."

"Yes, he did. The first time we took Asa to Stump's, he ate four sandwiches. You know, he'd been hungry a lot growing up. It used to fascinate me to watch him eat. He told me prison was the only time he knew he was going to eat three meals in a day."

Doodie slowed the SUV behind a tractor pulling a wagon filled with field hands to the next drop off. It gave him time to drum on the steering wheel and talk about more pressing matters.

"How's Asa's case coming?"

"He has a good lawyer. Molly Kincaid is sharp, one of the best criminal attorneys in the south. She took over the practice of the guy who gave me my first job out of prison. Kincaid says it's just a matter of doing what's best for Asa. He'll have the funds to live wherever he would like, but you know Asa likes his life right where he is."

Doodie nodded. "He has a cottage 'family,' a job, and purpose. That's all he could ever hope for."

"Well, whatever he needs, he'll have. I'm officially his guardian as of last Friday. We're going to wait on the civil suit until after the criminal trials are complete. The state has already set up a trust for Asa's care and assigned a judge as his advocate through the process. So, all that is moving forward smoothly."

"What about your record? When are they going to clear that up?"

I shook my head. "I don't know. Kincaid, she's representing me too, she said JP was about to sign a plea deal, which would include admitting that he planted the drugs on me and set Asa up."

"And malicious prosecution," Doodie said.

"Yeah, that too. The sticking point is his attack on Asa. JP doesn't want to admit that happened."

Doodie chuckled. "I hear he's more than willing to give his sister up, though. That shouting match they got in at the jail was enough to put Cindy in prison for the remainder of her life. Hains should be commended for spending just a little more and installing that security system with audio."

"He should also get a star on his forehead for having enough sense to recuse himself and call the Attorney General's office and the Justice Department immediately."

"I heard they're giving the old judge a pass because he has no clue what is happening."

I grunted. "I'd stick a pin in him to see if he's lying. Malingering is something he certainly has the expertise to pull off."

We rode along a few more miles, passing weathered sheds with rusty tin roofs and only remnants of the tarpaper skins that once covered the graying wood planks.

I broke the silence with a sigh and my comment, "I hate that Hains had to resign and leave his home, but I get it."

"You definitely get it," Doodie agreed. "You left Doe's Ferry for much the same reasons—so you could live your life free of scrutiny."

I laughed loudly while saying, "And away from nosey old friends who check up on you while you're on a booty call."

Doodie slapped the steering wheel and grinned. "I knew you were sleeping with Tommy Lynne. She's just too damn happy these days, and a few of the local married women's attitudes have soured."

I grinned back at him. "We're not exclusive, so she's welcomed to continue life as it was before my return. I have no intentions of moving back here, not full time."

"Oh, I hear a crack in the armor. 'Not full time' isn't 'never,' which is where you were three months ago when you came home. She's a great gal. You'd make a good couple."

"Don't marry me off, Doodie. I enjoy Tommy Lynne's company. Let's just let it go where it goes."

We rounded a big sweeping curve, which opened onto a vista that included soybean fields and a view of a wide bend in the Roanoke River. Doodie put on his signal light and slowed the vehicle, before pulling into a hard packed sandy parking lot next to a small block building with ancient gas pumps rusting out front. When I opened the door, the smoking pit out back filled my nostrils with the smell from my childhood I associated with feeling happy. We were always in the best of moods at Stump's.

If my happy had a taste, it was Stump's barbecue. As we walked toward the picnic tables in the back, I imagined four barely clothed, tanned kids running ahead of Asa and John Doe, laughing and carefree. We sat in out back of the diner where the black folks were required to sit for decades. As children, our bonds overcame what others saw as insurmountable differences. I loved my childhood and those blood brothers who lived it with me.

When the picnic tables came into view, I saw the real reason Doodie stopped. Hains stood and walked toward us, leaving another man standing by their table.

"Jane, I'm glad you came," he said. "I think we have some things we need to clear up between us."

I looked up at him and saw a relaxed and content guy with the sparkle back in his eyes.

"Hains, you look like a ton of weight has fallen off you."

"I have you to thank for that. Without that push, I might still be trying to decide if I had the guts to leave that life behind."

"It wasn't my intention to blow up your life. I had no idea Cindy killed Mali."

"I was married to her, and all those years I thought she and JP did something to cover for their father. And of course, they all threatened to out me, which I spent years in therapy trying to overcome."

"I understand, Hains. It was a different time for all of us." I looked over at Doodie, to include him in my observation. "We all have scars, but we made it to the other side."

Doodie's man-giggle made us all laugh, as he said, "Mali would say, 'It sure as hell took y'all long enough.' "

Hains looked over his shoulder and smiled at a gorgeous man who looked a lot like a middle-aged Shemar Moore.

I asked, "Who is he? How long have you been in love with him?"

Hains smiled so easily, I wanted to hug him. Joy poured from his being. The last time I saw him that blissful; he had run for the winning touchdown with time running out and the conference championship on the line. This was what love looked like.

His introduction had just enough shy boy mixed with chest-swelling pride, when he said, "That's recently retired Navy Colonel Joel Adams, my future husband, and the love of my life. We've been planning this escape for years. Four saw us together at Christmas. You showed up. The world went crazy, and this seemed as good a time as any to cut the ties and go. We're moving to Santa Barbara."

Doodie spoke before I could, extending his hand to Hains and then pulled him in for a bro hug. As he patted his shoulder, Doodie told Hains, "Congratulations, man. You deserve to be happy. Go live your life."

I patted Hains on the back and said, "Go do you with no apologies, buddy."

Out of Doodie's grasp, Hains said to us, "At eighteen, we were forced into situations in which we had no control. I tried to live a lie, to keep my father and everyone else happy. Doodie's parents tried to involve him in a crime. Jane, you were the only one that had a parent who genuinely understood his kid."

"Don't make him a saint. He was still a drunk with PTSD. Not the joyride one would like as a child."

"I guess my point is," Hains continued, "We lost control of our lives forty years ago. I'm sorry it took this long to get it back."

Doodie nodded and reminded us of our mission today. "I wish Asa could understand what we've done."

"We'll tell him today, anyway," Hains said, and grinned down at me, "I think Asa and your dad would be proud of what you've done and who you turned out to be."

"I think they would be proud of all of us." I smiled at my giant friends. "And I know you both want to hug me, and I'm going to let you, but do not pick me up. I always hated that."

They both hooked an arm around me and lifted me into a group hug. With my feet dangling beneath me, I let my head fall back and laughed with the abandon of an anonymous child.

About the author...

Four-time Lambda Literary Award Finalist in Mystery—*Rainey Nights* (2012), *Molly: House on Fire* (2013), *The Rainey Season* (2014), and *Relatively Rainey* (2016)—and 2013 Rainbow Awards First Runner-up for Best Lesbian Novel, *Out on the Panhandle,* author R. E. Bradshaw began publishing in August of 2010. Before beginning a full-time writing career, she worked in professional theatre and also taught at both university and high school levels. A native of North Carolina, the setting for the majority of her novels, Bradshaw now makes her home in Oklahoma. Writing in many genres, from the fun southern romantic romps of the Adventures of Decky and Charlie series to the intensely bone-chilling Rainey Bell Thrillers, R. E. Bradshaw's books offer something for everyone.

www.ingramcontent.com/pod-product-compliance
Lightning Source LLC
Chambersburg PA
CBHW051256250626
47155CB00009B/3318